1,0   ,uuu books

are available to read at

Forgotten Books

www.ForgottenBooks.com

Read online
Download PDF
Purchase in print

ISBN 978-1-332-74601-9
PIBN 10237919

This book is a reproduction of an important historical work. Forgotten Books uses
state-of-the-art technology to digitally reconstruct the work, preserving the original format
whilst repairing imperfections present in the aged copy. In rare cases, an imperfection in
the original, such as a blemish or missing page, may be replicated in our edition. We do,
however, repair the vast majority of imperfections successfully; any imperfections that
remain are intentionally left to preserve the state of such historical works.

Forgotten Books is a registered trademark of FB &c Ltd.
Copyright © 2018 FB &c Ltd.
FB &c Ltd, Dalton House, 60 Windsor Avenue, London, SW19 2RR.
Company number 08720141. Registered in England and Wales.

For support please visit www.forgottenbooks.com

1 MONTH OF FREE READING

at

www.ForgottenBooks.com

By purchasing this book you are eligible for one month membership to ForgottenBooks.com, giving you unlimited access to our entire collection of over 1,000,000 titles via our web site and mobile apps.

To claim your free month visit:

www.forgottenbooks.com/free237919

* Offer is valid for 45 days from date of purchase. Terms and conditions apply.

English
Français
Deutsche
Italiano
Español
Português

www.forgottenbooks.com

Mythology Photography **Fiction**
Fishing Christianity **Art** Cooking
Essays Buddhism Freemasonry
Medicine **Biology** Music **Ancient**
Egypt Evolution Carpentry Physics
Dance Geology **Mathematics** Fitness
Shakespeare **Folklore** Yoga Marketing
Confidence Immortality Biographies
Poetry **Psychology** Witchcraft
Electronics Chemistry History **Law**
Accounting **Philosophy** Anthropology
Alchemy Drama Quantum Mechanics
Atheism Sexual Health **Ancient History**
Entrepreneurship Languages Sport
Paleontology Needlework Islam
Metaphysics Investment Archaeology
Parenting Statistics Criminology
Motivational

TO THE DARK TOWER

BEING GERARD LINTON'S ACCOUNT OF ALL THAT
HAPPENED AT THE HOUSE OF JACQUES COUR-
NOT IN THE SUMMER OF NINETEEN HUN-
DRED AND SEVEN

Childe Rowland to the dark tower came.
—*Old Scottish Ballad.*

By
MARK S. GROSS, S. J.

ALBATROSS LIBRARY
NEW YORK, N. Y.

Copyright, 1922, By
P. J. Kenedy & Sons

MADE IN U. S. A.

MY MOTHER

2129713

CONTENTS

CHAPTER   PAGE

    I   I GO TO SEEK MY UNCLE   1

   II   I PICK UP A PRETTY COLD SCENT . . 14

  III   THE SCENT GETS WARMER 26

  IV   I GET A SCARE ON MY WAY TO JACK'S
        HOUSE 34

   V   I MEET MR. CLEMENT D. BLYTHE: SEE
        A FACE IN A WINDOW: AND GO GAL-
        LANTLY TO THE RESCUE 41

  VI   AN APPARITION OF THE NIGHT . . . 51

 VII   A PERILOUS NIGHT'S LODGING . . . 60

VIII   THE MADMAN AGAIN: AND OTHER
        MATTERS OF INTEREST 70

  IX   THE BUNGALOW IN THE GLEN . . . 78

   X   I WITNESS A QUEER SCENE AND MAKE
        A DECISION 87

  XI   THE LADY OF JACK'S HOUSE 98

 XII   I AM WELCOMED BY MY UNCLE . . 112

XIII   I BAIT AT THE ROYAL WINDSOR (SO
        DOES THE MAN WITH THE EMPTY
        SLEEVE), AND STUMBLE UPON A MOST
        SURPRISING TRYST 123

 XIV   IN THE PAVILION 135

  XV   WHAT I OVERHEAR IN THE MAPLE
        TREE 149

CONTENTS

CHAPTER   PAGE

XVI   I Become an Imaginary Burglar: and
         the Secret of the Bungalow is
         Revealed   162
XVII   The Encounter on Eagle's Nest .   173
XVIII   My Uncle Takes the Count . . .   184
XIX   William and I Stand Guard . . .   197
XX   I Run an Errand Perilous   206
XXI   I Talk to Father McGiffert: with
         Sad Results   214
XXII   In the Kidnapper's Den: and After   224
XXIII   The Conversation Below the Water
         Tank   237
XXIV   In the Boathouse   245
XXV   The Chase for the Chart . . .   252
XXVI   Tom Donkin's Prophecy Comes True   261
XXVII   My Flight Down the River . . .   271
XXVIII   Jack's House Again   282
XXIX   The Parley: Carver Makes a Pro-
         posal   290
XXX   The Parley: I Call the Tune . .   300
XXXI   I Dig for Buried Gold   311
XXXII   The Attack is Launched   320
XXXIII   We Explore the Tower Cave: and I
         Make Another Try for the Treas-
         ure   328
XXXIV   Dawn on Eagle's Nest   340
         Epilogue   353

TO THE DARK TOWER

I

INASMUCH as this narrative is to be the history, not of my whole life, but merely of an inconsiderable portion of it (as far as time goes), I must be brief in relating the circumstances that sent me forth to seek my fortune.

And yet, I cannot think back on that period without dwelling in a kind of museful tenderness and sorrow upon those last months which I passed under my father's roof. I can still see him coming in of an evening after the dusk had fallen (it was October then, and the farm lay under its first mortgage) and flinging himself into a chair before the open hearth; and I, sitting over my Cicero at the table, would know that the day had been a poor one at the mine. And I would say nothing, knowing his humor; and he would say nothing, but sit there before the fire, his head on his chest, lacking spirit even to pull off his boots. And presently my mother, guessing he had returned (she always guessed right), would come through the dining-room

from the kitchen where she had been preparing supper. She would take his hat off, standing behind
his chair, and then kiss him, and ask him if he were
hungry, and tell him what good things there were
for supper. And after a while his despondency
would leave him, his eyes would kindle, and the old
enthusiasm of a year since would shine anew in his
speech and manner.

"Never mind, my girl," he would say, taking my
mother's hand and looking up with an eager face,
"never mind. The ore's there—that's sure. We'll
get it out. You'll have everything money can buy,
my dear. And you'll go to college, Gerry, and be
a great man. And then you'll thank your old daddy
that he let the farm slide and stuck to the digging."
And then, dropping my mother's hand, and leaning
toward the fire, "Why, Jim Blandford said to-day
we'd strike it within the week!" he would exclaim.
"And Jim knows. He knows the rock all right.
You can't fool Jim. Only a little more waiting—
just a little." And my mother would put her arm
about his shoulders, and in her eyes was the love
of my father—and nothing else.

Such a scene, I believe, is the saddest memory I
have of those days, sadder even than when I saw
my mother's coffin lowered into the grave.

Well, shortly before Christmas of that year, my
father died, protesting his faith in the mine and his
love for us, almost to the end. But I imagine he
suspected, long before this, the will-o'-the-wisp he

had been following; for, at the last, after Father Krane (whom I had fetched those four miles from Pacific, and bitter cold it was) had given him the sacraments, he suddenly went all to pieces and asked my mother and even me to forgive him.

That was a dismal Christmas for mother and me, even though the wry-tongued, kind-hearted Mrs. Jessop made her fat husband drive her through the drifts to cheer us up. Now, I do not mean to draw out this sad period in any detail; I will merely state (a little baldly perhaps) that shortly after the holidays my mother took ill of a fever and passed away. But I must mention one incident which happened two days before she died. During the night she had been delirious—"talking upside down," as Mrs. Jessop said—but towards morning she had had a bit of rest, and when I came into the room about eight o'clock, she smiled right cheerfully at sight of me.

"Gerard," she said, as I took a chair at the bed-side, "Gerard."

"Yes, mother," said I, bending towards her.

"Gerard, I'm going to die, my child."

The word fell like a blow, making me wince. My eyes sprang full of tears and a tightening was in my throat. For all that, I made an effort to laugh.

"Nonsense, mother," I cried, gulping hard. "Why, you're looking a great deal better this morning; honest you are."

Her frail, white fingers closed on my hand. She shook her head sadly on the pillow.

"No, my son, . . . no."

I made no answer, but looked at her, my eyes smarting with tears.

"There, my child," she went on, after a space, "you mustn't cry. You mustn't cry over *me*."

"I'm not crying, mother," I declared stoutly, blinking with all my might. "You don't catch me crying."

She smiled faintly. "That's right, my dear. Keep a brave heart—you'll need it . . . How bright the sunshine is on that window!"

The clock ticked loudly through an interval **of** silence. Then,

"You'll be left all alone, poor child," said my mother. "And you won't have much to begin life on, I'm afraid. But I have a brother, Gerard, who was good to me till I married your father. Since then, he—he has forgotten me. But perhaps he will help you. Yes, Clement will be good to my boy, I'm sure he will. You go to him, Gerard."

"Where does he live, mother?" I asked. Then, bethinking myself, "Shucks, mother," I hastened to add, "I won't have to go to him because you're going to get well. Sure you are."

But she paid no heed to my encouragement.

"In Chicago, child. But whereabouts in that great city, I don't know. But I know he's ex-

tremely wealthy, and has a kind heart at bottom.
You'll go to him, my son?"

"Uncle Clement Blythe—all right, mother, I'll
find him."

I knew my father had mortgaged the farm a second time, and I dreaded to think how deeply he had
gone into debt. As it proved, the mortgages
amounted in reality to a complete lien; and when,
a month later, Mr. Wilcox, the lawyer from Pacific,
and another man with a hard, bloodless face drove
up to our gate and I had brought them into the sit-
ting-room, I was informed, with little ceremony, of
the extent of my misfortune. The land and barns
and live stock, the house and furniture—all were
gone: and I sat there, nodding my head at the two
blurred figures across the hearth, and thinking of
my mare Nellie, and thanking God my mother was
dead.

After this I went to live with the Jessops. These
good people received me as one of their own boys—
nay, even better; for I was allowed regular wages
for farm work, whereas Jem and Lou got nothing.

But I had not forgotten my mother's word about
Uncle Clement Blythe; often and often I thought
of him, and whether he would treat me kindly after
casting off my mother. But, owing to this un-
brotherly act of his, and because, too, I was pretty
well satisfied with my present lot, I could not decide
whether to appeal to him or no.

In this frame of mind I continued till the twenty-second of June—I remember the date well, for it was my birthday. That afternoon I was shocking wheat in the lower field (the harvest was a bumper that year, too) and had got around to the fence which borders the county road. Just on the other side of the road is the Frisco track; and as I paused for a moment to wipe the sweat from my face and to watch a meadow-lark singing on the thatch of a shock not twenty yards away, here comes the afternoon Flier from the west, booming down the track, its great engine rocking and plunging and looking as big as a mountain.

Now, you must know I had seen the trains go by every day without giving them so much as a second thought; hence, you will marvel (not more than I did) how greatly my spirit was stirred by this particular train. And yet, it was not the train so much, with its long line of speeding cars, that upset me, as that which was at the end of it. For at the end was one of those large platforms with a shiny brass railing, called "observation platforms," and seated there was a company of ladies and gentlemen. And one of the ladies, as the coach swept by, leaned over the rail and waved a fluttering handkerchief. I didn't have gumption or courtesy enough to answer her salute, but stood there like a gawk, watching them fade down the track.

And as I stood there, a kind of wistfulness came over me, a wistfulness and then a downright hankering after that bright gay world of the city, to which the smartly dressed people yonder on the flying train belonged.   And at a clap, as it were, the charm of my country life fell broken about my ears.   Was I to spend all my days in this monotonous grind of humdrum toil, in this dull routine of farm work? The world of progress and action and enterprise was off there beyond the hills whither the train was speeding.   There lay achievement and success, and big things doing and to be done; here was only stag-nation and the slow circle of daily drudgery.   There was my uncle, and though he had treated my mother harshly, yet almost with her dying breath she had bid me seek him out.   Besides, I had reached my eighteenth year to-day; I was getting old (so I thought), and a few more summers of this kind of life would leave me branded forever as a horny-handed, fat-witted yokel.   In short, that fluttering handkerchief had aroused within me the spirit of adventure and the fire of ambition—and forthwith I resolved to seek my uncle and El Dorado.

Though I had been to St. Louis once before in my life, I felt pretty small, I tell you, when I stood under that great, roaring shed at the Union Station. My brand-new clothes, and my handsome leather grip, and my roll of banknotes (all of which I was so proud of at Mr. Jessop's) seemed no great shakes at all in this place.

Well, when I boarded the Chicago train, I found the coach pretty well filled.   Doubting whether I could get two seats to myself, I decided to try the coach behind.

So soon as I set foot within the door I knew I was in one of those Pullman sleeping cars, for I had heard tell of them and, of course, had often seen them flying along the Frisco and Missouri Pacific tracks. But this was the first time I was ever inside one; and it did look rich and handsome, I tell you.

On both sides of the aisle were tall green curtains falling from the roof of the coach, and embroidered on them, as I could see, were numbers. The floor of the aisle was covered with a thick carpet, just like a parlor, so that you couldn't hear your own footsteps. Indeed, what with the carpet and the curtains I could hear nothing save a low, murmurous talking from the other end of the coach; and the subdued light added to the restfulness of the place.

I was glad I had come early, and thus could get my pick of the berths (behind the curtains were the berths, I guessed). Not that I was over-nice about it; for, the first one I tried being empty, in I crawled, valise and all; said my beads (which I did every night, as my mother had taught me) and, though it was pretty dark, doffed my duds and was sleeping like a log ere ever the train pulled out.

The next thing I became aware of was a blinding light, and for a second or two I didn't know where I was. Then a voice on the other side of the light (which proved to be a lantern) spoke up somewhat apologetically.

"You're in the wrong berth, I believe, sir. Got your check?"

"Check?" said I, and the same moment I noted brass buttons on the sleeve of the hand that was holding the lantern. Then I recollected my whereabouts and knew it was the conductor. "Oh, you want my ticket. Wait a minute. It's in my coat."

"I want that too," he answered, and his voice sounded less apologetic. "But I want to see your sleeper check first."

I sat up straight.

"Sleeper check!" I cried. "What's that?"

At that the conductor made a sudden lunge over my head (I confess I ducked), and next moment the berth was flooded with light.

"Come, now, young fellow, that talk won't do. Show your check or bundle out of here doublequick." I saw his face plainly now, and let me tell you he meant business. But for my part he must show me I had no right to my comfortable bed before I surrendered it; my back was up too.

"Look here," said I, "I guess I was the first one to claim this berth. Nobody else had it, and I'd like to know what right you've got to throw me out."

These words had a startling effect on the conductor. He gazed at me with widening eyes, and then swore—not angrily, but softly and in great wonderment.

"What do you know about that?" said he, addressing some one behind him. And then, for the first time, I became aware of others standing in the aisle. "He thinks it's first come, first served."

It began to break upon me now that the taking of a Pullman berth was a more complicated business than I had supposed, and that, perhaps, I was not altogether in the right of it. With the conductor was a white-jacketed porter and a gentleman in his shirt-sleeves. The gentleman was smiling and that gave me courage; for he was smiling not only with his lips but with his eyes, which were dark and humorous and kindly.

"Maybe I'm all wrong," said I, feeling dead sure I was, "but I thought anybody was welcome to a berth. So I just took the first empty one I found. I haven't got any check. The only thing I've got is a ticket, and here it is."

The gentleman's smile broke into a chuckle, and the conductor, who was stout, mopped his brow with a very towel of a handkerchief.

"Well," says he, "you *are* an innocent. I'd like to know what your mother was thinkin' of, lettin' you travel."

"My mother's dead," I responded, resenting his mention of her.

"Oh," says he, and I noticed that the gentleman's smile vanished. "Well, now, you just put on your clothes and take the car ahead. You've got to *pay* for a sleeper. Remember that next time."

Though I wouldn't have paid for one back in the

station (had I known it), now I was only too willing to do so; for I suspected the conductor thought I had been trying to cheat him out of some money.

"That's all right," I answered. "I've got the cash. How much is it?"

The conductor began to get angry again. "It's two dollars. But that don't make no difference. You've got to turn out of that bunk. It belongs to this gentleman."

"One moment," interposed the gentleman, stepping forward. "Porter, is there another lower?"

"Yessuh. Two ob 'em. Ain' ve'y crowded dis trip."

"Well, then," said the gentleman, turning to me and smiling again, "you just pay for it, and you're welcome to that berth."

"I'm sorry for it," said I, looking up (for he was a tall man). "I didn't know."

His hand came down upon my shoulder, and the grip of it was strong and friendly. "Right as right. Forget it and go to sleep."

Next morning when I reached the wash-room and saw all the rich-looking men smoking and chatting I could hardly bring myself to enter: they seemed to fit there so perfectly, and I felt that I didn't fit anywhere. Then, as I still hung at the door, a man at the end of the seat opposite me dropped his newspaper and looked up.

"Good morning," says he quite heartily; "so you had a good sleep after all, eh?"

It was the gentleman whose berth I had pirated, and I was thankful to him for his words; for at once I felt I had a friend there—or at least an acquaintance—and this put me at my ease.

When I had completed my toilet, he made room for me on the seat, and we talked together most agreeably. What I liked best about him was the fact that he didn't patronize me at all, but talked to me just as he would have done to the prosperous gentleman in the white linen suit on the other side of him. And he was a man of the world, too, just as much as any of the others, and knew all about city life and spoke of far-away places with so much familiarity that I could not doubt he had been all over the United States. And he took for granted, too, that I knew as much as he did; so much so that I found myself speaking up in a manner that but yesterday would have made me blush. By and by, however, I let out that I came from a farm down in Missouri (before we had done I was itching to tell him my whole story, though I never did), and then how he talked crops and soil and fertilizers and stock—it did my heart good to hear him!

Since I have said so much about this gentleman I may as well go a step further and tell you what he looked like. He was a tall man, as I have mentioned, with the darkest, merriest, kindliest eyes I have ever looked into; and, though tall, he wasn't lanky, but had a chest and pair of shoulders quite as strapping as Lou Jessop's. Last night I had

thought him oldish (likely on account of his height),
but this morning I could see he was on the sunny side
of thirty.   Take him for all in all, he was just the
sort of a man I hoped I should grow up to (though
little chance of it, you would have said, had you seen
me) ; ănd, what was not least either, in my eyes, he
wore a handsome gray suit, the exact replica of
which I resolved to purchase so soon as I should
begin making my fortune.

After a while the porter came in with a whisk
broom (prodigious long), and each of the gentlemen rose in turn and had his clothes brushed:
though, for my part, I couldn't see that they needed
it.   Nevertheless the porter was very earnest in
the matter, and laid on the whisk broom with a positive gusto.

Every gentleman, as I was sharp to notice, gave
him a coin, and before my turn came I had a dime
ready in my hand.   This was a ratherish big tip
for a mere dusting off, but then, the porter had
shined my shoes and otherwise made himself agree-
able; and besides, I wished to put on a little style,
for, you see, I had caught the contagion of my rich
surroundings.   And indeed when I dropped my
dime into the darky's palm (with a dash of swag-
ger), and heard his unctuous "thank you, suh," and
realized that I was tipping a Pullman porter just
like any other nabob, I felt pretty expansive, I tell
you, and only wished Mrs. Jessop were there to
see me.

I PICK UP A PRETTY COLD SCENT

WELL, Chicago was a most tremendous place: buildings the size of mountains, trains roaring over your head, street-cars banging below, automobiles honking and darting about, and a million people on the sidewalks: I could hardly get my breath.

But, for all this confusion, I had wits enough left to set about finding my uncle. I consulted a city directory in a drug store, and cut the long column of Blythes down to two: "Clement D. Blythe, 60-- Sheridan Road" and "Clement W. Blythe, 59-- Lakewood Ave." (I purposely refrain from giving the entire addresses for the sake of the people who may now be living in these houses.)

Next, thinks I, to find a policeman. And hurriedly leaving the drug store, I had the good fortune to bump smack into one: a whale of a man with a great red face. Drawing him aside, I poured out my whole tale.

"Well," said he, with a grin, "if ye don't know which wan iv thim it is, the best thing to do is to **thry** bot'. They're close enough togither. La-ake-

wood is jist two blocks wist iv th' Road.   Take the
'L'—"

"Take the what?"

He pulled a comical face.

"Glory be to God now!   What a dear greenhorn
it is!   The helyvated, to be sure.   Come along
wid ye.   I'll bring ye there meself."

After making a block we came to a pair of stairs
which led up to those overhead railroads.

"Now," says the officer, "go up here an' git on
a thrain marked 'Evanston Expriss'.   Kin ye ray-
mimber that?"

" 'Evanston Express'?   Yes, sir."

"Tell the gua-ard to dthrop ye at sixty hundthred.
Thin walk east—to yer right—a couple iv blocks.
That'll be La-akewood.   An' th' R-road is jist be-
yant.   Do ye undtherstand?"

"Yes, sir."

"Thin God bless ye f'r a good la-ad."   And his
big hand rested for a moment, affectionately, on my
shoulder; the next he was making his way back
through the crush.

Well, I had no difficulty in locating Lakewood
avenue and the home of Mr. Clement W. Blythe.
It was a beautiful house; but all the good its beauty
did me—it was untenanted.

My heart beating a little faster, I struck over for
Sheridan Road.

If Mr. Clement W.'s house was beautiful, the
mansion of Mr. Clement D. was the next thing to

a palace. Of pure white stone it was, with an uncovered stone veranda and two stone lions on guard
at the top of the steps. Between the balusters of
the veranda were set squared shrubs in boxes, the
green looking very rich and aristocratic against the
white. The plate glass of wide windows gleamed
icily at me, and I wondered if they were symbolic
of my uncle's heart.

I rang the bell and waited. Again I rang. I
rang a third time. And then—then a lump came
up in my throat; was this house likewise empty?

"Dog-gone it," said I, out loud, "they're gone
too, I guess. Gee, if I only knew where they went!"

"I know where they went."

I span round. Before me, on the veranda, stood
a little, curly-headed girl with a jumping-rope in her
hand. She was a very pretty child, perhaps ten or
eleven, and her bright blue eyes were looking me
all over, and not disapprovingly either.

"Why," said I, "do you live here?"

She shook her head and pointed with a handle of
her jumping-rope.

"I live next door. My name's Cissy Carton, and
my daddy's got a brand-new Pierce-Arrow. He's
got three cars now. He's goin' to take me and
mamma out ridin' this afternoon. Oh, an' he drives
so fast—ever so fast. I like to go fast."

I noticed that one of the handles of her jumping-
rope—the one she had pointed with—had come off.

"Won't you let me fix that handle?" said I.

"There, we'll sit right down here on the steps, and I'll fix it in a jiffy."

She wasn't a bit shy of me, but seated herself at my side.

"Now," said I, "where did Mr. Blythe go? You see, he's my uncle and I've got to find him."

"Well," said Cissy, primly smoothing her dress over her knees, "she said her papa was goin' to take her to his country home in M'Gregor."

"McGregor! Where's McGregor?"

"In I'way. That's what she said—M'Gregor, I'way. Is I'way very far away?"

"Oh, not so far away," said I; "not as far as I've traveled already. I've come all the way from Missouri, and Iowa's just on top of Missouri.— But you said *she* told you. Who's she?"

Cissy opened her eyes in grave astonishment at my ignorance.

"Why, Domini. I come over to see Domini all the time. Don't you know Domini?"

I shook my head, wondering what my cousin Domini was like. I hoped she was as nice a little girl as Cissy Carton. But what an odd name— Domini!

"Now, Cissy," said I, "there's your jumping-rope as good as new. I'll have to be going along; I have to find my uncle and Cousin Domini."

Cissy and I walked out to the sidewalk together, or rather I walked whilst she skipped through her rope.

"You don't know how to get to McGregor, do you, Cissy?" I asked her, as we parted.

She lifted very serious eyes to me. "You take the train, don't you?"

"Sure enough. I might have known. Well, good-by."

Straightway I decided to go to McGregor. Of the two Clement Blythes, this Clement D. was at least the more tangible. Of Clement W., save for his house, I knew no more than I did of the hinder part of the moon.

Looking back on this journey now, I can see what a wild-goose chase it must appear to older eyes. But I was a boy then, with a boy's love of adventure; and dogging a man about the country, who might or might not be my uncle, was a business spiced with hazards and uncertainties: besides which, was the lure of new scenes. Just the same, there were times, too, as you shall hear, when all my heart went out of me, and I called myself a fool for ever having left the kindly Jessops.

Of course I had no idea just whereabout, in Iowa, McGregor might be. But after spending the rest of the day in seeking the right railroad station (I must have questioned a hundred people in that wilderness of roaring streets), I was finally told by a ticket agent to take the Burlington to Prairie du Chien, Wisconsin, from which point I was to board a ferryboat and cross the Mississippi to McGregor.

Of my journey that night little need be said, save

that ere ever I got started, my handsome new valise was filched from me. I was playing havoc with the sandwiches and pies of the station lunch-counter, and when I had done—lo, I was valiseless! This was pretty hard lines, because that grip contained every last stitch of my clothing except what was on my back. Anyhow, I reflected, I still had my roll of bills: which was a comfort.

But I fought shy of Pullmans this trip, you can bet; and slept like a top, too. Indeed, when the conductor knocked me up at Prairie du Chien (some time before dawn) I could have pounded my ear straight on through to St. Paul.

It being yet dark, I missed seeing this town. (But perhaps I didn't miss much.) I remember only a long street which led down to the ferry landing at the river. Here, in a ramshackle, all-night restaurant, I breakfasted; and then immediately dropped to sleep again.

When I awoke, it was broad day, with the sun streaming through the windows. Hurrying out, I beheld before me a mighty reach of water which, I was told, was the Prairie channel of the Mississippi river. On the other side of this channel was a long piece of wooded lowland—an island—and beyond that again, though invisible to me, was the McGregor channel, or the Mississippi proper. That part of the river evidently hugged the line of immense bluffs that were straight over against me, and that extended both up and down the river as far as I could see. These bluffs took my eye at once. Although from where I stood, they were a good mile off, I judged they must have been from four to five hundred feet high. Solid green they were, save where a vertical slash of white, here and there, betokened a bulging cliff. And above the bluffs, away off there in the far blue sky, were a couple of drifting specks which, I knew, were buzzards.

Well, by and by, here comes the ferry puffing up the river. It was a tidy little craft, a stern-wheeler, with "Rob Roy" painted in large letters under its bows. When we got under way I moved up into the prow and kept my eyes open for things to see.

First, we passed under a railroad bridge that spanned both channels and the island lying between. This island we skirted for upwards of a mile, but long before we reached its lower end I could see where the two channels met, with the monstrous big bluffs towering above. It was an amazingly wide river there—our Meramec was but a creek in comparison; and the bluffs,—the closer we approached, the higher they seemed to lift themselves into the sky. To me, indeed, they were not bluffs so much as mountains; I had never seen anything like as large; our St. Louis county hills would hardly reach half-way up them.

As we chugged past the extremity of the island I caught my first sight of McGregor. It was tucked away in a narrow defile or gorge between the hills, so packed with trees that all I could see were snatches of white and red amidst the greenery. Only at the margin of the river was the view unobstructed; and here several boat houses and raft-docks and no end of skiffs were moored; and above them, on the embankment, one or two buildings showed. So completely was the town ensconced in this natural pocket that I wondered a good rain didn't wash the whole of it into the river.

When we landed, and I had made my way up the embankment through old spars and cables and heaps of mussel shells and other odds and ends that clutter the shore of a river town, I was surprised to find a railroad track. The track, thought I, must skirt the river, for I didn't see how it could get out through these hills to the open country beyond— if, indeed, there were any open country beyond. The town itself, now I was in it, appeared to be even more closely walled in than I had supposed. It lay in the shape of a V, with a single street extending away from the river to the apex of the letter, where it brought up dead against a hill, like a blind alley; and on either side the town was barricaded with cliffs, almost perpendicular, that were studded with trees and bushes.

But it was no backwoods town, not by any means. There were electric arcs above the street, and along the curbing several automobiles; and the stores were very smart-looking indeed. Besides this, I saw several ladies who were dressed just as stylishly as any I had seen in Chicago.

Well, now that I had reached my destination at last, the business before me was to inquire after Mr. Clement D. Blythe. I had no apprehension that I shouldn't find him; the town was small, even tiny, and so tightly hemmed in that I couldn't escape the suggestion that I had my uncle cornered.

I walked on up the street for fifty yards or so, on the lookout for some native who should be apt to know the personal history of every denizen. At length I boarded an old fellow and put my question; but he only spat out into the street, wiped his tobacco-stained chin, and said, "Nup, I hain't never heerd o' him."

Then the thought occurred to me to make inquiry at some of the stores; and turning my head, I saw that I was standing in front of a saloon. I should have known it was a saloon, even if I hadn't seen the display of liquor behind the plate glass; for right in the middle of the window was that famous picture of *Custer's Last Fight* before which I used to linger in admiration outside Peitz's saloon in Pacific.

I had never been in a saloon before, but I surmised that the bartender would have the acquaintance of every man in town; and, though I didn't suppose my uncle frequented saloons, yet I made sure, knowledge of him must have reached the bartender's ears.

The saloon was a big one, long and high-ceilinged, and pretty wide, too. Distributed over the sanded floor were tables at which patrons sat smoking and drinking beer. In the middle of the room stood a knot of men, some of whom, upon my entering, flung me a glance and then went on talking.

There were two bartenders in white aprons, and as I came up, the nearest jerked his towel over his shoulder and, leaning forward with a deferential air, inquired: "What'll you have, sir?"

His manner, no less than his words, tickled my vanity, I suppose, for, though I hadn't intended taking anything, I now put my foot on the rail, just like an old-timer, and said: "Oh, I don't know. I guess I'll take a glass of beer. It's pretty hot."

"Yes, sir," he replied with a nod, as though my order pleased him.

I took a swallow of the beer and found it very good.

"I suppose," said I, reaching for my purse, "you know most of the people living here in McGregor?"

"Well, I guess I do, yes, sir. I was born and raised right in town. I *ought* to know 'em all."

Thinks I, this is my man.

"Did you ever hear of a Mr. Clement D. Blythe, then?"

Now, as I uttered these words an odd thing happened. I was looking point-blank into the bartender's face, but beyond him in the mirror I could see reflected the group of men who stood in the middle of the room. I had no sooner mentioned my uncle's name than one of these whisked round and stared at me.

Upon the instant I, too, had turned; and crossing over to him,

"Are you Mr. Blythe?" said I.

He lifted his brows.

"Blythe?" says he. "I'm afraid you've made a mistake, my boy." Then, stepping apart from the rest, "Why, what made you think my name was Blythe?" he asked, smiling.

"Because you jumped when I mentioned it just now."

"Did I?" says he. "Well, that's funny. I'm sure I wasn't aware of jumping. Nervousness, I guess. Or maybe because your voice sounded like the voice of a very good friend of mine." And he continued to smile in simple good nature. But he was lying, I made sure; for his excuse was too thin. Besides, I didn't' like his looks: his sallow face, his narrow lips and dark, secretive eyes repelled me.

"But maybe you know Mr. Clement D. Blythe?" I urged. "He's out here for the summer. Maybe you can tell me where he lives?"

He shook his head slowly, his mouth pursed.

"No-o," he replied. "No, I don't think I ever heard of him before. Are you a relative of his?"

"Yes," said I. "I'm his nephew; and I traveled all the way from Missouri up to Chicago only to find him gone. Then I heard he was in McGregor; and now I'm here, nobody seems to know him."

"Come, come," says he, quite friendly, "that's too bad. You're sure out of luck. Here . . . here's my card. I'm stopping at the hotel across the street, and if you want any help, at any time, you mustn't hesitate to ask me."

"Thanks," said I, taking his card. On it was engraved 'Clarence F. Carver'. "My name's Gerard Linton, Mr. Carver." I shook his lean hand with as much grace as I could muster; for, I confess, I felt an instinctive dislike of the man. Then, before I could protest, the bartender, at Mr. Carver's order, had set two tumblers of beer before us.

Carver raised his glass.

"Here's hoping you find your uncle, Mr. Linton," said he. And I, feeling somewhat foolish, drank his toast. I could not but think, or fancy at least, that he was poking fun at me. How far wrong I was, and whether I was to look back with pleasure on this treat of Mr. Carver's, the remainder of this narrative, if ever I can finish it, will make decidedly plain.

III

THE SCENT GETS WARMER

AT the door of the saloon Mr. Carver and I parted, shaking hands anew, this time with a degree of cordiality on my part due to the mellowing influence of the beer. Owing also to the beer, I now began to feel pretty hungry; and accordingly, spying a lunch-room several doors up the street, I went in and ordered my dinner.

My reflections at table were not of the rosiest. Here I had traveled all this way only to find that my wealthy uncle, who certainly should have cut some feather in a little burg like McGregor, was not only not known by the inhabitants but unheard of, even. True, it seemed altogether likely that Carver had some knowledge of him; of this, indeed, I was convinced; but from the circumstance it was no obvious or even warrantable conclusion that my uncle was on the ground. After all, the only sure evidence I had to go on, of my uncle's being here, was the word of a little girl: and was this evidence sure? Then came the thought, for some time in the background, that, even if I did find Mr. Clement D. Blythe, as like as not he would prove to be the

26

wrong man. Faint as the trail already was, the chance of its leading to so unfortunate a goal gave me a sudden shake all over; so that I sat up with a start, took out my purse, and counted my money.

The counting of my money put me in heart again, for I had, all told, one hundred and two dollars and seventy-five cents. Thus cheered, I brought a good appetite to bear on my lunch; and then, having paid my score, left the eating-house and continued on up the street.

At the top of the town, to my surprise, I spied a Catholic church, with what looked like the priest's house, standing at one side. Here at last was somebody to steer me aright! Before approaching the rectory, however, I thought I would pay a visit to the church and ask our Lord to favor my search; for the priest was, so to say, my last shot; I made sure if the priest knew nothing of Clement Blythe I should be at my rope's end altogether.

Presently, as I knelt there, a man in a long linen duster came in from the sacristy and drew down the sanctuary lamp to see, I supposed, if there were enough oil in it. As he thrust it up again, I had a better look at him and saw that he wore a Roman collar. He was a priest.

Forthwith I bounced out of the pew and made for the sanctuary. When I reached the altar-railing he had disappeared; but I overtook him just as he was leaving by the outer door of the sacristy.

"Father!" I blurted.

He whirled round, eyeing me in astonishment.

"Father, can I see you for a moment or two? I want to ask you a question."

His look, which at first had something in it of hard shrewdness (for I was a total stranger, you see), softened by degrees but never left my face. As he still stuck at an answer, and did not budge, I advanced a step.

"Father," I plumped out desperately, "I'm up against it. If you can't help me, my name's mud."

At this his blue eyes suddenly twinkled. "And what will it be if I can help you?"

"I mean—" I began.

"Yes, yes, my lad, to be sure," says he. "But what name have you got besides this possible one of mud?"

"Gerard Linton, Father."

"And I'm Father McGiffert, Gerard," says he, extending his hand and smiling. "Come, you're not in so bad a scrape as you think you are. Let's go over to the porch, and you can tell me all about it."

We walked across the stretch of flat sward between the church and the house, and in those few yards my spirits revived at a bound; for I felt I had found a friend indeed. And here I may as well give you some idea of what Father McGiffert looked like, for he will appear again in this narrative, as you shall hear in due course. He was a man past forty, I surmised, as the flecks of gray in his curly black hair seemed to indicate. But his stature, though only medium, was strong and stocky, and his complexion, instead of being palish, like most priests', was brown as a nut.   About the corners of his eyes was a web of tiny wrinkles which gave his face a cast at once canny and good-humored.   His speech was the Irish kind, though not anything like so broad as the Chicago policeman's; but with a burr (as they call it), quaint and pleasant to hear.   And he was muscular too, as I had reason to know; for the grip of his hand had been like iron.

"Now, Gerard," says he, taking a chair and waving me to another, "out with your story, lad.   Sure, if I can help you, I will.   But I have old man Sullivan a-dyin' up Bloody Run, and if I'm not there this afternoon to send him to Heaven, sure, it's him that'll be mean enough not to remember me when he joins the saints.   So be quick as you can, my lad, but take your time too."   With which concluding and rather contradictory injunction, he leaned back in his chair, pulled a black pipe out of his pocket, and began to smoke.

I'm afraid I took my time indeed, for I told my tale from the beginning; and, being naturally long-winded, I doubt but I tried the good Father's patience grievously.   But he was a good listener all the same, and by a gesture now and then or an exclamation, gave me to suppose that he was interested.   And at the end,

"Well, and so it comes to this," says he, knocking his pipe against the railing of the porch: "you've traced one of these Blythes here to McGregor, not being sure. whether he's your uncle or not. (And a pretty uncle he is, treatin' your mother like a heathen.) And you can't find him here. Nobody's heard of him. Well, and neither have I, Gerard. And it's ten to one, *you* won't either."

He bent forward suddenly and put his hand on my knee. "There, there, my lad, keep those tears back. Don't mind what I say. I'm the very devil himself for bluntness."

He paused, blowing hard through his pipe, while his eye studied the street below.

But, for my part, I wasn't crying at all; I was more of a man than that, I hoped; though, I must own, his words brought a hard lump of disappointment up my throat.

"This Blythe would be a pretty wealthy man?" he suddenly asked, giving me a sidelong glance, his pipe still held between his lips.

I leaped at the hope. "Oh, yes, Father! His house in Chicago is a regular palace!"

"Well, I tell you what then, Gerard," he replied, bending forward. "I don't. say you will find your uncle there—maybe you will, maybe you won't—but you try Jack's House."

"Jack's House!" I echoed. "What's that? A hotel?"

He laughed.

"No. It's an old trading-post, about five miles down the river—that is, it used to be a trading-post.

Now it's a summer home belonging to some rich fellow from Chicago. Four years ago the whole place was rebuilt, and I understand the tower wing of the old post was preserved. Sure, it must be a magnificent place altogether."

"But Jack's House?" said I, wondering and a little crestfallen, too. "Why Jack's? Is that this Chicago millionaire? You see, Father, my uncle's first name is Clement."

"No, no, no," says he, smiling. "This man's name isn't Jack; at least, if it is, the house isn't called after him. For all I know, his name may be Blythe; and I'm hoping it will be. That's your chance. As for him, ye see, nobody knows him in McGregor. He's been here only two summers— for a month or so, and keeps mighty close, by all I hear."

"Well," said I, "who's Jack then?"

"Ah, that's a long story," says he; "but to make it short, Jack was the old French trader who built that post nearly a hundred years ago. Jacques Cournot was his name, though some say 'Tournot,' and some again 'Sarnot.' But it doesn't matter. Well, he carried on a big trade with the Indians all through this western country. Sioux they were, too, mostly, and the Sioux aren't parlor Indians, or weren't, not by a jugful. Folks say Cournot built that tower as a kind of citadel in case of attack; for though the redskins were friendly to him, they were a treacherous lot, and he knew it—no man better, I guess. And sure enough, one night they dug up the tammyhawk, or whatever you call their heathenish weapons, and massacred Cournot and the whole outfit. All the good the tower did the poor fellow.

"And so," he wound up, "that's Jack's House, and from that day till four years ago the ruins of it stood there untouched."

"But," said I, more interested now in the old Jack's House than in the new, "wasn't there anybody to come to their rescue? Wasn't anybody living here then?"

"Well, not right in this house," said he, his eyes a-twinkle. . . . "No, the nearest whites in those days, I'm told, were across the river, in Prairie du Chien. And Prairie wasn't any more than a row of log shacks along one of those sloughs, about where the Sacred Heart College is now. There was a fort over there, too,—Fort Crawford: but I imagine by the time the soldiers got started, the Sioux had pretty well finished their job.

"But that's neither here nor there," he added, getting to his feet and looking at his watch. "God bless me, it's nearly three o'clock, Gerard! We'd both better be off." He paused, giving me a queer look. "But it's a long tramp, my boy. I'm sorry I can't take you in the buggy. Perhaps—"

"O shucks, Father," said I (for though my accomplishments were slender, I could use my feet), "that's nothing. I've got good legs. I can walk

all day.   That's nothing at all.   Just tell me how
to get there."

He gave me directions.   And then,

"Now, God bless you, lad," says he heartily, laying his hand upon my shoulder (we had already de-
scended to the street below).   "And when you see
that uncle of yours, tell him to come to Mass.   And
look here, if he isn't your uncle, come back for supper.   You'll spend the night with me."

I thanked the good man with all my heart (there's
nothing finer than the kindness of a Catholic priest),
and struck out up the road.   But, in the event, I
didn't take advantage of his invitation; indeed, ere
ever I set eyes on him again I was to run a gauntlet
of adventures, as puzzling as they were perilous;
and the upshot of them was, that Father McGiffert,
for all his friendliness, was the last man in Mc-
Gregor I wished to see.

IV

I GET A SCARE ON MY WAY TO JACK'S HOUSE

A DREADFUL hot tramp it was; that much came home to me ere I was many minutes on the road. But I cheerfully put up with the heat, for, I must confess, the romance and mysteriousness of my quest began to prick me. Here were the ruins of an old post which once had rung with the wild yells of savages; where the flames had leaped ruddy to the midnight sky; where white men had been massacred, but not till many a redskin had bit the dust: here, in a word, was a chapter out of Cooper. And here, too (which was a nearer thing), a man who might be my uncle had built a splendid mansion: what motive had he to build it upon the tumbled walls of Jack's House, and why was he chary of showing himself in McGregor? Last of all, here was Carver, who, I made sure, knew my uncle and who yet, for whatever reason, denied that he knew him. That there was some secret mischief about this new Jack's House I could not but feel; but this, as I say, only set my curiosity on edge and put a spring into my lagging step.

At length I hit the lane, which, as Father Mc-

Giffert had mentioned, struck off from the main road towards the river. But I had not got far when I saw that, instead of continuing straight, the lane began to bend round and ascend a side of the hill whose one end rose up steeply on my right. But the walking was not difficult, for the lane, running sidewise along the hill, lifted at a very gentle grade.

The further I got up this hill the more incongruous it seemed to me that a house of Father McGiffert's description should be situated anywhere in the vicinity. For now, more clearly than before, I was enabled to view my surroundings; and standing here, half way up the hillside, I seemed to be in a very sea of hills—they were all about me, like tumbling billows suddenly solidified. On my right the wooded slope still rose for a hundred feet or more; far forward the hill dipped slightly, bending eastward toward the river, and then climbed so high that the great trees along its comb looked, against the sky, like an unkempt hedgerow. Through a gap in the dense foliage along the road I commanded a fair sweep of the gulch below me and the opposite ascent: a vast green scoop embossed with treetops and flooded with the hot sunshine. In the quarter I had come from were more hills, some high, some low, some standing out boldly like rounded knobs, others shrinking away as it were and peeping timidly from behind their bulkier neighbors—but all of them, big and little alike, richly robed in their garments of summer green.

Now, as I stood there looking out over this billowy waste of woods and sunlight, I was suddenly struck by the stillness and the solitude. Both seemed out of the ordinary. Give ear as I might, I could hear not a sound. No bird sang. Not a leaf rustled. All that host of small woodland voices, discernible by the wonted ear, was dumb. Nothing stirred. The very air hung motionless. There was only the sunshine and the sea of verdure. For leagues around, for all the evidence I had, there might have been no other life than mine. Often ere this I had been in the woods alone; but never had I experienced such a sense of being so utterly by myself.

Wondering at this (and not a little uneasy about it, too, foolishly or not), I was just on the point of pushing on up the lane, when two things occurred which, though trifling in themselves, gave a new and almost violent turn both to the loneliness of my surroundings and to this strange voiceless quiet. From just beneath me in the valley arose the high, clear whistle of a cardinal; but no sooner had the cheerful and familiar notes begun than they ceased —broken off, you would have said, as though the bird had been frightened by some sudden and hostile presence. Then, as I still hesitated, half expectant of the rest of the song, sure enough, away down at the tail of the hill the whistling struck up afresh, floating fainter and thinner but almost magically sweet and airy through the dead summer hush. The next I knew, I had skipped clean across the road like a skittish colt: above me on the hillside a boulder had dislodged and rolled a few yards down the slope.

Now, I was not nervous—anything but; nor imaginative, as you already know; nor was I superstitious, reading odd meanings into commonplace incidents. Hence, I squared my shoulders boldly and told myself that it was mere folly to think there was anything ominous in a cardinal whistling in one spot and then in another, or in a stone rolling down a hillside. But it was no go: maybe I had taken the redskin story too much to heart; or maybe that modern paleface, Carver, had something to do with it. Anyhow, try as I might, I could not rid myself of the weird and even frantic fancy that the hills and valleys all about me were swarming with a multitude unseen but watching, and that the sleepy stillness of the afternoon might, at any moment, be shattered by the roarings of a thousand throats.

This crazy quirk of imagination, you will say, is hardly of a piece with the character of the stolid country boy who began this narrative; and, in truth, for my own part I could not but wonder at myself for the extravagant thought. All the same, I could not banish it either; for all my care-free whistling and my brisk step, the nightmarish notion stuck in my head and would not be ousted. And, as you shall see immediately, it was not altogether groundless, but indeed partook rather of an auspice than

of a figment.   For, within the next fifty yards, here
is what fell out.

On the near side of the road, and flush with its
very edge, extended a particularly dense brake of
sumac.   Now, I wasn't especially apprehensive of
this thicket, but noticed it merely on account of the
buckeye-trees (sometimes called horse-chestnuts)
which lifted their round, leafy bulks right behind it,
and which were the first I had seen up in this country.   I had just got about to the middle of the
sumac, when, lowering my eyes from a cluster of the
prickly nuts, I saw, framed in the green foliage, a
peering, human face!

It was a man's face, black-browed and brutal; so
much I glimpsed ere it disappeared; for in the turn
of a hand, while yet my breath was caught, it vanished.   So   quick,   indeed,   had   the   apparition
whipped away that I could scarce believe my eyes,
but stood staring in amaze.   What added to my astonishment was the utter silence.   I heard not a
sound, not the snapping of a twig.   Nor was there
a single quiver of the sumac leaves.   The spot where
the vision had appeared looked as innocent as any
leafy square foot of the whole thicket, and as stirless.   Was my freak of mind making me see things?

My first impulse, while surprise alone still
gripped me, was to plunge plump into the bushes and
so to the bottom of the mystery.   I took one step
forward, but only one; and then fear, like a hand
of ice, came clutching at my heart, and all my blood

ran cold. I couldn't, even had my life depended on it, set foot within that sumac.

Instead, I wheeled about and put off again up the lane. I went quickly, you may be sure, for the dread of what was back there on the roadside had got into my very marrow. Indeed, I didn't know I could be so pigeon-hearted, and kept reproaching myself, as I hurried along, for an arrant coward: so that, though my heels were itching for it, I refused to run. But I walked fast—I tell you I walked fast! I didn't turn my head either, for it was enough for me to know that the evil, lurking face was behind me.

For five minutes, perhaps, I pushed rapidly on till I gained the crest whence the lane, dipping at a plunge, bowed round to the high hill lying toward the river. By this, my fright had greatly abated; and so, ere I struck on down the incline, I halted and looked back. Not a soul was in sight; the lane was deserted and lonely as ever. Away back there, —a matter of two hundred yards or so—I could make out the fringe of sumac bordering the road— as sweet and peaceful a spot as you could wish: so that I began to doubt if the murderous visage among the leaves were not, after all, a mere mad coinage of my brain.

Whether it was or no, seeing I was now well past the rencounter and no harm come of it, I grew much easier in my mind: indeed, my spirits rose at my every step, for somehow or other—account for it as you like—the hunch came strong upon me that now at last I should find my uncle.

The lane, curving through an ángle of forty-five degrees, mounted by a gradual slope to the chine of the next hill.   Here, along the level summit, I was surprised, now and again, to note among the oaks and hickories a pine-tree's soaring spire and the dark, thick-set pyramid of a hemlock.   Presently the pines and hemlocks crowded up; the other trees fell away; and on either hand the somber, gray-green walls so closely hedged the lane that I was in a twilit canyon, it seemed, instead of on a hilltop. For the afternoon sun, though still high in the heavens, had no access here; and the needle-carpeted lane, hushing my steps, was all in shadow.

It would be ten minutes, I suppose, that I kept crisply on my way.   Then, the lane taking a sharp turn, I stopped in my tracks and gazed.   In partial view before me lay the goal of my long hike.

V

I MEET MR. CLEMENT D. BLYTHE: SEE A FACE IN
A WINDOW: AND GO GALLANTLY TO THE RESCUE

IT was a charming scene, especially from where
I stood. Beyond the shadowy canyon of the
lane ahead of me (as you look forth from a
railroad tunnel) I saw a grassy, sunlit area of perhaps four acres, spruce and comely as a park, sloping gently upward on all sides round; and in the
very center, plump upon the eminence thus formed,
the towered flank of Jack's House, all mantled with
green ivy as with a garment.

The tower was round and of a massy bulk;
pierced with small casements no better than port-
holes, except about middle way up where a modern
window was set; rearing high over the rest of the
house and crowned with a fretwork of stone, called
(I think) a machicolation. But this last was a
mere flourish, added by the present owner just for
appearance' sake; for you could see, up there
through the thinning ivy, where the new masonry
began.

Passing the tower, I spied a brace of gentlemen
standing on the gravel walk beyond the stone porch.

One was an old fellow, but, to judge by his sporty rig, quite a fashionable, if decayed, dandy. The other, of a powerful physique which was well set off by knickerbockers, appeared to be a guest. If here at last stood my uncle, it was no guess which of the twain he must be.

"Have I the pleasure," I began, addressing the old man in my well-conned exordium,—"have I the pleasure of speaking to Mr. Clement D. Blythe?"

He nodded, and my heart gave a leap of joy.

"Why, yes," says he, with a crackle of a laugh; 'and that's a cheap enough pleasure too, eh, Gordon?"

"Then, sir," said I, still speaking by the card, "I will make bold to ask if you had a sister named Katherine. For if you had, I am your nephew, Gerard Linton." And I held out my hand.

He took it, without an instant's hesitation; but his face, even before he uttered a word, dashed my hope in pieces.

"Well, Mr. Linton," says he, a simper upon his lips, "I am glad to make your acquaintance. But I regret I am unable to fill the rôle of uncle. I have no such sister."

Upon these words all my backbone turned to water, it seemed, and I stood, or rather hung there, limp as a rag.

"Aw, gee," I desponded, forgetful of my fine phrases, "then it's the other one, and I came all the way out here for nothing."

"I beg your pardon?" queried the old gentleman in his precise and piping tones.

Then I told him of Mr. Clement W. Blythe, of Lakewood avenue; how I had first gone to his house, but found it closed and deserted.

"Why, that's old Clem of the stock exchange," volunteered the man in knickerbockers. "I know him well. He and his family have been doing Europe since last fall. But he was to be back by the first of this month. In fact, I have an important engagement with him on the fifteenth."

These words gave me fresh heart, and already I had opened my mouth to express my thanks, when Mr. Blythe cuts in.

"Ah, you must pardon me, Mr. Linton. Meet my friend, Mr. Crowninshield."

Mr. Gordon Crowninshield put forth a hand that I couldn't help but look at twice: it was big like the rest of him, hairy as a bear's paw, and blotched with great freckles: and the grip of it made me wince.

"Well," said I, prying apart my fingers behind my back, "I'm very thankful to you, Mr. Crowninshield, for what you've just told me. I'll go straight back to Chicago. I guess I can catch a train to-night."

Then, as I still hesitated, wondering if Mr. Crowninshield, too, might be returning to McGregor, and so accompany me (in the back of my head was the recollection of the face I had seen), the old man spoke up nervously.

"I—I wish you good luck, Mr. Linton. I think,

if you hurry, you can catch the St. Paul to Mil-
waukee."

This was as good as telling me to go; accordingly,
I took the hint and, raising my hat, wished them
both good-by.   Down in my heart I was really glad
that Mr. Clement D. Blythe was no kinsman of mine,
after all: certainly, so far as I had observed, he
bore no resemblance to my mother.

This last thought had just crossed my mind, when,
lifting my eyes to the tower (I was repassing the
north end of the house) I brought up short, with
half a gasp: from one of the loopholes of that old
bastion my mother's own dear face was gazing down
on me!

I rubbed my eyes and looked again: the face was
gone.   I turned: the two men had also disappeared.
For a moment or so I stuck in my tracks, in two
minds whether to go back and ask who the lady
might be.   Then, realizing that I had been dismissed, and that no good could come of my inquiry,
I went on down the drive.

But at the mouth of the lane I halted under the
pines and scanned the tower again.   All the loopholes, like dead eyes, stared at me vacantly.   The
wide window, halfway up the stronghold, was empty
too.   And then, ere I turned almost sadly away, a
sudden gust of air lapped the tower round; all the
ivy shook and twinkled; but no dear face looked out.

I moved onward, but my step was slow.

To be sure, the lady was not my mother.   My

mother was in her grave; and besides, the face I
had seen was that of a much younger woman—of a
girl, in fact. But for all that, the face was the dead
image of my mother's picture which used to hang in
our parlor. The cast of the head, the snowy brow,
the very eyes and nose and mouth, were my mother's
all over. Certainly, this was my day for seeing visions; but here indeed was a vison that touched me
more nearly than ten thousand ugly faces peering
from the roadside.

Trudging along beneath the pines, I turned this
business over in my mind. So far as I could judge,
it came to this: the girl's pat likeness to my mother
was either a mere, if marvelous, coincidence, or else
it betokened kinship. There was no other way
about it. Now, strange as it may seem, I was loath
to believe the latter alternative; for if the girl were
related to my mother, then that sporty little ancient
was my uncle, and he had been stuffing me with lies.
Nay, in this supposition the whole affair assumed a
mysterious, not to say sinister, complexion. Doubtless there was more behind, and what this might be
I had little stomach to discover. (You are to remember, please, that I was but a country lad, with
no very keen relish, at bottom, for the darkly ad-
venturous.)

All in all, I preferred to think that the resemblance was pure chance; though, to be sure, I hoped
my cousin, should I prove to have one, would take
after my mother as closely as the girl in the window.

Then I remembered that she would be Domini, or more likely Domini's elder sister: for little Cissy Carton, at least, had told the truth.

My train of thought was here derailed by the sudden dimming of the sun; and looking up through the trees, I beheld the whole western and southern skies overspread with cloud: a vast gray blanket, fringed with masses of sullen, ominous blue. A storm was brewing, even imminent; I must mend my pace if I hoped to make McGregor before it broke. Just then a puff of air fanned my cheek, and the trees all about me heaved a long sigh, as it were, and then fell still. There was rain in that whiff—I had smelt it; and knew now it was odds but I should get a good soaking, leg it as tight as I could.

By this, I had emerged from the belt of evergreens and was come to where the lane began to drop down and curve to the opposite hill. Now, I had by no means forgot the villainous face among the sumac, as any one of you may guess. Indeed, seeing I must pass the ambush again, my former fears returned upon me not one whit abated; so that (whether it show me a coward or no) I resolved to give the spot a comfortably wide berth. To do this, I would follow the lane to the top of its climb, whence I had looked back (as you remember), and then fetch a compass higher up the hill, striking the trail again below the sumac brake. This detour would cost me valuable minutes, per-

haps a wetting into the bargain; but I had no mind
to be reviewed by skulking presences, were they
never so harmless.

To make up for the time I should lose in thus
fighting shy of the sumac I now began to run.   I
remember to this hour how still the air was, and how
my footsteps, pelting down the stony lane, rang
through the woods.   All about me, under the trees,
the dusk seemed already to have gathered; the day
faded visibly as I ran, and the shadows of the underbrush on either side deepened into darkling
patches, like holes.

Then, once more, the lane brightened.   I was la-
boring uphill now (and fairly winded, too), and
the foliage, being less rank, admitted more of the
light.   I had all but gained the cope of the rise,
when I pulled up, deeming it safest not to expose
myself to the view of that long reach of road, but
merely to peer over the crest and then commence
my slant ascent.

But I never made the ascent, and this is why: as
I raised my head over the clump of bushes I was
using as a screen, I descried far down the lane the
figure of a man.   He was footing it my way at a
crisp pace and, as I could tell by his manner, was
wholly unaware of any danger.

Now, this wayfarer's presence changed my plan;
for, seeing him coming so confidently up the hill,
I could not but feel shame for my silly fears—as
who of you would not?   Accordingly, I decided to

stick to the lane; and so, jumping out of the bushes, put off boldly down the hill.

As we drew nearer—though still several hundred yards apart—I began to remark something familiar about the man. Not that I could see his face, for his head was bowed with the toil of the ascent; but only that the outline of his person hinted at one whom I had seen before.

On a sudden, then, as I was engrossed in this guesswork, and even laying a wager with myself that I should, upon a closer view, know the man well—on a sudden, I say, there fell a turn that stopped me like a blow, with all my heart pounding in my throat.

This is what I saw: I saw a crouched figure steal out upon the lane some feet behind the wayfarer and come creeping up. Then, as my tongue stuck to the roof of my mouth (though I tried my best to let out a shout), the intended victim, who, luckily, must have caught a warning sound, wheeled like lightning and smote the footpad down with a single smash of his fist.

At the same instant, from either margin of the lane, two more robbers leaped out to the assault. Quick as thought the stranger sprang aside and, with his back to a tree, faced both assailants. For a breathless interval not a move was made, except that the first robber lifted himself heavily to a sitting posture, leaning on one hand. Some parley then ensued by which, though I heard not a word, I

guessed that the highwaymen were urging their prey
to give in. But he bravely stood his ground, defiantly alert and evidently daring them to come on.

At this point it came over me strong that I should
indeed be a craven did I not lend a hand and balance in some measure the odds that stood so desperately against the lone stranger: for already the
first ruffian had risen to his feet. I was afraid, I
must own, and a coldness crawled up my spine;
nevertheless, I cried out at the top of my lungs and
bolted, full-speed, down the lane.

All four men jerked round and looked my way:
and then, in a trice, the attack was renewed, the
three footpads falling on, tooth and nail. But I
marveled, as I sped along, how gamely and agilely
my man defended himself (and this lent me courage) : his fists flashed in and out, and he seemed in
ten places at once; while, often enough, a robber's
head crooked back with the jolt he had got.

The closer I approached, the faster and more
furious waxed the fray. I understood now what
the highwaymen were up to: they wanted to get at
grips with their victim. More than once they came
to a clinch, but always he broke away, landing in the
act, head-rocking punches. He was making a stand,
and no mistake.

· I was now but twenty yards off, but no more heed
was being paid me than if I were a butterfly. Then
I caught a glimpse, momentary but clear, of the
stranger's face; it was pale as marble, with a trickle

of blood across one temple; and I recognized it. It was the face of the man who had surrendered his berth to me on my journey to Chicago! Quite at the same instant his eyes met mine: you should have seen how his grim look went all glad.

"Don't give up!" I cried, chock-full of fight now; and with the words I flung myself upon the shoulders of the nearest robber. Down we went on the hard stones in a tangle of arms and legs—and me on top. Crack! his sconce strikes the ground!. I felt the jar of it. His muscles all relaxed. I still spraddled his back, but he was lying quite stirless. Satisfied that he was knocked out of commission, I jumped to my feet and turned to mix it again!

But a thousand sudden stars, shooting from a central glory, met my vision: and I knew no more.

VI

AN APPARITION OF THE NIGHT

WHEN I came to life again, still half dazed, my first sensation was a hot thrumming in the back of my head; then I felt water slapping against my face; then I opened my eyes. On all sides around was inky darkness, and I wondered, vaguely, where I was. But at the same moment, almost, came a glare of vivid, bluish green, and, as the thunder crackled and roared, I saw before me an ascending road all streaked with rivulets, like glistening snakes, and on either side gleaming leaves, and slanting silver rods of rain: and, in a flash, memory returned, and I knew I was still lying in the lane where the robber's blow had felled me.

What I did first (if you will believe it) while yet I lay in the mud and water, was to clap my hand to my pocket for my purse. It was still there, and my money, too, as I could feel. This knowledge (though the strangeness of it didn't come home to me then—I was merely glad I wasn't robbed) greatly cheered my spirits, so that I struggled to my feet and stood for a moment, the rain streaming down my face, at a stick whether to push on to

McGregor or to seek a night's lodging at Jack's House.

Jack's House was closer by a good deal; besides, what with the knock I had got, and what with lying in the rain, for there was no telling how long, I was faint and wondrous dizzy. Jack's House it should be, then, and I set my face up the lane, with a heart vastly stouter than my legs. This was by far the worst plight I had ever been in; but, as I stumbled ahead in the dark, I murmured a prayer to our Lady and made sure that with her help I should win my way out.

The throbbing in my head, the further I trudged, seemed to grow in intensity; at times I felt my whole body, as it were, spinning round. When this occurred, I would stop till the fit was spent; for I knew that straying from my path was the one danger I must be on my guard against. Once in the bewildering tangle of the underbrush, with not a glimmer to guide me, I should have the devil's own time finding the lane again. You are to bear in mind that the night was black as forty cats, and that the electrical phase of the storm (though the rain continued to pelt) was mostly overblown. Only at long intervals could I discern my way by the glare of the heavens.

But luckily two circumstances kept me in the right track: the continual lift of the ground beneath my feet, and the thick foliage of the roadside. Time and again I would be warned of my first false steps by the wet leaves, like kindly hands, brushing against my face.

At last I gained the crest whence the lane began to dip and curve. This I could tell not only by the ground underfoot, but the lightning, at that moment, flashed far in the north and by its quivering gleam I saw the pine-wood hill above me (dark and daunting it looked, too) and below me, on my left, the gorge of treetops, glistening and shaking in the rain like monstrous heads impatient of the wetting.

From now on I held the road as unerringly as any horse. Sure, our Lady must have been piloting me, for the gloom was like solid, and my poor head was sadly a-whirl. Once, I remember, I stumbled and pitched prone on my face, and was like to have lain there the remainder of the night, so bootless a business it seemed, was the putting of one foot before the other. But a trickle of water got into my nose, which strangled me somewhat, so that I sat up and coughed and with the movement my brain cleared, and I again fought on.

After reaching the top of the second hill, where the pines were, I kept warning myself of the sharp turn the lane made just before it ran into Mr. Blythe's. There especially was I in danger of being sidetracked. But this bend I negotiated quite nicely—and mind, you couldn't see your hand before you—only to encounter, at the very end of all my labors, an obstacle that caused me to lose my bearings entirely. Here, then (and I don't blush to tell you my scare, either), is what befell.

You will recall that I said the lane under the pines was thickly overlaid with a carpet of needles, so that my footfalls were quite deadened. Well, for all I was drenched to the skin and though my head still sorely ached, I was shoving forward with a lighter heart, for I knew that warmth and shelter were now close at hand. I saw no light ahead indeed; but I remember saying to myself that the household must be retired to rest, and that a few round raps on the door would fetch them up. I was even then cudgeling my weary wits for some proper words of apology, when, with an astounding suddenness, the whole hilltop shook with a dazzle of light and a very avalanche of sound and I, my heart pounding in my throat, leaped back like a shying horse. Before me—I had all but trod upon it, as you would upon a snake—was the form of a man, hunched low and squatted like a toad. He was turned the opposite way, towards Jack's House; and luckily for me, for I believe if I had beheld his face too, in that first glare, my heart must have jumped clean out of my mouth!

But to see his face I had not long to wait. Hard upon the first flash of lightning succeeded a second (these were the last two bolts of the storm, worse luck!), and at the apparition that now met my eyes the hair of my head lifted in stark terror.

It was scarce more than a wink the light endured, but this is what I saw. Crooked back over one shoulder, a hatless head of long white locks, all matted and plastered by the rain; a pair of eyes that glowed like living coals; horribly sunken cheeks, and a beard like a prophet's. And yet, I don't think it was the face so much that chilled me through with fear as what this dread creature did. For no sooner had those fiery eyes beheld me than the mouth popped open prodigious wide in a' wild cackle of laughter—a weird, mirthless laughter that froze me where I stood. It was a hideous thing to hear there in the black night, but its ending was more hideous still; for the laugh rose in pitch higher and higher and then suddenly broke off in a piercing scream, as of anguish and despair, like a lost soul's.

Up to this I had felt rooted to the spot; but now the awful spell was snapt, and with that unearthly cry ringing in my ears, I turned tail and dashed headlong into the wood.

What happened next I might have expected, if I had had my wits about me. For I had not covered a dozen yards (as I judge) when I smashed into a pine, glanced spinning off, and rolled over and over upon the needles. By great good fortune I had not killed myself, only barked my knees and left shoulder; and after a stunned moment or two, I sat up and rubbed my bruises. My terror was now greatly abated—knocked out of me, you may say; still, as I sat there in the pitch dark, nursing my knees, I began to entertain the horrid suspicion, or rather fancy, that perhaps the maniac (for such I deemed him) was stealing up on me. I listened with all my ears: there was only the sighing swish of the rain through the pines, and the beating of my heart.

Then, by degrees, some horse-sense came back, and it dawned on me that if the old hobgoblin was invisible to my eyes, I at least was invisible to his: and this was a very comfortable reflection. Accordingly, I dismissed my recent rencounter (or tried to) and turned my attention to recovering the lane.

But here was a fix. The summit of the hill was wide and level; there was not another lightning flash that night; and, owing to my tumble, I had fairly lost all sense of direction. So that, to give you the upshot of this misadventure, I wandered clean abroad and having got off the hill (how, I cannot tell) and become involved in a perfect maze of climbings and descendings—and all in utterest darkness—decided at last, in sheer desperation, to cast myself down in the first likely spot my feet should touch.

But luckily, ere I must adopt this extremity, I spied through the night what appeared to be a lighted window. Sure enough, a lighted window it was; and presently I knocked on the door of what, for the darkness, I guessed was a log-cabin. Again and again I knocked, and then hammered loudly; but got no response.

It was plain how matters stood—the cabin was

empty: if I wanted shelter I must take it uninvited.
But, before I turned the knob, I deemed it the part
of prudence to have a look inside; so I stole to the
window and peered in.

It was a mean, foul-looking hole, low-raftered and
smoky. A fisher's hut, thinks I; but could spy no
tackle anywhere about, either on the ground or upon
the walls, which latter and the ceiling were decorated
mostly with cobwebs. As to the floor, it was of
planks, but it might just as well have been of earth,
for it was tramped all over with dried mud, and
filthy to a degree. A rough table stood in the midst
of the room, and upon it a gallon jug and a litter
of dirty cooking utensils. Some old clothes were
flung across the backs of a couple of chairs, and in
one corner was a mess of straw and blankets. Besides the chairs, were three or four pine boxes which,
though empty now, looked by their comparative
whiteness as if they had contained provisions. The
only really inviting feature of the whole cabin was
the fireplace; it was filled with a couple of great logs,
and the flames, tossing and leaping in the chimney,
shed a ruddy, dancing light over the squalid scene,
rendering it half cheerful and almost cozy.

But of man, woman, or child the cabin was void.
Whoever occupied it was now abroad; and as I had
no fancy to await his return, I pulled wide the door
and stoutly crossed the threshold.

The smell of kerosene, like a blow, hit me in the
face. The cabin reeked with it. You might have

cut it with a knife. So strong was it, indeed, as to be positively choking; and I hung at the open door, letting in the fresh air.

The cause I spied at once. Close to the front wall stood a can, but the whole contents of it had leaked out, soaking the base log and all that quarter of the floor. Well, the odor was disagreeable enough, but unless I preferred to bivouac in the drenched woods, I must brook it.

Bar this kerosene stink (to which, by and by, I grew accustomed) and a ladder in one corner sticking up through a black hole in the loft, little else was revealed by my entrance. At first, my eyes lighting on this ladder, I was in half a mind to climb it and explore the loft. (And would to God I had done so! I had thus put an early period to the whole tale of these tragic events). But I wasn't very keen just then for further investigation. If the owner of the cabin was above, he must be deaf or a wondrous sound sleeper; and if he desired an explanation of my intrusion he might get it in the morning—the fire was what my chilled flesh wanted now.

Without more bones, I dragged the largest of the boxes before the hearth, its open side fronting the flames, so that, lying in it, I might get the full benefit of the heat. Then, taking off my coat, I wrung it fairly free of water and hung it across one end of my bunk for a face shield. It was a pretty hard bed, I suppose, but I thought nothing of that, as you may imagine; the box was clean—about the cleanest thing in the room, the straw and blankets over in the corner, though I cast them a glance of consideration, being too begrimed to touch, let alone sleep upon. And indeed, as you are soon to hear, it was mighty lucky for me that I disturbed nothing more in the cabin.

Well, into the box I crawled, wet clothes and all; and, what with my dead weariness and the comfortable warmth, dropped off, I think, before you could count twenty.

VII

A PERILOUS NIGHT'S LODGING

I HAD made no guess as to the manner of my awaking; but if I had I should have missed it a mile: for here is what happened. (And I cannot tell you about it, even now, without a twitter at my heart.)

The first thing I became conscious of was a dream —I knew it was a dream: it was wheat-threshing time at home, and I was taking a spell on the feeder's stand. The roar of the separator was in my ears, and the crunching grind of the cylinder as the bundles disappeared. Then, suddenly as I fed in an uncut bundle, there was a terrific explosion (though uncut bundles are really no matter); machinery seemed to fly in every direction; and I awoke in my box, trembling to my toe-tips.

"Why not? You just take an' tell me why not, Bill Short! If I want to cook, you ain't the man to stop me!" This declaration was followed by an oath and a thwack on the top of the box that made my head rattle.

"Looky here, Blue Island," said another voice, "you can go and cook your fool head off. It don't

60

make no never-mind to me, only it ain't breakfus' yet.   But let me tell you this: if you're gonna bust that fryin' pan, you're gonna buy us another one outa your own money."

By this, I had come alive to the situation—the occupants of the cabin had returned.   And, though they were a trifle the worse for liquor—to judge by the row and the strong smell of whiskey—I was just on the point of revealing myself, when Blue Island's answer brought my heart to a standstill.

"Money!" cried he.   "You're the fine bird to be talkin' o' money, ain't you?   If it wasn't for you, we'd 'a' *had* money—money to burn, too. That kid had a hundred and two bucks in his jeans— fat a roll 's I ever lifted.   But you're moral, ain't you?   Yes, all of a sudden moral, an' I don't get it.   But your moralness don't go with me, Bill Short. Don't I know you cooled 'n ole paper woman just to cop her pennies?"

The other laughed.

"That's all right, Blue I—that talk don't hurt me none, I guess.   So long's you don't bust that fryin' pan, I should worry."

"Oh, damn your fryin' pan!" rapped out Blue Island.   "That's for your fryin' pan!"   And he sailed the skillet clean across the room; I heard it ring against the logs and clatter to the floor.

"Easy there, Blue," soothed the other voice. "Old Fiddles ain't done nothin' to you.   An inch lower and you'd of took him square on the bean.

You got to be careful. Old Fiddles is a peaceable yegg. He ain't lookin' for trouble—not now he ain't, anyhow."

"Oh, I wouldn't hurt Fiddles," said Blue Island quickly. "Not for nothin' I wouldn't. He's a harmless ole bar-fly. He wouldn't scratch a pimple. All he wants is a bellyful o' booze, an' he's satisfied. He ain't worth the powder to blow him to Bride-well. But I kinda like him just the same."

And with these words down he plumps upon my box. I saw the slats warp inward where he sat, and all over the skin of my body puckered.

For look at my fix. Here was I, trapped in this den of brigands, and a hundred to one I should be detected any moment. That they were the very rogues who had floored me in the lane I made no doubt: the man called Blue Island had blabbed as much. Why they hadn't robbed me then I did not try to bottom; but it was a cinch, if they caught me now, they wouldn't be so forbearing a second time. I was in a tight place, and don't you forget it!

It was extraordinary they hadn't smelt a rat thus far; but what with the liquor, I suppose, and the unkempt condition of the cabin (to which they were accustomed) it had not crossed their minds to re-mark the position of my box. Besides, my coat, which they must have spied, in drying had slipped from the box and now lay in a pile before my face. With infinite care, as the one knave above me sat and talked, I drew it noiselessly against my breast.

For a space, however, after Blue Island had taken this ticklish seat of his—ticklish to me—there fell a silence. I durst hardly breathe, the cabin was so still; but more loud than breathing was the beating of my heart, which seemed to bounce around in my chest like a rubber ball, and to set the whole box quaking. Half a minute, maybe, passed in this manner, and then itches began to break out all over my body, till it was almost an agony to lie still. But I clenched my teeth and held on, staring into the red embers of the fire. Then, suddenly, a prolonged snore sounded across the room, and my heart gave a greater leap than ever; but in hope this time, for I saw in the snore the manner of my escape. But next moment my hope was dashed: I heard the gurgle of a man drinking, and then a jug or bottle clapped down upon the table.

"Phew! Ratgut, that's what that is! But it's likker anyhow. Take a pull, Blue, old top, and don't set there like you lost your best gal."

The ruffian above me cursed his luck.

"I wisht I was ole Fiddles, I swear I do," said he enviously. "Look at him. Just look at him. Stewed and snoozin' and happy. He's happy anywheres, Fiddles is, s'long's he's got likker. But I ain't. I ain't built that way. I wisht I was back in little ole Chi, that's what I wish. I tell you what, Bill Short, I don't like this here country stuff; and what's more, I don't like this job—no way you take it, I don't. When a man can't cop a wad that's

same as throwed at him, then it's time to pull stakes,
I say."

At this Bill Short gave a prodigious yawn.

"Blue Island," says he, sleepily, "you'll never
learn nothin', you won't.   Orders is orders, buddy.
And you can bet your bottom dollar Reed ain't the
man to trifle with."

"Reed be hanged!" cries Blue Island.   "I know
Reed, a' right, a' right.   I know that bird from way
back.   He'd squeal on the whole jingbang, in a second he would, just to save his own stinkin' hide—
I know Reed.   An' looky here, Short"—he smote
the box such a blow that I wondered his fist didn't
come through the wood—"here's another thing I
don't like—goin' to that town to-night!"

"Oh, dry up," growled the other.   "Didn't we
have to get grub an' likker?"

For answer, Blue Island, who had a monstrous
foul tongue, called his companion a name you would
blush to hear.

"Yes, an' I mean it, too," he went on.   "Why,
you ain't got the caution of a cockroach, Short!   An'
you bossin' this job!   I'm supprised at you, I declare I am.   S'pose that kid had 'a' got back an'
told the sheriff—it'd 'a' been a warm time for us.
An' ba-lieve me, it's gonna be a warm time for us
still, don't you forgit it, all becuz o' that same kid.
I wanted to plug him for good; it'd 'a' been smooth
as Mich'gan Av'noo then.   But not you.   No, orders is orders, you says.   You're the brains o' this

here little party, ain't you?"   He spat fiercely on
the floor.   "Brains!   You got about as much brains
as a boiled chicken!"

Here he paused in his tirade; and I, if I had been
dismayed before, now fairly wilted through sheer
terror.   For I saw that in the lane it had been the
toss of a penny whether I should die, and that, even
now, my life in this brute's hands wasn't worth a
rusty nail.

"Snoozin', eh?" he muttered, after a bit.   "Well,
snooze away, Bill Short.   Wakin' or sleepin', you're
about the same.   You couldn't run a kinnygarden,
you couldn't.   Lemme tell you right here, I'm
through.   This here's the last job I'm on with you.
I'm through, see, through!"   Whereupon he gets
to his feet and lurches across the room.

Now was the crisis of my peril (so I thought),
for I knew that if he took to roving about the cabin,
sure as death he would stumble on me: the suspense
was like an iron band around my chest, so that
breathing was a pain.

But presently, returning to the box, he resumed
his seat.   He had risen to fetch the jug, for now
I heard the liquor bubble in it as he drank; and then,
with a smack of relish, he jounced it down upon the
box beside him.

Followed then a long interval of silence, broken
only by the popping of the firelogs and the intermit-
tent snoring of the two slumbering crooks.   My
hope of escape rested now in Blue Island's sleeping

too; and you may take my word for it that I had every sense stretched tight upon the listen.

Ten minutes, perhaps, crawled by; and yet Blue Island gave no sign of turning in. Not a move did he make, at least that I could detect; and indeed were it not for the sag in the boards above me, I had almost believed he had stealthily quitted the cabin.

At length, however, it dawned on me that maybe he had dropped off where he sat. This seemed likely enough, for a man can sleep without snoring; and so, wary as a weasel, I twisted my body about till I was able to raise my eyes over the edge of the box. I gulped in dismay: one inch from my nose was the black butt of a big revolver sticking out of the desperado's tail pocket. You may fancy how pleasant I felt!

The man himself was bent forward, as though with his chin in his hands; and at his side was the jug of liquor. But whether he waked or slept was more than I could read.

For a minute, maybe, I sat there, leaning on one hand, my eyes fixed on the man's hunched shoulders and my ears straining for a snore. Any one of you may guess what a delicate business it was—nay, desperate is the better word. But I must tell you this: somehow or other, now that I had begun to act, all my fear—the kind that makes you tremble and bungle things—had left me. Afraid I was still, you can bet I was; but I was cool, too, as cool as any of you right now, and steady in every nerve.

Well, as I say, about sixty seconds might have been ticked off by a clock, and then, judging Blue Island indeed asleep, I began cautiously to edge myself clear of the box.   Just when I had got out and was rising to my knees, Blue Island lets off a snorting kind of grunt and flings out his right hand for the jug.   Quick as a lizard, down I pop on my belly, and at the same instant, bang! the jug hits the floor and the liquor begins to gurgle out.

Still as still, I lay and listened; but the man never budged.   And all the while the whiskey continued to spout with a kind of jerky, choking sound, to my ears as loud as a cataract.   Then, all at once, I felt an icy dampness about my knees, and screwing my head back, saw the liquor stealing under my legs and out upon the hearthstones, where it spread in flat shiny pools, red as the fire they mirrored.   In a flash, then, the realization of a new danger struck me all of a heap: if the alcohol—for that's mainly what it was—should reach those living embers, it was all up with my escape.

This dire prospect, as I say, unmanned me, or nearly so; but with a great effort I got a purchase on myself, and resolved to try it for the door.   It was now or never.

Softly I rose to my feet and tiptoed around the box.   But six or seven steps lay between me and

safety; if my luck only held out—crack! like a gun-
shot a board creaked under my right foot. I halted,
balancing myself on my toes, both arms stretched
out, and my heart going like a sledge. With the tail
of my eye I stole a glance at Blue Island: he hadn't
stirred a peg but sat bunched forward on the box,
his head on his knees and his arms dangling: dead
to the world, if ever a man was.

At the table, which I had to pass, slept another
bandit (Bill Short, I supposed), the upper part of
him all sprawled out among half a score of pack-
ages. And here I did a thing which for pure nerve
quite surprised even myself: out of his very grasp
(you might almost say) I took half a stick of
bologna: in spite of all my peril, my mouth watered
at sight of that good sausage, for I was as hungry
as a harvest hand.

Then, having got so far without mishap, I plucked
up fresh heart, and renewed my sneaking. And
now all went towardly; the flooring sounded no
alarms, and the brigands slept like logs. But at
the very door (as I saw) there was like to be dis-
aster. Here the man called Fiddles lolled, or rather
hung like old clothes, on a chair; and though I had
no special fear of his awaking (for be was drunk as
an owl), yet his legs were lying in such wise that I
must step over them to reach the door.

Well, there was nothing for it now; I must go on.
As I gingerly thrust one foot across his knees, he
rolled his head around, so that I saw his face: all

blotched and boozy it was, with a dirty bandage about one temple. Then, as I hesitated, straddling his shins, "Don't go," he said (as distinctly as I am telling you now), "don't go. Wait a minute." You may imagine what a turn he gave me!

But by this, I had the door ajar, and felt the cool air upon my cheek. Then, ere I slipped out, I took one last look around. Though the fire had somewhat fallen, the room was still faintly ruddy, with dark patches in the corners. Bar the snoring, everything was silent as the tomb, and except for the flames and the wavering shadows, there wasn't a stir. Beyond the bowed shoulders of Blue Island I could see the liquor shining on the hearth like molten gold; and then, even as I looked, a quivering blue flame leaped out upon it and began to spread; and I knew I had escaped not a moment too soon.

VIII

THE MADMAN AGAIN : AND OTHER MATTERS OF INTEREST

WELL, but maybe you think I wasn't glad to be quit of that cabin—glad's no word for it! Thankful I was, too, though but a green, heedless lad; and there in the black night my heart went up to God for his care of me, without whom, as the Bible says, even a sparrow doesn't fall.

My cue now was to put as great a distance as possible between me and my enemies; and so, striking out at random, after much wandering I spied, at length, through the trees a vast stretch, black as ink and glittering with the starlight. It was the river, sure enough; and having climbed through a barbed-wire fence, I came down on a railroad track that ran along the bank. I was out of the woods at last.

Now, thinks I, a crack at this sausage, and then to McGregor. But I had no more than begun to cast my eye around for a place to sit down, when my gaze was caught by a bonfire, burning brightly

high up on a cliff about half a mile or more down
the river. What this might be I wondered, but
hadn't the shadow of a guess. Campers were out
of the question, for even campers at this wee hour
were snuggled in their blankets; and besides, the location of the fire was scarce a likely spot to pitch
a tent. For (as I could plainly see) the fire was
not clear on top of the cliff, but upon a ledge just
below the brow: a giddy eyry, sure enough, for
pleasure-seekers, as the huge rock, like a giant shoulder, beetled out almost over the railroad—a plumb
drop of hundreds of feet.

Suddenly, then, as I was yet looking, a figure pops
out on the ledge like a gnome in a fairy-tale; and
snatching up a burning brand, runs back and forth,
waving it in circles over his head, like a signal. You
may fancy my surprise when I tell you that this figure was a man with a long white beard: you have
it, the very lunatic I had fled from in the lane! Of
this I was dead sure, for the flames illuminated the
whole upper face of the cliff and even the trees
upon the brink. I tell you, it was a weird spectacle,
that fire away up there on the black bluff, and the
old warlock flitting about it with his torch, and fath-
oms below, the mighty river sliding darkly, and for
leagues around the solemn hush that ushers in the
dawn. . . . I jumped—a fish had flipped from
the water, feeding.

And now, all at once, I heard other sounds: at
first, a solitary piercing shriek out of the hills, cleav-

ing the night like a rocket; then cries of men, wild and panicky, as in mortal fright. For five minutes, perhaps, the incoherent clamor continued; and then by degrees the line of treetops at the head of the glen above me began to be etched against a faint glow of rose. Presently the glow deepened and broadened: a great vermilion flare against the sky. Then, upon a sudden, the wide brightness seemed to narrow inward, and next moment a pillar of flames and sparks towered fiercely out of the trees.

But this fire was no mystery like the one on the ledge: I knew right off what it meant—the cabin where I had slept was ablaze, and the bandits, like so many wildcats, were being burnt out of their lair.

It was not long the conflagration lasted, and the leaping yellow column sank below the treetops almost as quickly as it had mounted. The shouting, too, died away, and presently only a stillness and a dim glimmering remained. And the stars, as I was surprised to note, even they had most of them disappeared; the ones that were left looked all shrunken, and glittered but feebly: and turning, I saw the dawn welling up, olive green, in the clear eastern sky, and the day-star, like a jewel, throbbing in the midst of it.

At this first peep of morn the fire on the cliff had likewise subsided; for when next I looked I could descry no one, only a wisp of smoke trailing upward against the rock.

Well, as I ate my breakfast, all the sky-line over yonder along the Wisconsin bluffs flushed up very prettily. And when the sun rose, I grew so warm and comfortable I fell into a drowse. It must have been more than forty winks, for when I opened my eyes again, the sun was away up in the sky, and the mist had vanished from the river. Its broad surface was no longer smooth, but tumbled into a million glancing waves, bright as quicksilver, by a gentle upstream breeze. But it was a lonesome scene; bar three bobbing skiffs far up in the bend—clammers, doubtless—I was the only bit of humanity in sight. Just below the skiffs was what I now saw to be the mouth of another river: in the twilight of the dawn I had mistaken it for backwater. It was a river, sure enough (the Wisconsin, I guessed), for now I could make out, a mile or more above the confluence and behind some low islands, the red beams of a bridge. I was to know more of that bridge, as you shall hear; and if then I could have foreseen events, it is likely I had strained my eyes out.

But of the real future I had no inkling; indeed, by my way of it, nightfall should see me on the train, bound for Chicago, having first discharged my duty of reporting the presence in the neighborhood of highwaymen and their assault in the lane. For, while my several adventures had been stirring enough, the sum of them, too, spelling out mystery, as to the first I frankly owned I had my fill of perils and alarms, and for the second I felt I had no call to busy myself in a matter that didn't concern me. A clout on the head was the whole of my grievance against the robbers; they hadn't touched a penny of my money; and, for all there was some foul work behind their strange forbearance (as the conversation in the cabin clearly indicated), it was work I should do well not to meddle in.

For my own part, indeed, the object of my journey to McGregor had been attained; at least I knew now that my uncle must be the other Mr. Clement Blythe, and maybe by the time I got back to Chicago he would be there.

You may wonder I could turn my back thus stolidly upon a business that had about it so many points calculated to prick my curiosity; and, in truth, I must confess there were two such circumstances that gave me a little pause. The girl's face at the window of Jack's House still stuck in my mind, although, as I have already stated, it was long odds but her likeness to my mother meant nothing in the way of kinship. And as to my Pullman friend, I could shake off neither the misgiving that his had been a far worse fate than mine, nor the scruple that it was up to me, even yet, somehow to lend him a helping hand. Still, girl and man together, however doggedly they tracked my thoughts, could not overtake my desire to hasten back to Chicago, find my uncle, and begin my grand new way of life.

Well, ere I set out for McGregor, thinks I, I'll jump into the river and freshen up a bit.

Owing to the strong current, I had to swim like a steamboat. Even then I could only keep abreast of my clothes; and when I struck back for shore I found I had been sheered out further than I thought. Now, the result of this was not that I had a fight for my life and a narrow escape from a watery grave and suchlike (as you might expect, and as I might very easily weave into this dull chapter were I just pulling a long-bow and not recording facts) ; but as I swam on my side, I espied, some hundred yards downstream, a very trim-looking, green-and-white boathouse, freshly painted. Rather an anticlimax, you will say; but, if I hadn't seen that boathouse, this book had never been written. (Which doesn't mend matters much at that, maybe.)

Right off, it jumped into my head to notify the folk who owned the boathouse of all that had happened. Like enough, they were people of substance and well known in these parts; with the magistrates in McGregor their influence would go a longer way than my mere statement; and dwelling so close to the scene of the crime, they would make a point, for their own sakes, of seeing that the countryside was well scoured for the brigands. Last of all, I should probably get a ride back to town.

Having thus made up my mind, I hurriedly donned my clothes and struck out down the track for the boathouse.

This structure, on a nearer view, was larger than
I had supposed; indeed, to judge by its size, it
housed a craft of goodly proportions—maybe one
of those big motor launches, I thought. A three-
foot dock girdled the whole of it, and a stair with
bannisters led down the embankment to a padlocked
door.

But the spot seemed deserted just at present, so
I turned and walked up through the trees along a
well-beaten path which, I supposed, led to the dwelling. The path rose very gently, the whole place
(as I had remarked from the railroad) being a wide
glen scooped out of the bluffs; but the rankness of
the vegetation was such that you wouldn't guess
there was a human habitation for a mile around.

Up this glen I had pushed on for forty or fifty
yards when, the path deflecting suddenly to the right,
I spied, beyond the mouth of the green alley, the
front door of a brown bungalow, and before it a
slice of sun-flecked lawn with white flags running
up to the very steps of the veranda. It was not the
kind of house I expected to find, for it was evidently
the quarters of some family who were out here just
for the season—summering, as we say. This was
rather disappointing, and for a moment or so I
halted, at a doubt what to do.

But, during that short pause, an incident befell
that knocked my immediate object into a cocked hat:
further up the path, almost at the rim of the open

lawn, a man cautiously thrust his head and shoulders out of the bushes and peered toward the bungalow. On me the sight of him burst like a thunderclap; for it was the head and shoulders of Mr. Clarence F. Carver!

IX

THE BUNGALOW IN THE GLEN

YOUR watch would have ticked five seconds, maybe, while I stuck in my tracks, gaping like a fool in sheer wonderment. If the man had but turned his head he certainly would have caught me; but he continued to gaze, for all the world as if he were spying on the bungalow and its occupants. Then, at last, my sense of danger (which, you will own, my recent hazards had rendered canny enough) jogged me hard, and I skipped behind the foliage.

But you may guess I peeked out again pretty quick. There was Carver, still eyeing the bungalow; so far as I could observe he hadn't moved a hair, forward or backward. Half a minute passed, he studying the bungalow and I studying him.

Studying is the word, for while my eyes rested on his slim shoulders and gray-capped head, I was racking my brains for some coupler that would yoke him up with last night's doings, and that would, above all, explain his lurking here. But I had nothing to go on, bar only my dislike of the man and my suspicion (pretty thin, on second thoughts) born of the saloon incident. After all, for what I knew,

78

Carver himself might live in the bungalow and merely be playing now at hide-and-seek with his children: though this too was pretty thin.

Well, about thirty seconds, as I say, stole by, and I was more hopelessly muddled than ever, but watching like a lynx. Then, of a sudden, a fresh turn was given the situation, a turn even more startling than the appearance of Carver. The front door of the bungalow was opened—and you might have knocked me over with a feather. Forth into the summer sunshine, a cigar between his teeth and a fishing-rod in his hand, briskly strode Mr. Gordon Crowninshield!

Like a rat at his hole, Carver vanished; and myself like a second rat. I don't know to this day what impulse prompted me to whip back into the bushes; perhaps it was a kind of shame I had—and something of fear, too—of being caught at playing the same game as Carver: if he was spying so was I. For all that, directly my eyes lit on Mr. Crowninshield, I knew he was the man to inform of the robbery; for, though he was no native, he would see justice done. But, to show you how far up in the air I was, I didn't stir a finger; only flinched under cover, like the veriest crook, and let Mr. Crowninshield go by. In a minute or so you will hear what a dunce I was; but if you listen clean to the end of the tale you will see that I was pretty lucky, too.

Well, Mr. Crowninshield swung on past, as I say: so near me that the white smoke of his cigar came drifting through the leaves just above my eyes. When his footfalls died away, I peeped out to see what Carver was up to. But I didn't poke my head clear into the open, and it's mighty good I didn't, for there was Carver, half out in the path, looking my way and as alert as a squirrel.

But pretty soon he seems satisfied that the coast is clear. Quick as a wink he whisks round, glides up to the veranda, tiptoes up the steps, and tries the door, putting his weight against it, carefully, to deaden the sound. But it's no go, and next moment he flits to the window on the right; peers in, softly thrusts up the screen and, while I yet crouched there with mouth agape, presto! he's inside.

But I found my legs at last and my wits too (or, so I thought). I concluded now, what I had guessed all along, that Carver was indeed a knave and a rather cheap one at that—a common housebreaker. No sooner had he disappeared from the veranda than I had made up my mind—a foolish resolve—to sneak up on him, take him red-handed, and give the alarm. There was little credit in the act for me, for I figured, you may be sure, on running scarcely any risk whatever; all I proposed to do was to reach the window, slam down the screen, and yell like bloody murder. In two shakes the whole bungalow would be about Carver's ears.

Of course I had sense enough not to go straight up the flags to the front door, for I knew he would have his weather-eye open for Mr. Crowninshield's return. So, keeping under cover, I stole along the edge of the lawn to a point just opposite the corner of the house, where, as I thought, I couldn't be seen from the room he was in. On this side of the bungalow, however, was another window which likely gave into the same room; and this stumped me for a moment. But here, luckily, a strip of trumpet-vine, climbing to the roof, would be a sort of shield and so, taking my chances, I slipped across the grass, noiselessly mounted the balustrade and stood with a fluttering heart on the veranda itself.

Within was dead silence.

Then came the thought that maybe Carver was looting some other room: in which case it would be folly for me to try and trap him in this one. Accordingly, instead of going round to the open screen, I got down on all fours and crept to the nearer window. Very cautiously I raised my head, just edging my left eye above the sill. The burglar was at his work.

But pretty queer work it was, it struck me right off; so that my curiosity got the better of me and kept my face glued to the sill. Carver was lifting out, one after another, the three framed pictures that hung against the opposite wall and prying behind them. Then, rapid as a mesmerist's passes, his hands flew over the whole partition as high as you could reach, but pressing every foot of it too.

But nothing seemed to come of these strange manœuvres, and the man stepped back, flinging a

glance out the front window. I ducked, you bet;
for I knew he would be keeping an eye on my window too.

When next I looked, he was slewing out the desk
(which stood against the same wall) and a second
after, down he pops behind it, feeling of the plaster-
ing again, I guessed. But presently he gets up,
nicely slides the desk back, and then, as though he
remarked it for the first time, makes a sudden lunge
for the telephone.

I, of course, had seen it all along, and was a little
surprised to find a telephone away out here in the
woods. It wasn't a clumsy, double-boxed affair,
either, like the one in Mr. Peter's store back home,
but the modern nickel-plated kind you can pick up.
Carver lost no time in picking it up, I tell you: he
snatched the receiver off the hook as if his life depended on it. The man must be crazy, I was thinking, to go talking through a telephone; but that's
just what he didn't do. He left the instrument un-
hung and sat himself down in the desk chair.

Quickly, then, he ran through the drawers, finger-
ing every book and paper there, but, as I noticed,
at pains to replace each one. And every now and
again during this search, he cocked his head and
gave ear. By this, I had begun to marvel greatly
that he did not try to rifle the small safe that stood
on the floor beside the desk. If money was what
he was after, it would be in the safe: that was cer-

tain. For all his cleverness, it seemed to me, as a professional burglar Carver was rather a poor hand.

But next moment, as though he had read my mind, off the chair he slips and is squatted on one knee before the safe, his ear laid close to the steel knob. I could see his hands plainly: he had no tool of any kind; merely kept his finger-tips just touching the safe door, and slowly turned the knob: and all of a sudden the door was wide, and Carver and I were peering within.

And now comes the part that clean amazed me. Straightway Carver draws out a little compartment just chock-full of banknotes. Big notes they were, too—the yellow kind: I saw them, for Carver counted the whole packet, flipping the edges against his thumb. But just as I imagined he was going to pocket the swag (as he would call it), what does he do but put the whole of it back and continue his mysterious hunt!

To say that I was puzzled is putting it mild: I think I was almost staggered; so that by now I must have had all my head above the sill, staring openly into the room. Luckily for me, though, Carver was so desperately intent upon his purpose that he himself got off his guard and didn't keep a watch; had he but looked around, my goose had probably been cooked right there. But, as it happened, I wasn't observed; and stuck at my post, in a fool's security, all eyes and no brains. And yet, it came upon me,

too, even then, that these were singular thieves and
highwaymen hereabouts who sought other spoil than
gold: but what this new kind of spoil might be was
more than I could fathom.

Then, all at once, Carver's swift fingers came to
a standstill—so suddenly it made me blink: he half
rose to his feet, all ears, as I could see. For a
breath or two he stayed that way; then down he
dropped to the safe, and, while I was yet getting my
wits together, he had all things restored and the
safe locked and was thrusting one leg through the
front window.

It was then I woke to action.

"A thief!" I roared. "Stop him!" and went
tearing around the corner of the veranda.

Carver had disappeared.

So quick was his vanishing it brought me up dead,
like a stone wall. While you might count a slow
three I gazed round, plumb bewildered. Then it
burst upon me he must be hiding in the room, and
at the thought I wheeled and thrust my head through
the window.

A heavy hand fell on my shoulder. "Oh, ho!
I've got you, have I!"

Instinctively, like a trapped cat, I leaped away;
but that steel grasp plucked me back, knocking my
head against the window sash.

"No use, my young Johnny, no use," warned a
large person, with side whiskers, whose expression
of stolid triumph already told me I should have the

deuce to pay to square myself.   "Better step in here
now, nice and quiet."

Though the merest ass must have seen I wasn't
the culprit, I had sense enough not to fly off the handle with my captor, but to try and keep calm and
show him his mistake.

"Wait a minute," said I, coolly.   "You haven't
got the thief."

"Oh, haven't I!" says he, lifting his eyebrows and
grinning.   "Maybe I haven't got both, but I've got
one."

This speech, for all my effort at composure, put
me a little out of patience.

"Why, look here!" I cried, "didn't you hear me
give the alarm?   Didn't you hear me yell, 'Thief!
Stop him'?"

"To be sure," says the fat-headed gump.   "And
a very cute trick it was, too."

Then I recollected that Carver, all the while, was
probably in the room, listening to this farce; and
the thought made me half frantic.

"For God's sake, man," I pleaded, "don't be a
fool!   The thief's right in that room.   I'm willing
to bet you he is.   I scared him back when I
shouted!"

But the big oaf kept grinning his assurance.

"Like enough," says he.   "Like enough he's here.
He'll step out soon and hand me his card and ask
the favor of being jailed."   Then the fellow's face
suddenly set hard.   "Come, we've had enough of

this. You can say your say to the judge—if they have judges out here in this howling wilderness. Step in here now, or I'll drag you in, you thief!"

But all in a breath, what with my chagrin at the man's cruel stupidity and my overwhelming sense of his rank injustice, I whipped my head around and buried my teeth deep in his hand.

One screech of pain he shrilled, and as I sprang away I felt his blood, warm as tea, within my mouth.

Whether he pursued me, I am not certain; I only know that I fled that bungalow like one possessed. And as I ran, his scream was in my heart, and the blood that was bubbling on my lips trickled down upon my chin, and a shuddering came over me, and a cold sweat broke upon my brow: for I felt I had done an awful thing.

X

I WITNESS A QUEER SCENE AND MAKE A DECISION

SHAKEN as I was with my fit of savagery, I paid scant heed to direction, but plunged through the cracking brush, driven onward not less by horror of my deed than by dread of my pursuer. And yet, with the alarm of it all, I had had wit enough not to cut straight down the flags (for I had thus offered a clear shot), but to dodge round the house and dart for the shelter of the woods.

On through the clinging thicket I staved, stumbling, lurching, floundering, falling and picking myself up again, still smashing on, till at length my heaving breast felt on the point of bursting, and I flung myself down by a moss-covered log, gasping for air.

I must not have been pursued, for I lay there a good fifteen minutes at least, and all the while heard nothing but the quick thumping of my heart. This gradually slowed to normal; then, getting up, once more I put off for McGregor. I was still in the glen, but I considered it safer, ere I ascended the bluffs, to retire farther from the river. By and by I began to observe that the ground under my feet, instead of lifting (as it should be doing, for I must now be come pretty near to the top of the glen), was falling perceptibly away. Marveling not a little at this but pushing ahead all the same, I presently brought up before a kind of pocket, rank with a mass of oily weeds and surrounded, except for my side, with a towering concave slope. I had reached the head of the glen at last.

It was now my business to take to the hills, and without a moment's hesitation plump across this pool of greenery I started. But at my second step I sank above my ankle in mud, and when I tried to pluck my foot free, the mire clung to it like a living clutch. Indeed, as it was, I just made out to struggle loose; it was mighty lucky for me, I tell you, that my other foot rested on a log.

I knew now what I had run into, even before I took a long spar and poked apart the weeds and trailers. It was a quagmire or black bog, like the one at the south end of old man Hooker's timber down home which we called the Devil's Hole. I tell you the cold sweat started when I probed through the leaves and saw that slimy surface pimpled over with air bubbles! Then, just to test it, I pitched out a chunk of rotten limb. It was as I expected: no sooner had the limb struck the quag, which quaked all over and then wrinkled up like a loathsome skin, than it began to draw out of sight— not as in ordinary marsh but quickly, as though the deadly morass, like some live monster, were sucking

a victim into its maw.   I turned away in a kind of
nausea : you are to remember that I had escaped the
fate of that bit of wood by the skin of my teeth.

Well, after this encounter, you may be sure I got
up on high ground as fast as my legs could carry me.

Having followed the line of bluffs for a half mile
or more, I thought I would go out to the brink and
steal my first look below; if nobody was in sight I
would take to the railroad track.   But if I had
hoped to see the railroad track I was certainly disappointed; all beneath me were sloping treetops, like
a falling carpet, and the river.   This bluff must
have been tremendously high, for the river didn't
look to be much wider than our Meramec and the
Wisconsin hills over against me seemed to have
drawn a good deal closer.   Northward the whole
country stretched away flat as a table, with a number of sloughs, or side channels, weaving like silver
braids through the dusky green of the bottom timber.   A large, sweeping view it was, and came very
grateful after the sweating toil of fighting my way
through the thick brush.   And what, doubtless,
added to the pleasingness of the scene was the clar-
ity of the air and the deep sky, like a calm blue sea,
with a couple of fat clouds floating in it, soft as
pillows.

· Well, I was sitting there on a rock, drinking in all
this and resting up a bit, when suddenly, away down
below there, a milk-white motor launch slides out
from the trees and heads upstream.   It hadn't come

home to me how high I was above the water till I spied that launch. The whole river seemed all at once to sink lower; and the launch itself looked like a toy boat I once got for my birthday and sailed on the duck pond. And yet it must have been a big launch, too, for the two silver streaks of cloven water were plainly visible.

Now, at first, I didn't pay very much thought to that launch, except, as I say, to marvel at the height it helped me to realize, and except, too, to understand that the coast wasn't clear below. But, after a minute, I saw it make a sharp swerve inshore and disappear under the trees. Then it came over me, quick as winking, that the launch was Mr. Crowninshield's and that, ten to one, he had caught a glimpse of me from the river and was bent on heading me off. My guess, as you shall see directly, didn't quite hit the mark; but it was near enough to set me moving.

I wasn't very anxious, though, for it seemed to me it would go hard indeed but I could slip by one or two pursuers in all this desert of trees and rocks and bushes. So I just hit up a lively gait, kept my eyes about me, and every now and again paused to listen. My plan was to withdraw a hundred yards or so from the brink of the bluff and then strike north again.

For about ten minutes all went well: I saw no one, nor heard the least untoward sound—though, as to the matter of hearing, on account of a fresh-sprung breeze that kept all the foliage astir, it became increasingly difficult to detect anyone speaking or walking.

After crossing two or three ravines, all rocks and briars, I began to think myself a fool for taking such an arduous course, when perhaps the man in the launch hadn't been Mr. Crowninshield at all. Accordingly, in the bed of the next ravine I decided to steal down toward the river and see what was what; for, once on that railroad track, and nobody in sight, I promised myself to leg it to beat the Dutch.

I was making my way down this ravine as sly and watchful as a mink (and a picture of a place it was, all moss-clad rock and sleeping pools like mirrors) when, coming to a sharp turn and peeping round the corner, I saw, just at my feet, a sheer drop of perhaps two rods, and, beyond, a great broadening of the ravine into a thinly wooded glade, and away down at the end of it a pantomime that first dismayed and then set me gawking.

For there were Mr. Blythe and Mr. Crowninshield, as plain as my two hands, facing each other in earnest speech; though never a word reached me, owing to the rustle of the trees. My first impulse, as I say, was to hustle back and fetch around them, as I might easily have done; but all of a sudden Mr. Crowninshield makes a vehement scornful gesture, as though dismissing not only the topic of their talk but Mr. Blythe too, and turns on his heel.

Upon this what does Blythe do but grasp the spurning hand and, plumping down on his knees, begin to plead for dear life. I was out of earshot, as I say, but I had a full view of Mr. Blythe's face, and even at that distance I could mark the piteous look of it. If ever a man implored mercy that man was Mr. Blythe; if ever there was a picture of abject, crawling servility and palsied terror that picture was before my eyes. The old man's hat had fallen to the ground, his white hairs blowing in the breeze; his uplifted face was ashen; and the one beseeching hand (with the other he clung to Crowninshield) shook like an aspen.

For a little Mr. Crowninshield seemed to hesitate, then he whipped about and rapped out something, straight as a gun, to Mr. Blythe. Whereupon the old man threw up his right arm, to a dot as if he were taking an oath. Mr. Crowninshield nodded and put out his hand, and Mr. Blythe, seizing it in a transport of joy, jumped to his feet and began pawing his thankfulness all over Mr. Crowninshield. Both, apparently, were satisfied, and in this frame of mind they locked arms and went on down toward the river.

Well, here was a funny business, as good as a page out of a story-book; and I leaned back against the rock, clean graveled. In fact, all my adventures thus far seemed to possess neither head nor tail, and I have to laugh now, seeing the simple pattern these crazy pieces made, at my extreme perplexity. You are to think I could only guess a tie of the various scenes I had witnessed. But there was one point, even then, common to them all, and this should have soothed the itch of my curiosity: every incident had been outside my own contriving; I was a mere looker-on; and the few knocks I had got were such as a man might take who was bowled over by the belt of a thrasher. There was something going on in these hills, something even crookeder than was devised by a nest of bandits: of so much I made sure. I had turned into Queer Street: that was certain, and the least to be said. But—and here's the cold water—I had nothing to do with it; the whole af-fair was quite apart from my interests. I knew which side my bread was buttered on, you bet; and this meant my getting to Chicago as fast as steam might carry me.

And yet, there was my Pullman friend . . . and yet, there was the girl at the window of Jack's House. I hope you will not think me a feather-head for having so often made and unmade my mind. But it's my opinion you too would have wavered, even as I did, had you seen Mr. Blythe and Mr. Crowninshield stage that pantomime. In short, as I stood there in the ravine, with my hands jammed into the pockets of my mud-bespattered pants, it was a toss-up whether I wouldn't strike out for Jack's House and blurt the whole business to the girl. She might have a different tale to tell.

I started up the ravine, still in two minds what

to do; anyhow, I must get back a piece from the river.   Supposing, thinks I, the girl did have a different tale to tell; supposing this dandy, terrified old gentleman were my uncle after all: what was I to do about it?   Go whining and truckling to him as he had whined and truckled to Mr. Crowninshield? The bare thought was like a slap in the face, and I brought up short with smarting cheeks.   Drawing a deep breath, boy-like I took a big resolve: before ever I played the whimpering poor relation to my uncle or licked his boots, he and his money and my rosy prospects might all go hang . . . and the girl, too, that looked so like my mother?   Well, of course, she wouldn't be to blame; and, if she wished maybe to write to me, I would tell her to send the letter to Pacific, care of Mr. Jessop.

You will see I had already decided to go to Jack's House, more to set my mind at rest than from any other motive.   For, if Mr. Blythe had lied to me, then he didn't want to acknowledge me for his nephew; and you can bet I wouldn't press our kinship!   But I was curious to know if he really had lied.

The general direction of Jack's House I thought I had; and when I got back to the summit of the bluff and climbed up into an oak, sure enough I spied, away yonder over the treetops, the battlemented cap of the tower shining in the sun.   It wouldn't be a far hike, on a bee-line something over half a mile; and down I shinned, pretty eager now to get to the bottom of all this mystification.

I thought, at first, I must break my way through the brush, up hill and down dale, just as I had been doing. But, as luck would have it, I had gone but a little distance when I came upon the traces of a road and, what's more, in the fresh earth of a gopher mound, on the blocked stamp of an automobile casing. That an automobile should have found its way to this outlandish place surprised me not a little; but I made a guess it was from Jack's House and that Mr. Blythe himself had driven it. And sure enough I was right; for now and again, as I hurried along, I detected the markings of the tires; and at last the road—really no more than a trail—after many windings, but keeping cleverly on the ridges all the while, led me to the ring of pines that circled Jack's House.

I paused, considering what I had best do. Sure, if I was going to address a lady, I must try and tidy up my person; and after a rueful inspection of my bedraggled clothes I took a stick and began to scrape off the mud.

But I didn't scrape long. Chancing to look up, my eyes lighted on an object which here, in the good broad daylight, was more of a curiosity than a terror. About a squirrel's jump off the road and half hidden in a clump of young pines, was my hoary warlock of the night before. Crouched on his hands and knees, he kept turning his hairy, haggard face, now toward the house, now toward me, for all

the world like some shy wild creature on the point
of flight.

I wasn't in the least afraid: darkness and light
have a vast deal to do with fear. On the contrary,
I observed him, as cool as you please, wondering
what the poor lunatic was up to. Certainly, what
little sense he had left was centered on Jack's House;
for no man, cracked or sound, would have braved
last night's storm as he had done just for the fun
of the thing. And here he was again, watching with
such a devouring intensity as would make you think
the house was all of a sudden to blow up. But what
his interest might be, whether hostile or friendly, or
merely mad, was more than I could tell.

Thinking to clear up this mystery at least,

"What's the matter?" I demanded, and strode
boldly toward him. At my first step, back he
springs through the pines, flinging his hands, palms
outward, before his face and uttering breathless gut-
tural noises like one who is tongue-tied. But his
meaning was plain enough, for all that: the tables
were turned indeed, and he was now as daunted and
scared by me as I had been by him.

"Look here," said I, "I don't want to hurt you.
Just tell me why you're staring at that house;" and
I gave my hand a backward wave. But at the harmless gesture he turned tail and bolted. I didn't try
to follow him—that had been useless; and besides,
old as he was, he had the legs of a deer.

Returning to the road, then, I resumed my prim-

itive toilet, marveling greatly at this fresh quirk in
the riddle.   Twice now I had caught this old crazy-
quilt spying upon Jack's House.   Had he evil designs upon the inmates?   Or could there, by any
chance, be a secret link between him and—say, the
girl?   Was he skulking here to await some signal,
or perhaps to give one?   (I raised my eyes.)
There was the tower, stern and formidable for all
its ivy; with a start I remembered that the girl had
looked upon me from a window in that stronghold.
Then my fancy vaulted clean away from me plump
into delicious romance; and in a flash, I beheld the
maiden languishing in that fast donjon, prey to a
villainous crew, whilst her aged father, demented
with grief, prowled the vicinage and fixed ever a
longing eye upon the keep: and myself the fearless
knight who should smite the dastards and achieve
the rescue.

But next moment, with a sudden and wholesome
bump, I hit the earth again.   Forth from the front
door came the captive heroine of my fiction, dressed
all in white and fresh as a daisy, with a guitar slung
by a lilac ribbon from her shoulder.

XI

THE LADY OF JACK'S HOUSE

D OWN the lawn between roses red and white she came, idly thrumming the guitar and humming a snatch of song, her snowy dress radiant in the sunshine and her chestnut hair glinting golden. After all the dangers I had run, after the terrors of the night, after robbers and thieves and madmen, after all the dark hints and stirrings of an ugly deed afoot, she appeared before me, moving among the flowers and across the green grass, a bright vision of loveliness and purity and honest kindliness; so that the sweetness of her took me by the throat, and for a little I saw her as a glory in a mist.

Ere I could accost her, or even recover from my emotion, she had passed out of sight, toward the rim of woods to my left. Thither following, I spied, just within the belt of pines, a kind of pergola or latticed pavilion all mantled with a thick cloak of wisteria, such as covered our front · porch at home. The lady (for in my eyes she was no longer a mere girl) had doubtless sought this retreat; but, just as I was about to approach, there

trickled through the curtain of vines the silver tinkle
of plucked strings and the soft clang of chords—
and then the sweetest voice I ever heard: not one
of that shrill, treble kind, but full and rich and low,
yet soaring too, now and again, as graceful as a
bird: altogether, a voice so melodious and airy as
minded me of a poem I had read called "To a Skylark":—though, to be sure, her song wasn't about
a skylark at all.

> Oh, the frolicking sunbeams kiss the flowers
>   And dance away, dance away.
> But on you, poor maid, the darkness glowers,—
>   A fettered thing, mewed up for aye—for aye.
>
> And the rivers flow on where the world's end gleams,
> A city of gold, like shining dreams,
> And roseate visions clad in beams,
>   That are sealed from you, my captive fay,
>   Sealed for aye—for aye.

I tell you, it was pretty! and, though somewhere
in the back of my head was the prick that I had no
business thus to eavesdrop, I could only stick there,
gawping like a zany, while the harmonies of the
guitar purled through the greenery. And then,
"Oh, deary dear!" sighed a voice behind the
vines. "Roseate visions and my captive fay!" and
there followed a bubble of laughter accompanied by
a sudden jarring clash of the strings. "Well, anyhow, *I* think it's a nice song. And if you don't like

it, ladies and gentlemen, please don't express your
opinion till I've done.   So there!"

You may suppose I started!   Had she spied me!
But already she had twanged the guitar anew and
floated off on a quite different air.

> But oh, my laddie, what care I—care I?
>   Deep in my soul a jewel sleeps,
>   More lovely than an opal sky,
>   Or radiant towers piled on high:
>   'Tis that my heart her freedom keeps,
>   Her freedom keeps.

> So ho, my laddie, ne'er hint to me
>   Of gyves and locks and prison bars
>   That cage me from the splendid stars,
>   Because my heart is free—is free,
>   Because my heart is free.

By the time she reached the last note my face, I
imagine, must have been the color of a turkey-cock's
wattles.   She seemed to have sung straight to me
(think of it!); and, what was worse, the words fell
so pat to my egregious conceit of Beauty Thralled
and the Rescuing Knight!   Through sheer power
of will, I do believe (for my heels were all for
flight), I forced myself around to the arched opening of the pavilion and presented—the picture of a
perfect booby.

"Oh!" she cried, giving a little start and looking
up at me in unfeigned wonder.

"Pardon me," said I, with about as much composure as a newly caught sunfish, "you—I—that. is,
are you Miss Domini Blythe?"

"At your service," says she, with a smile that
wasn't on her lips but in her eyes—dancing eyes that
seemed hugely to enjoy me: which put me a little
on my mettle. "And you," she went on, "are the
boy who was speaking to papa yesterday. Dear
me,"—with an unabashed survey of my person—
"what's happened since? Forgive me, but you must
have had an exciting time."

Now her 'boying' me put me clean about, so that
in my pique I quite forgot I was bashful and spoke
out slap:

"I'm no boy and I just came—"

"Oh, excuse me," says she sweetly, her face all
apology, except for her eyes, which were wicked
still. "But then, you know, Mr.—Mr.—"

"Linton," said I, with some hauteur.

"Mr. Linton, papa said you were a boy, though
I asked him yesterday what that *man* wanted. I'm
glad I was right."

Here we were landed square on the business!

"And what did he say?" I asked eagerly.

Her fingers wandered over the strings. "Oh,
that you had mistaken the house, that's all. Did
you"—with another mischievous glance at my
clothes—"did you mistake other houses too?"

But this shaft fell harmless, for I was thinking.
'Mistaken the house' was true enough, if Mr. Blythe

wasn't my uncle; but the phrase sounded like deception.

"Is that all he told you?" said I.

"What else?" says she. "You did mistake the house, didn't you?"

"I did and I didn't," said I. "It all depends."

Her eyes widened in laughing wonderment, but with a dash of seriousness too.

"Oh, my goodness! The plot thickens. Explain your enigma, sirrah."

"Well, this way," said I. "Have you an aunt named Katherine Linton?"

"Aunt Katherine Linton?" Her unrecognizing repetition sent my heart into my shoes. Then, quickly and merrily, "You would be my cousin?" she cried. "Come, that's jolly!"

"Jolly it would be," said I. "I'd give anything to call you Cousin Domini. But I guess your father told me the truth after all."

There was tact for you! Oh, my blundering tongue!

The change in Miss Blythe was not only instant but shocking, like coming out of a firelit room into zero weather. She rose to her feet, staring me up and down. I felt cheap, I tell you; I couldn't meet her eye. And when she spoke her voice was like ice.

"You guess my father told the truth after all? What do you mean?"

"Please let me explain," said I, glancing up at

her, and down again at my mud-stained shoes.
"Maybe if you heard what I've got to say, you
wouldn't think I was such a—such a skunk." I
didn't mean to say "skunk," but now it was out I
let it go.

She was silent, so I started in to tell her my story
from the time my father died. At first, I was half
afraid to look at her; but by and by, when I come
to where my mother urged me to seek my Uncle
Clement, she sits down, and I raise my eyes and see
her gazing at me, a red spot in either cheek and her
mouth a little open. She was interested, I could
see that. I didn't forget Cissy Carton, either, which
fetched a small "oh!" and a flicker of a smile. But
about the robbery in the lane and all subsequent
events I was mum. Just then I could see no good
in telling all that; besides, maybe it would frighten
her. "So you see," I wound up, "I didn't doubt
your father's word" (which was a gracious fib).
"I came back—well, to see you, Miss Blythe, because you were the very picture of my mother—that
is," I hastened to add, "when my mother was a
young lady like you."

She smiled, and I knew I had got the better of
her indignation.

"Well," said she, "it's very nice of you to say I
look like your mother, but so far as I know I haven't
an aunt or uncle in the whole creation. In fact, I
fear papa and I have no kindred at all. Your uncle

must be that other Mr. Blythe. I'm sorry you came all the way out here for nothing."

"Oh, that's all right," said I. "I'm pretty well fixed. I've got a hundred and two dollars in my—" My face, I suppose, must have startled her like a sick ghost's, for she uttered a little cry.

"What—what on earth's the matter?"

"Nothing," I gulped, "nothing much." (Which was my second fib.) "Only I've lost my money." And it was all I could do to keep from blubbering like a boy right there in her presence. As it was, some confounded tears did steal to my eyes: I felt one sneaking down alongside my nose.

But at this juncture a very trim-looking young woman in a white cap and apron suddenly appeared under the archway.

"Luncheon, Miss Domini," says she, and starts to retire.

"One moment, Mary. Lay another cover for this gentleman."

Mary so far forgot her manners as to give me a stare: I didn't blame her. Then she withdrew.

"This is very kind of you, Miss Blythe," said I, and I meant it; for luncheon sounded mighty good to me; "but I can't accept your invitation."

"Why not?"

"Why not!" I cried. "Just look at me!"

She did, and laughed. "Oh, but this will be a very informal affair—between cousins." Her eyes were dancing again.

"Well," said I, "but I wouldn't want to meet your father again, after yesterday. It would look kind of funny, wouldn't it?"

She stood up. "Why, no. You're my guest. Anyhow, papa won't be home. He and Mr. Crowninshield have gone fishing. Come along."

The house, as I believe I have mentioned, was of stone and two storeys in height. The old trader's original dwelling—or what was left of it—comprised the ground floor on the side next to the tower. South of the porch my eye was caught by a row of casement windows, some swung open, leaded with small diamond panes, very pretty and quaint. That was the dining-room, as I was soon to learn: and there fate sat waiting for me.

We entered by the front door into a kind of hall where there was a polished curved staircase, a tall mirror, and plants in green and crimson jars. On my right, behind a portière of bead-work, was a large airy room—the "post-room," Miss Blythe called it—where (as I glimpsed) stood a shiny center-table with books upon it and a vase of flowers, and in the back wall an immense screened fireplace hung about with no end of Indian trophies, and beyond, over a closed door, a mounted stag-head.

Whither should Miss Blythe take me but to her father's own apartment where, after she had laid out fresh towels in an adjoining bathroom and bid me "remove the stains of my cousinish travels," she

left me to my toilet and the cheerful reflection that
I hadn't a penny in the world.

Dead broke! That was my pickle (or my
tragedy), and what was I going to do about it?
Selecting the least spotless of three chairs, I sat
down to think.   One thing was sure right off: I
wouldn't give up the search.   By hook or by crook
I would get back to Chicago and find my uncle yet.
In any event, and no matter how much hard luck
came my way, nobody should say I was a quitter.
I set my jaw and glared at myself in the dresser
mirror.   (But behind all my grim and game resolve,
those pavilion tears, I'm afraid, were lurking and
peeping.)

Of course, there remained the chance that I might
recover my lost purse—a tight chance, sure enough,
but still a chance. . . .

In the dining-room, before ever I sat down, my
mouth watered to see all the good things to eat.
But I sternly reminded myself, I remember, that I
mustn't give my hunger free fling, but dawdle along,
taking a bite now and then, and be more interested
in Miss Blythe than in the food.

"I don't know whether you're a Catholic or not,
Mr. Linton," says she, when we were seated, "but
I say grace before meals."   Which she did at once
and aloud.

"Amen!" was my hearty response; for sure, here
(if Miss Blythe would only step out of the room)
was something to be thankful for.

"So you're a Catholic too," she remarked, as
Mary put a dish of chops under my nose; of which,
in an heroic burst of manners, I selected the small-
est. "Why, that's one more piece of common
ground—and a big one too."

"Yes, so it is," I agreed elegantly. "Thank you,
just a wee bit;" and I delicately placed upon my plat-
ter a thimbleful of a delicious-looking concoction of
cheese and cream and potatoes.

"You have a beautiful place here, Miss Blythe,"
said I, gallantly trifling with my chop.

"*Isn't* it lovely!" says she. "Papa bought it only
this spring—all furnished, just as it is."

I suddenly found myself looking down on stuffed
green peppers whose wondrous good odor shook my
heart. But I stood by my guns; nay, I made a
sally!

"No, I thank you," said I, haggardly polite.

"Will you have your tea hot or iced, sir?" asked
Mary.

"Whichever is convenient," I replied with a lofty
but painful detachment, though I was hoping she
would make it iced.

But here Miss Blythe came to my rescue at
last.

"You don't appear to be hungry at all, Mr. Linton. You're really slighting my perfectly nice luncheon. What's the matter, did you have a late breakfast?"

"No," said I, feeling a little foolish. "I—the

fact is I haven't had anything to eat—to speak of—
since yesterday noon."

"Well! Of all the—You poor starved boy!
['Boy' went unresented this time.] Here, give
me that plate of yours. Was it hot or iced tea you
wanted?"

"Well, iced," said I, humbled but happy.

My heart rose to see the quantity of food she
loaded on my plate; and, though I feebly protested,
I was glad she paid not the slightest heed to my
hypocrisy.

"That will do, Mary. I'll ring for the dessert,"
says Miss Blythe. "Now then, the decks are
cleared. If you don't eat now, I shall be mortally
offended, honestly and truly."

Well, you may take my word for it, I didn't of-
fend her! For the next fifteen minutes or so it
would have done your heart good to see the way
things vanished from that table. It did my heart
good, I know; and I am pretty sure, to judge by her
looks, it did Miss Blythe's heart good, too.

"Now," said she, after I had got fairly started,
"*I'll* do the talking. You may say 'oh,' or 'indeed,' or look interested if you wish. That'll be
quite enough. Let's see, what were we talking
about? No, don't stop. I've got it. You said
this was a lovely place, and I said papa had bought
it ready furnished. Well, he did, and it was lucky
too. All we had to bring, practically, were our two
selves and the British Sovereigns."

"British Sovereigns?" I echoed huskily, through chop and potatoes.

"Yes. Our servants, William and Mary. It's rather hard on them, but it's cute, don't you think? —No, pardon me, don't think!—Papa's sick, you know. There's something wrong with his heart, the doctors say. So, a couple of weeks back he came out here for a complete rest, and told me not to tell a soul where we were going." She smiled. "And I didn't, except for Cissy. You see, we didn't want to be invaded by our friends. I thought it would be dreadfully dreary, only papa and I together. But one morning, about ten days ago, Mr. Crowninshield turns up. He's out for the summer too, and has a bungalow down near the river—the prettiest spot! Papa and I have been there several times. He's been awfully nice to—to Papa. He and papa are quite old cronies.

"There's the butter, right behind the sugar-bowl. Aren't these peppers good? I love them done this way. Do take another one. There.

"Still, it's not a very exciting life. Why, I don't even get any letters! So, you see, your arrival was quite an event." She leaned her elbows on the table, giving me a sudden quizzical look. "If you don't mind, what *did* happen to you since yesterday afternoon?" And then abruptly, and with a smile, "No, no," she cried, as I laid down my knife and fork, *"mea culpa!* That will be your after-dinner story. Do go on with your luncheon."

You may suppose her pleasant chatter interested me more than she might have guessed; though you may suppose, too, I obeyed her injunction and didn't let it interfere with my meal.

"May I ask a question?" said I, when the dessert had been served—some whipped-cream affair that looked mighty dainty and toothsome. "Then I'll tell you what happened since yesterday."

"Certainly," says she.

"Then," said I, "did you ever hear of Clarence F. Carver?"

She shook her head. "Who is he—the villain of your story?"

"Well," said I, "he's one. The truth is, they're most all of them villains, so far as I can make out. But this Clarence F. Carver is the top-sawyer. He's a dark one, he is."

"Oo-o-o!" She shivered in mock terror. "False, fleeting, perjured Clarence, that stabbed me in the field by Tewkesbury!—No, he didn't stab me. I'm so interested I dropped into poetry, that's all. Do go on."

"Well," said I, "I'll ask you just one more thing. Who is Mr. Gordon Crowninshield?"

Now, when I said this, something flashed across Miss Blythe's face that I find it hard to put a name to. Perhaps I can express it best by saying that the gayety in her eyes vanished for an instant, like a quenched candle. But next moment it shone again, and her simple reply disarmed my suspicion.

"Mr. Crowninshield?   He's a friend of papa's. Papa met him several years ago in business; though he's been out to dinner, too, lots of times.   Now then, for your story."

"Well, all right," said I, finishing off my dessert and leaning back in a comfortable glow.   "To begin with, after—"   But the tale was stricken from my lips.   In the doorway facing me appeared Mr. Blythe!

XII

I AM WELCOMED BY MY UNCLE

D OMINI, seeing my amaze, turned round and jumping up with a little cry, ran to her father and kissed him.

"What's the matter, dear? Wouldn't the fish bite?" cried she. "I didn't know you would be home so soon, or I'd have waited luncheon for you. Or did you eat those nice sandwiches I made up?"

But Mr. Blythe answered her never a word—didn't even look at her; but kept eyeing me with an expression of surprise and growing anger. Under the stress of such a stare, naturally I rose to my feet, prepared for an explosion. It was not long in coming.

"Oh, here's Mr. Linton, papa,—" began Domini, noticing his look.

But he, gently seizing her two wrists (her arms were about his neck), put her aside and came teetering toward me, his indignant demeanor, I must say, much discounted by his effeminate gait and slightness; so that, to tell you the truth, I wasn't any more daunted by him than by a yapping spaniel.

"To what, sir, am I indebted for the pleasure of this second visit?" says he, pompous and possessed, but the color burning high on his cheeks all the same. He was angry all right enough, I could see that: but I gave it back to him in kind.

"To the kindness of your daughter," says I, meeting him stare for stare.

"My daughter!" exclaims he, wonderingly, and looking round.

Domini's wide eyes were glancing from one to the other of us in sheer bewilderment, the fingers of one hand pressing her white cheek.

"Why, papa!" cries she. "What has he done? You—you never told me. He came this morning, and—and I invited him to luncheon. I—I don't see—"

"Of course you don't see, Domini," he cut in, not unkindly. "But"—and he faced me again—"if I had been here, you would never have seen the inside of this house, sir! What have you been doing since yesterday? Prowling about my premises, I daresay, waiting a chance to slip in for a bite to eat, like a tattered tramp. Tramps," he added, "usually apply at the kitchen door; they're not entertained at my table."

I was pretty hot, I tell you; but here was a capital opening, and so I said:

"But this tramp did better than that, Mr. Blythe. He had the privilege of brushing his rags in your own room." And while he gazed and gulped, I couldn't help marveling at my neatness of speech; and felt pretty cockish over it, too.

Then, all at once, he swings round and flings out his arm toward the door.

"Get out!" he barked, in a treble of passion. "No cub of Jim Linton's shall stand here and insult me in my own house! There's the door——"

"Oho!" cried I, and thwacked the table. "So you're my uncle after all, eh? This *is* a discovery! But I might have guessed it; no man in his senses would have kicked up such a row about a stranger."

He had blabbed his secret, sure enough: but it didn't seem to disconcert him one whit.

"Yes," he cried, "I am your uncle—unfortunately I am. There's the door, just the same. But before you go, take this away with you: Your father is the dirtiest blackguard that ever stood in two shoes; and Kate Blythe ceased to be my sister when she fouled her honor and draggled her skirts in that——"

All my heart whirled up in a blaze.

"You lie!" I roared, leaping forward. "By Heaven, you lie!" and would have taken him by the throat, then and there, but for my cousin Domini, who looked round from his shoulder with wild, pity-ing eyes.

I believe my outburst cowed him for a little, for he only blinked at me, mumbling his lips. But sure, nothing he might have said could have cut me more cruelly.

"Oh, sir," I went on, with a steadier grip on my

feelings, "you have blackened the memory of my dear parents. I do not know what quarrel there was between them and you; but I know that my mother was a saint, and that my father was a hundred times the man you are. Nothing you may say, thank God, can alter that. They are dead, and as high above you as Heaven is. But I am their son, and oh, sir, your words stabbed me!" I must confess that some tears, not unmanly, I hope, had sprung into my eyes.

The old man disengaged himself from Domini, drew from his pocket a silver cigarette case, selected a cigarette, lighted it, and tossed the burning match into a glass. And all the while his hands were shaking like the palsy.

"My stars!" says he flippantly, "the beggar is eloquent enough. You *are* a beggar, I suppose. For of course your father and mother died penniless—that's always the way. I had no idea they were dead, though. Well, they're better dead, that's sure."

He paused, and I, scarce able any longer to brook such talk and fearing to do the bad old man a hurt, was just on the point of bidding my cousin Domini farewell, when he checked me.

"One moment. Of course, being left a beggar, you sought me out to get a living from your rich uncle."

"O papa, papa!" cries Domini. "For shame, papa!"

You may imagine my face was burning like fire. His words had so squarely hit the mark—and yet had missed it, too, in a right manner of thinking. ·

"Ah, I see I am right. You did come a-begging, though you're blushing for it now. Of course, I'd sooner house a monkey than any brat of Linton's, but—well, well, perhaps that darling mother of yours told you to go to your nice Uncle Clement. In that case, we'll have to see what we can do. Why, yes, here's a dollar, a generous bit for a beggar. Take it." And plucking the coin from his pocket, he suddenly held it forth to me.

Will you believe it! Smarting as I was under this humiliation, I reached out my hand and took it! Then, seeing what I had done, in a fierce crack of rage I flung that dollar plumb through one of the dining-room casements. Clean as a bullet it pierced a diamond pane; and in the pulsing silence, before I could find my tongue, I heard it roll and ring on the porch floor without.

"That's for your favors!" I cried, and felt my lips all quivering on the words. "Oh, it's true my father died a—a pauper, if you like. It's true I came seeking my uncle's help. But I expected to find a man,—not a devil. And oh, sir [though how I could 'sir' him still is beyond me], if you taunt me with being a beggar, then there are two beggars in this room. This very morning I saw you crawling like a worm to Mr. Gordon Crowninshield. You groveled there—" I stopped. My uncle had

gone a sickened white, and clung crumpled to a chair,
as though I had struck him, not with words, but with
my fist.

But next moment he rallied, came erect, and
pointing to the door, "Go!" he ordered, in a quavering voice; "go, boy!"

I bowed to my kinswoman.

"Good-by, Cousin Domini," said I; "I thank you
for your kind heart. In the goodness of you, maybe
I can forget your father."

And without a word more I left them there, and
strode down the drive with never a look behind, and
on into the pine-wood; my mind all a-seethe, but my
legs bearing me to McGregor. I had no thoughts,
I do believe: only trampled pride, and anger hot
and tingling, and a great bitterness: which made me
walk on with high head as in a trance. But, ere I
had reached the tail of the pines, I was gnawing my
knuckles in a struggle with my tears. It was all
over with my fond dreams; but this I could have
borne, with as stiff a lip as any of you. What was
worse, far worse, than my toppled castles was the
nameless smirch put upon my sainted mother.
Slander it was—oh, I knew it!—slander as base and
foul as the rotten polecat of a man who had uttered
it. For all that, it rankled in my heart, and sent
the hot tears smarting to my eyes—to think that
this was the man whose fireside and kinship I had
sought!

If then I had met my uncle on the road, I think

I should have taken a terrible delight in knocking him down and trampling on him—Domini's father and all. And in lieu of his actual person, I invented one. Happening to see an odd blotchy growth on the trunk of a tree, I made believe that was his face; and seizing a large stone, jagged at the innocent bark till my fingers bled. This isn't pleasant to relate, nor does it show me a model youth; but, for one thing, I don't set up to be a model, and for another I put it to you whether you yourself wouldn't have gone me one better and punched the real face.

A sudden roaring rush of sound came out of the pinewood hill above me (I was already on the downward reach of road where my Pullman friend had fallen among the robbers) and looking back, I saw a gray motor car flying at top speed behind the tall black stems on the chine of the hill.

Wondering what this should portend, I halted and waited for the automobile to overtake me. No doubt it was my uncle's car; no doubt he was after me; and no doubt, too, (by the Lord Harry!) he should get his fill of me before he was done!

Next moment the car topped the crest of the lane and came plunging downhill. But it was not my uncle; behind the steering-wheel, her hair a-flying, sat my cousin Domini.

I stepped aside, and the car with a loud grinding crunch came to a breakneck stop. A door flew open, and Domini jumped to the ground.

"Cousin!" she cried, her hands outstretched, "oh, my cousin!" and broke off, leaning back against the fore mud-guard, her eyes all red and her breath coming fast.

This was her magnificent amend for her father's unspeakable insult; and it took me all of a heap.

"Cousin Domini," said I, my hard resentment all run to tenderness, "it's all right. For your sake I'll forget it—I'll try mighty hard anyway. I will, honest."

"Oh, but come back!" cries she. "You mustn't go away like this. You must come back."

She had heard all. She had heard the thing her father said. I looked at her.

"Can you ask me, Cousin Domini?" said I, and felt a pity for her even as I spoke.

She dropped her eyes, the color mounting on her cheek. Then, giving me a swift eager look,

"There's some terrible mistake in all this," she said hurriedly. "Oh, I know there is. There must be. Papa couldn't have said such things without being deceived. Oh, give him a chance, Cousin, to take back what he's said."

"Cousin Domini," I declared, and I meant it— and she knew I meant it—"for you I would go a long way and do a big thing. But to go, back to your father's house would bring only shame to me and unhappiness to you. For many years now— since before I was born—he has had time to con-

sider the black lie he flung at me to-day. That lie
stands between him and me forever."

Her head was bowed, and I saw she knew it was
hopeless to try to persuade me further. But when
she looked up there was a kind of sad smile playing
at the corners of her mouth.

"So you're going back to Mr. Jessop's?" said
she. "And without even telling me your name?"

"Oh, my name. It's Gerard."

"Well, Cousin Gerard," says she, holding out her
hand (which I grasped eagerly enough: and a lump
was in my throat too), "*we* are friends, anyhow,
aren't we? [I gulped my assent.] And if I
wrote you that papa was wrong and admitted his
error, you would come and live with us, wouldn't
you? [I looked away.] Wouldn't you?"

"Maybe," said I.

"Well, and if I wanted you to do me a favor,"
she went on, "would you do it?"

"You bet I would!"

"Then I want you to borrow fifty dollars from
me. Here it is. You can't walk back to Mr. Jessop's, you know." And the old merry light peeped
out of her eyes, like a ray of sunshine between
clouds.

Of course I took the money; took it with a heart
full of love and gratitude toward this incomparable
girl who had befriended me from the first.

"Good-by, Cousin Gerard," says she, and gave
me her hand again in frank affection.

Then, mounting into the car, she deftly put it about and with a farewell wave shot away up the road.

Once more I headed for McGregor. Should I return to Father McGiffert's? This would entail an explanation, and I boggled at telling even Father McGiffert of my kinsman's currish conduct. As to my lost money, you can bet I wasn't going to give it up without a search. To-morrow I would return along the railroad to the spot where I had gone swimming, for I guessed I had dropped it there while stripping for my plunge. But I would make no report of the assault in the lane; this would mean delay, and the sooner I was quit of the scene of my misadventures, the better.

When I reached the town at last and came down under the trees to the main street, I remarked some folks going up the stone stairs to the church; and, thinks I, I'll drop in, drabbled clothes and all, and pay a visit to Our Lord, and say a prayer to St. Anthony, too, to help me find my money.

Inside were more people, mostly scattered in the rear pews; and after I had knelt down and looked about (as one will), I observed a queue of five or six standing near the confessional; and it broke upon me, for the first time, that to-morrow was Sunday. Seeing the folks going to confession, and remembering that I hadn't been to Holy Communion for a month, I thought I might as well take the opportunity and go to confession too.

To forgive my uncle called for a tough wrestle with myself. But, kneeling there before Our Lord, who had forgiven me so many times before, I finally succeeded; and then confession was easy—dead easy: not only easy but refreshing. When I came down into the street again I could have flown, had I.wings, all the way to the hotel!

XIII

THE Royal Windsor Hotel, according to its modest advertisement, was "the best hotel in town."

"I want to put up here," said I to the young fellow behind the desk.

He looked at me a moment, somewhat doubtfully as I thought; so, to set his mind at rest, I drew out, in an absent-minded way, my cousin Domini's roll of bills.

"Yes, sir," says he promptly. "Will you register here, please?"

I smiled to myself, thinking what an open sesame money was. But my smile suddenly vanished—my eyes had lighted on the signature, "Clarence F. Carver, Memphis, Tenn.," the third name from the top of the page. I suppose my face betrayed dismay, for,

"Is anything the matter, sir?" inquired the clerk.

"Oh, no," said I, recovering. "My, you've got lots of guests, I see."

"Yes, sir, we're doing pretty well," he agreed.

123

"Which same," he added, with a second survey of my person, "can't be said o' you, if you'll excuse me saying so. Been a-roughing it, have you, sir?"

I nodded to his guess (roughing it was right!) and thereupon, a bright idea striking me, dipped the pen into the inkpot and wrote without a hitch, "John P. Jones, Cuba."

"Cuba!" exclaimed the clerk. "You've sure come a long way, ain't you, Mr. Jones? You ain't a native down there; now, are you?"

I see I had cut it too fat.

"Oh," said I, "that's Cuba, *Illinois;*" and hoped there was such a place.

The inquisitive clerk led me along a short corridor just off the lobby, where the smell of supper a-cooking took me in the face like a caress.

"Here you are, sir," says he. "There's the bell for anything you want. Just touch it like this. See? That's something new we installed this year," he added proudly. "The dining-room's right down at the end of this hall, and supper will be ready in half an hour. I guess that's all. They ain't nothin' more I can do for you, is there?"

That was all, I assured him; and sat down on the bed to take stock of Carver. Whether the burglar had seen me at Mr. Crowninshield's bungalow was a matter of doubt; I inclined to think he hadn't, for he had got away too quick. Of course, were he lying hid in the room while Mr. Crowninshield's servant held me at the window, then he had heard my

voice and doubtless recognized it.   But in that case
he had probably been laid by the heels, as the servant would naturally examine the room after my
escape.   At all events, it was my tack now to fight
shy of him, for (as I suspected) he was deep in
some game I had blundered into and was like to have
spoiled; and when it came to shady maneuvering,
I had sense enough to own that Carver was too many
for me.

Enough, therefore, for me to find my money and
clear out: meantime, keep out of Carver's way.
To this end I was for ringing that electric bell and
having my supper served in my room; but upon second thoughts, seeing this would make me rather con-
spicuous, at least in the eyes of that nosey clerk, I
changed my mind and decided to brave the dining-
room.

Here everything went swimmingly.   I got a table
to myself where I was partially screened by an angle
of the wall but could keep an eye on the door, too.
But Carver didn't show up the whole time; and
though you may think I couldn't enjoy my supper,
seeing my mind was sitting on thorns, you would
have thought differently had you seen me plying my
knife and fork.   There were waffles, as I remember, piping hot, with maple syrup; a big ear of
boiled corn, a juicy broiled steak with parsley around
it, and any number of hot buttered buns—I ate
seven.   The Royal Windsor didn't belie its name;
it did the honors royally.

Well, after such a supper, I was willing enough to go hiding in my room; besides, though the long summer evening had but just begun, I was already ripe for bed. So, after saying my beads (and pinching myself at the end of every decade to keep awake), I rolled in and slept like a top.

But, no matter how tight you may sleep, a beam of light beating steadily upon your eyelids is almost sure to fetch you out of slumber; and when to the beam are added voices—and one of them like a steamboat whistle—you are bound to come awake. I did; and for a long second or two wondered where on earth I was and what on earth had roused me.

"Mr. Simon Doumie? No, sir, I ain't heard of him in this town.—See here, sir, here's the electric bell. If you want anything, just push it."

Of course my whereabouts was plain now. The clerk was in the next room with a new-come guest; and the pencil of light issued from a crack in the partition. I turned over and closed my eyes again.

"Well now, that's a setback, sure enough," bellowed the guest; and I could feel my bed quake with his voice. "And you got a pretty good line on the folks hereabouts too, eh, my son? Well, well, now. Blow me but that's disapp'intin', that is."

"Well, sir, to tell you the truth," said the clerk, and I heard him pull up a chair (I was to thank him later for being such a curious dog), "the only Simon I know of is Silly Sim. I don't know his last name—nobody does: he ain't got none, I guess.

But, o' course, you can't be visitin' him. He's nobody, and besides, he's plumb nuts—loose in the
loft, he is, sir."

You may be sure I pricked up my ears. Sleep
might wait. Here was a chance to learn something
definite about the crazy old man of Jack's House;
for, ten to one, the clerk meant him.

"Screw loose in the turret-deck, has he?" boomed
the guest. "Shiver my timbers, that's a pretty
howdydo, Mr. Simon Doumic! What else, my son?
Heave away till the anchor strikes."

"Sir?" said the clerk.

"Spin the whole yarn o' this here party called
Silly Sim."

"Oh. Well, sir, they ain't nothin' *to* it, much.
He ain't your man. He's just a foolish ole loon't
lives down on Eagle's Nest. Everybody knows
about *him*. He's crazy, but he don't do nobody any
harm."

"Has he been here long?" asked the guest.

"Long! Well, I reckon he has! He was here
before I was born, and years before that. Some
folks says he come down here from Canada, before
they cleared the Indians out—when they was soldiers across the river yonder in old Fort Crawford.
They's a heap o' stories about him too," the obliging
clerk went on, apparently warming to his subject.
"Some says his cave down yonder on the bluff is
packed plumb full of gold. Some says he murdered
his wife, and she ha'nts him every night. Some

says he never had no wife, but murdered somebody else's wife, and *she* ha'nts him. He keeps a big fire burnin' every Friday night, and waves a torch over his head ever so often—yes, sir, I seen that time and again, I have, sir! And some says it's to keep the bad spirits away—as *he* thinks, o' course, sir—and some says no, but it's a signal he's givin' to the steamboat *'Louisiana'* that sunk down there round the point years ago. And some says no again, but he's waitin' for a pardner o' hisn to come up the river one o' these nights, and it's a signal for him. But it's all such a tangle o' nonsense, sir, 't I don't believe a single bit of it—no, nor nobody else does either, to my mind. People just like to hear their-selves talk, that's all."

"Int'restin' old party, this here Silly Sim," bassed the other voice. "But he ain't my Sim. My Sim's a lawyer man—Mr. Simon Doumic, A—ttorney. He's a regular bigwig, he is, my son."

"Why," cried the clerk, "they ain't but two law-yers in town—ole Toppy and Mr. David Worth!"

"Well, now," growled the other in a crestfallen tone, "don't that beat a swab's luck. And his let-ter said as clear as clear, 'McGregor, Ioway.' How-somever, my son, I'll shake out a sail to-morry and cruise around a bit, and maybe I'll sight his craft. You just jump up now, like a good boy, and fetch me a pot o' b'iling water and a bit o' sugar: and put this slip o' tin in your pocket."

"Thank you, sir," said the clerk, and came back presently with the water and sugar; and shortly after I caught the aroma of spirits, and knew the old fellow was mixing himself a nightcap.

For some time I lay there, thinking of my fellow lodger next door and of Silly Sim down on the river, and of Mr. Crowninshield and my uncle and Domini, and of Carver and the three bandits and my Pullman friend, and of Jack's House and the old French trader who had dwelt there nigh on a century ago; and wondered what strange destiny it was that jostled all these people together in such a bewildering puzzle.   And my last thought, before sleep took me for good, was why my uncle hated me and my parents.   To this question I was to receive an answer much sooner than I expected; and, what was more, the manner of that answer was to pass my wildest imagining.

Next morning when I awoke the room was bright with sunshine, and I sprang out of bed all in a flutter lest I had overslept and so missed the chance of receiving Holy Communion.   I didn't take time for any prinking, but dressed in a jiff, tossed some water in my face, raked the comb once or twice through my mop of hair, and bolted out the door.

And bolted spang into a man that seemed to fill all the passage!

"Avast, there, my young hearty!" he roars, and claps down on my shoulder a hand like a vise.

"Excuse me, sir," I gasped, flinching under his tremendous grip. "I didn't mean to run into you. I was just in a hurry. Have you the time, sir?"

Upon this, he lets go his hold of me, and hauls up from the depths of his clothes a silver watch big as an alarm clock. And as he looked at the watch, I looked at him: for I made sure he was the burly-lunged customer who had occupied the next room. A gorilla of a man he was, dark and shaggy, and towering above me like the genie in the fairy-tale. Upon a pair of shoulders that seemed to graze both walls of the passage was planted a head of prodigious bigness, the broad pate, bald as a bladder, beaming like a halo within the rim of grayish locks. And the face matched the rest of that Gargantuan sconce: for size, a very dishpan of a face, brown as mahogany, and all creased and crinkled like an old shoe; and in the midst of this expanse of leathery wrinkles, under brows like hedges, glinted two small gray eyes, shrewd and hard as tool-steel.

"This here old turnip o' mine p'ints to seven ten," says he, in his resounding tones, and as he put back his watch I noticed for the first time that his left sleeve hung empty. "But looky here, young lightnin' streak, you take my advice and keep them deadlights o' yourn on the lookout, and don't be a-rammin' of parties amidships. Some day you'll maybe bust your bows, you will." And rolling out a rumble of laughter that shook the house, he heaved himself down the passage like a tidal wave.

Well, I had nearly an hour before Mass, so I went back to my room and slicked up some; so that, when I came forth again, I made a tolerably personable appearance. But all the way to church (and even while there, I'm afraid) I was thinking of the one-armed man and wondering what could have induced such an old salt to stray so far away from the sea. For an old salt he was, plain as pumpkins: so much even I could tell who had never laid eyes on a sailor before, much less on the sea.

After breakfast (which was an amazing fine meal —even better than the supper), I felt in such rare feather that I up and bought a cigar—a fat, red-banded ten-center (which properly impressed the clerk); and puffing mightily, strode off down the street to the railroad track. But, being a youth of a fair store of sense, I tossed my cigar away in good season. I knew the symptoms from a certain deadly experience; but was beforehand with them this time.

I was off to search for my lost money, the glad upshot of it being that St. Anthony (if I may be pardoned a sporting phrase) ran true to form. There lay my purse in plain view on the bowlder where I had stript for my swim.

But that the purse had been dropped just here, and not elsewhere, was indeed a lucky stroke. Had I lost it back in the hills, where hunting it would have been a hopeless task, my adventures, I guess, had hit a period: on such touch-and-go chances rests the material of this history. But, if I may point a

moral once in a way (and I promise not to do it
often), many a man's life is altered for better or
for worse by circumstances equally as trifling.
Mine, I know, was altered for the better, though the
improvement was not to be without its thrills: for,
on the nail, while yet my heart glowed with the joy
of my regained wealth, I decided to revisit Jack's
House and pay back her generous loan to my cousin
Domini.

The bluff at this point was too steep for ascent;
I would retrace my way up the railroad to the first
draw, and then cut through to Jack's House.
Downriver the next hollow held Mr. Crowninshield's bungalow, and you may suppose I meant to
steer clear of that.

Half a mile or more, maybe, I had to walk—
almost to where the river begins to bend round toward McGregor—before the bluff fell away. Here,
to my surprise, after stooping through the wire
fence, I came upon a kind of path winding upward
through the glen. Lucky for me there was a path,
as the scrub-oak, which grew thick as jimson, would
have been tough stuff to plow through. For a couple or three minutes I followed this path, when all
of a sudden I found myself at the foot of a long open
area, with a waterfall and ferns at the upper end,
pretty as a scene in a play. I recognized the spot
at once as the glade where I had witnessed the pantomime of Mr. Crowninshield and my uncle.

It would be easy to make Jack's House now; all

I had to do was to strike yesterday's trail, and I put off briskly up the glade.

But, ere I had taken five steps, I popped aside behind a tree. Conceive my start! Not a stone's fling ahead, seated on a log dead in my way, was Mr. Crowninshield. Had he not been so lost in his own thoughts he must have observed me; but, though he faced me, he sat with his eyes upon the ground, poking into the sod with his cane.

A little, and my first jump of fear began somewhat to abate. After all, the only score Mr. Crowninshield could have against me was that I had bitten his servant's hand, and likely enough the servant's declaration that I had broken into the bungalow. But Mr. Crowninshield hadn't caught me at it, and it was long odds but he would be unable to identify me by the servant's description. Moreover, Mr. Crowninshield, whatever his faults, would be open-minded enough, no doubt, to listen to an explanation; and if I stepped out now and told him all—who the real burglar was, and how I tried to capture him—I might make a friend of the man whom I had somehow been considering an enemy. Add to this, that I should probably be doing Mr. Crowninshield a pretty large favor; for it was beyond question he possessed something of peculiar value, seeing he kept it thus close to his person instead of in a safety vault in Chicago, and seeing, too, that Carver had made such a long journey to steal it.

In effect, after a few minutes of rapid thinking

(I weighed the other side too, but relied on my fleetness of foot: if it should go to that, I could give Mr. Crowninshield cards and spades), in effect, I say, I was within an ace of coming out into the open, when a footstep on the path behind me froze me like a rabbit.

"You're late," said Mr. Crowninshield, rising and glancing at his watch.

Before him, dapper, jaunty, and assured, stood Clarence F. Carver!

XIV

IN THE PAVILION

"B UT not too late, I hope," said Carver. "Is it anything of importance?"

They had started leisurely down the path, Crowninshield leading. You may fancy what a taking I was in, and how I scarce durst breathe! With Carver a friend of Crowninshield's, there was mystification with a vengeance! I knew it would be folly now to show myself.

"Not particularly," answered Crowninshield. "Where's the boy?"

"Gone, I think, sir."

"Good." They were passing me now. I could have reached an arm around the tree-trunk and caught Carver by the ankle. But I had no such temptation, be assured!

"And Mitchell?" said Crowninshield, giving my tree a swipe with his cane. "All quiet and safe?"

"Absolutely."

And saying no more, they passed out of sight among the scrub-oak. But what I had overheard was quite enough to put me in a twitter of thought. Who the "boy" was, and who Mitchell, I had a

guess. If right, I had stumbled on as blackguardly
an intrigue as any you might find in a dime novel—
though, I must own, Carver's attempted burglary
didn't fit into this hypothesis. If wrong, then I had
no explanation at all and was merely at sea. But,
right or wrong, of one thing I made sure: Crowninshield and Carver were as slick a brace of rogues as
any going, and, for all Carver's housebreaking, were
hand in glove upon some scheme that shunned the
light.

Here was my way of it: I was the "boy" and
Mitchell was the gentleman who had been assaulted
in the lane. This, as you see at once, leagued together in the dirty work Crowninshield, Carver, the
three bandits, and one whom I had all but forgot—
Reed, the ring-leader, according to Bill Short, of
the robber gang. Who this Reed was, stumped
me. Could he be the man I had taken for Mr.
Crowninshield's servant? Or was he, by any
chance, the old sea-dog of the Royal Windsor, done
up in disguise and playing a part? This guess,
though striking my fancy, was not likely. The one-
armed sailor too genuinely smacked of the sea, and
besides (as I judged), was too forthright a character to be acting a double rôle.

All this while I had lain motionless in the grass.
Now, making sure the coast was clear, I jumped up
and struck out up the glen for Jack's House. Besides paying back her money, I had another purpose
now in getting speech of my cousin Domini: to find

out if she knew the man named Mitchell. If she did, then for a certainty Mitchell was my Pullman friend; for doubtless he had been on his way to Jack's House when the robbers fell upon him. Altogether, I was in quite a flutter over my Sherlock Holmes activity and clipped it hotfoot along yesterday's trail.

The closer I approached, though, the warier I got; it was no part of my plan to be discovered by my uncle. But this was my lucky day: up on the porch reading a book sat my kinswoman alone.

Of course I wasn't going to venture across that open lawn; so, screening myself behind the identical clump of dwarf pines in which Silly Sim had lurked, I began whistling like a cardinal. I meant to signal her, directly she looked my way. But my imitation must have been as good as the original, for she didn't even raise her eyes from her reading.

Then I tried a catch somewhat more human, and at the first strains of "Dixie," she dropped her book and turned such a look of surprise toward the woods as made me smile. I stood up and beckoned her: and you should have seen her face then!

Up she jumps and sails down the grass pointblank for my covert. But I flagged her down pretty quick and pointed to the pavilion. In a trice she was up to the dodge and, to cloak her tell-tale precipitancy, stopped and plucked a rose; then sauntered in the direction of my rendezvous. She was cute, was my cousin Domini, and a girl in ten thousand.

We met at the pavilion arch.

"What in the name of common sense, Cousin Gerard!" says she, giving me her two hands. "Signals and trysts—why, I begin to feel like a heroine in a play. There, I'm so glad you've come back. Come, we'll have it out with papa once for all. There'll be a scene maybe—only one, and—"

"Cousin Domini," said I, "you know I can't. That's settled. But I didn't come for that. Look!" I drew out my purse. "St. Anthony found my money."

She clapped her hands. "Hurrah for St. Anthony!"

"And now," said I, "I'm going to return your fifty dollars."

"But you're sure you won't need it?" she urged. "No? Then I'll give you this rose to commemorate our deal in high finance—and the honesty of my cousin Gerard." And she stuck the rose into my coat lapel.

"Also the cunning of my cousin Domini," added I. Whereat she bobbed her head, and,

"Oh, but I'm a slyboots, I am," says she, with a smile and a knowing look.

I made no answer, for I was trying to think of some way of broaching Mitchell and the plot afoot without alarming her. Besides, she was so frank and innocent and secure, it did seem incongruous and even a trifle foolish to suppose she could be on the brink of any danger.

"Cousin Domini," said I, sitting down beside her, and looking very serious, no doubt (for I caught her amused expression), "Cousin Domini, on my way up from St. Louis I met a gentleman by the name of Mitchell. Do you know him?"

She gave a little start, and then smiled.

"Well, but what was he like? There are no end of Mitchells in the country, I should imagine."

Though I made but a poor hand of it, I described him as well as I could; but ere I had finished,

"Why, that's Dan!" she cried, her eyes all shining. "Dan Mitchell, as I live! He's just the finest fellow going. Why didn't you tell him you were my cousin? But you didn't know of course. He and I——"

"S-sh!" hissed I, laying my hand upon her arm. I had heard some one cough in the direction of the house, and now, in the silence, detected the sound of approaching steps.

Quick as a wink I sprang up on the seat and grasped one of the cross-beams supporting the roof. Swinging up on this, I had just time to flatten myself on a plank that luckily lay athwart the rafters, when a shadow fell across the opening below; and peeping down, I saw my uncle.

"Excuse me, child," said he, "but I wish you would come up to the house. Gordon just dropped in, and I have asked him to stay for dinner. You're not busy, are you?"

Domini got up.

"Why, no, papa. Only—"

"Yes?"

"Only I hope my bird doesn't fly away while I'm gone. See that little finch?" Domini pointed out toward the pines; but I saw, right off, she meant me.

"Ah," said her father, "he's a pretty fellow, sure enough. Were you feeding him?"

"No," said Domini. "I was just talking to him. He had ever so much to tell me. But I'm going to feed him too, if he'll only stay."

"Come," said he, "he'll wait for you."

My uncle spoke truer than he thought: the wingless finch up on the rafters had already made up his mind to wait for her.

When they were gone, I took the rose from my buttonhole and pressed it in where my other treasure was—in my purse. Then, spying more planks standing against the rear wall of the pavilion, I dropped to the ground and hoisted the bulk of them across the rafters: if it came to a hiding-place I was going to play it safe. Climbing back on my perch, most unbirdlike I stretched out and gazed up at the leafy roof two feet above my eyes.

By and by I caught the sound of voices and a little after, Domini and Crowninshield entered the pavilion. Only fancy my dismay! Of all places, why in the world had she brought him to the very spot where she knew I lay concealed? But next second came a speech that almost took me breathless.

"Miss Domini—Domini—am I not worthy of a single word? Won't you speak to me? I love you, dearest. Body and soul and mind and heart, I love you. I've told you this before, but somehow you would not take me seriously. . . . Domini, if you only knew! If you only knew how I love you! God! I want you beyond anything in heaven or on earth, Domini!"

He paused, and I, fairly aghast, threw caution to the winds and popped my head over the brink of the planks. There was my cousin, seated, and Crowninshield bending over her in an attitude that made me long to whack him one on the backside.

"Domini, darling, is this silence—" He made to take her hand, but, before you could say Jack Robinson, she had somehow eluded the caress and risen to her feet, facing him with a kind of tender pity in her eyes that I resented. For I tell you the truth, had he so much as touched her, I would have broken up that love scene with a pine board!

"Mr. Crowninshield," says she (too gently to suit my taste), "you pay me a great compliment. But—but I am sorry for you. Will you take that for an answer? It is the only answer I can give."

I never saw a man's face fall so in all my born days. He tried to say something, but the words stuck in his throat; then, with a bow, he left the pavilion. For three seconds even I felt a bit sorry for him.

Three seconds, I say: for at the fourth (or thereabouts) I peered out through the leaves of the roof and saw him turn and look back: and I give you my honest word that the ugly leer on his great purplish mug made my flesh creep.

Silence. . . . Then,

"Has my finch been scared away?" came a low voice.

"No," said I, "he's still on his perch.   But—but—"

"Yes, pretty finch?"   And, though I didn't look down, I could swear to a titter.

"For heaven's sake, Cousin Domini," I blurted, "why the dickens did you bring him here?"

"Just because I knew my finch was here."

"Oh," said I: but all the dear trust of that reply didn't come home to me then.

"Anyhow," I went on, after a bit, "you treated him too nice."

"Nice?"

"Yes, you were sorry for him.   That's what you said—and you looked it too."

For a space she was silent.   Then, very sweetly,

"Cousin Gerard," she asked, "did you ever declare your love to a young lady?"

"Me!"   With blushing cheeks I spurned the insinuation.   "Well, I should say not!"

"Because if you did, you know, and she had refused you, you would want her to have a kindly feeling at least for what you had offered her."

I was willing to make some concession. "Well, yes; that would have been all right for 'most anybody else. But—but that son-of-a-gun—"

Rose a ripple of laughter.

"Oh, come, Cousin Gerard! Even son-of-a-guns deserve that much consideration, don't you think?"

But my tolerance couldn't make the stretch.

"No. sir-ee," I declared stoutly. "Why, Cousin Domini"—and this slipped out before I knew it—"Crowninshield's kidnapped your friend, Mr. Mitchell!"

"He's what? Kidnapped? Is Dan Mitchell out here? Come, Cousin, play me fair and square and tell me everything."

But I didn't reply. Lucky for me—for both of us—that I had but just taken a peek toward the house. My uncle was not thirty yards away, heading straight for the pavilion.

"Your father!" I whispered; and scarcely had I readjusted my planks when,

"Alone!" he exclaimed, standing before the archway. "But you were talking, Domini. I swear I heard a voice."

"Come in and sit down, papa. There. Now, let me fix your tie. You think you know how to dress, dear, but I must inspect you every time. So. Now then, I *was* talking." Sure, my cousin Domini had a cool nerve.

"To whom? I see no one. To yourself?"

"To one of my guardian angels." (I almost chuckled: a while ago I was a finch; what would she make of me next?)

"To one!" says he. "Why, have you two guardian angels?"

"Don't you think I need two, dear? I did just now. But—but he's gone at last."

I knew who it was she meant. So did her father, for he didn't answer immediately. Then,

"At last?" says he, and his voice was crestfallen. "Then you don't care for him one little bit? . . . Of course I asked him what you said before he went away. But I told him to take heart, because I knew my little girl would do anything I asked her. Wouldn't she?"

It was Domini's turn now to hesitate. But when she spoke, how full of love was her voice! And all for that half a man, that puny dandy she called her father. God forgive me, but I reproached her for it in my heart.

"Dear father," says she—it was the first time I had heard her use that word, too sacred for him, I swear—"I don't know why you wish me to marry Mr. Crowninshield. But I know you must wish it for my good. All my life long you have been generous to me—generous to a fault: you have given me everything I wanted. And now, if I refuse to—"

"Ah," said her father, like one who has solved a puzzle—but his tone was kindly, too, "then there's somebody else, and you never told me. Come, young Mitchell, I daresay?"

Positively my heart sank, for I was certain he had hit the nail on the head. But next breath, like a refreshing shock, Domini uttered a little peal of laughter.

"Dan Mitchell! Oh, papa! I would as soon think of marrying my cousin Gerard!"

Whereupon I inwardly heaved a sigh of satisfaction. I knew now that Mr. Mitchell was definitely out of the running, and forthwith resolved to free him from Crowninshield's clutches.

"Oh, that boy," said my uncle contemptuously (which only made me grin). "Why, Domini, I didn't know you disliked Dan Mitchell so thoroughly."

"Oh, but I don't!" cries she. "Dan's a perfect dear of a fellow. But—but, to tell you the truth, papa, don't you think marriage is far too serious a business to be gone at blindly? I mean, don't you think one should choose for one's self? A girl must certainly know her own heart better than her father knows it. Of course, papa," she added hastily, "I am sure you *think* it is a good arrangement; I am sure you *think* it is best for me: I know that."

There fell a little silence, and I wondered what was coming next. I wanted to scratch my right leg the worst way; but of course durst not: the least thing might make the old man smoke.

"Domini, child," says he at last, a tremble in his

voice, "you say I have been kind to you. I—I think I have. I have tried to be both father and mother to you. You have been a good child, too; you have responded to my kindness. I think I have your love. Like a good, dutiful daughter, you have obeyed me in all other things; will you not obey me in this one too?"

Through a chink in the planks I could see him; his fingers were working in convulsive little clutches along the bench.

For a moment Domini faltered; but when she replied, I thought I noticed a slight stiffening of tone.

"Papa, do you think this is a matter of obedience —quite?" Then, quickly, with all her former tenderness, "O papa," she said, "I know you think you are trying to fix a suitable marriage for me. I know you want me to be happy. But I—I can't help doubting your judgment here. Besides, there is one who comes before even you, dear father."

He popped about.

"And who—who is that?" he demanded brusquely, and almost defiantly.

"God."

"God?"

"Yes, Mr. Crowninshield isn't a Catholic."

I could almost see her father jump. "But, Domini, the Church allows mixed marriages. That's nothing new. Oh, come," he added, immensely relieved. "That's nothing—nothing at all!"

"That's everything," replied my cousin calmly.

He stuck at an answer; he must have seen she wouldn't budge: I saw it. At length,

"Domini," says he, "whatever else you may think of me for this, please don't imagine for a minute I have any axe to grind. I am looking solely to your welfare. Now, child, I am older than you. I have seen more of life. And while you may be right that a girl should choose for herself—because, after all, it is her own happiness that's at stake— I believe she ought to listen, at least, to the advice of her father. Now, you object to Gordon because he is no Catholic. Very good. But suppose he becomes one? Suppose for your sake he joins the Church? You will not only win a husband, but you will at the same time win another soul to Christ. [Of all the humbugs! him prating about winning souls!] And you may take my word for it, Domini, Gordon will make you an excellent husband. I know him. He's a fine, thorough-going character. I realize there can be no girl and boy infatuation in this marriage. Gordon is a man, a mature, level-headed man. The sort of love he offers you is what these romances all must come to in the end— that is, if a happy union is to result. Usually, the boy and girl romance is a rough road for both. It will be best for you, my child, to accept this love of Gordon's. You will come to appreciate him, never fear. And you will be happy; that is what I want."

"Papa," says she at once, "to be perfectly frank

with you, I haven't the shadow of any love for Mr. Crowninshield; more than that, I really don't like him. But to please you, dear, I am willing to do this: I am willing, if he promises to become a Catholic, to let him—let him take his chances. I mean—though it sounds utterly brazen to speak this way—but I must be straightforward—I mean that if he gives me his word to take instruction in the Catholic Church, I will be as nice to him as I would be to any other man who intended to propose to me. And if I can come to love him as I would want to love a husband, well and good—I will give him my hand. I cannot do more, dear papa. I am do—" —a pathetic little catch tripped her speech— "I am doing this much only for your sake."

"And that's very right of you, my child," says my uncle. "Come, give your old daddy a kiss—for I *am* old, I really am. There now, we'll go up to dinner, and you'll sing me a song afterwards."

They went away; but there was little music in Domini's heart then, if my guess was right. What she had let herself in for, neither she nor I entirely appreciated; but I at least had some pretty gloomy misgivings. And like a callow, rough-judging boy, I set it down as mighty foolish of my cousin to play putty to my uncle's touch; I thought she had been a girl of sturdier mettle; and had something yet to learn of filial piety and devotedness.

XV

WHAT I OVERHEAR IN THE MAPLE TREE

BEING pretty stiff with lying on my hard planks, I decided to get down and take a turn in the woods. But first I had a good lookout through the vines to be sure nobody was in sight.

It was a pleasant cool day, the air full of fragrant pine scent, and the needle-covered hill-top making fine noiseless walking. A little breeze was stirring in the tree-boughs too, for the sunlight flickered over the ground, swapping places with the shade. Of course I was mighty careful to keep well back in the woods; I knew it would be all up with my plans if my uncle spied me—or, for that matter, William or Mary, either. For plans I had, or rather a resolution: to stay near my cousin Domini as long as she wanted me, and to find Mr. Mitchell. Accordingly, I didn't stroll very far, but kept within easy striking distance of the pavilion. Besides, I must own, I hadn't forgot what Domini had said about feeding the finch.

Well, after prowling about for nigh on an hour, I returned to our rendezvous. I was a bit disappointed not to find my cousin, for I rather expected her to come back. But looking up, to my great delight I spied a corner of white napery hanging over the edge of my hiding-place. Quick as a squirrel I had whipped up on the rafters: there before me was a tray of covered dishes and a glass pitcher of iced tea with halves of lemons swimming in it. Bless my cousin Domini! she was as good as her word, and had fed the finch.

· Squatting Indian-fashion, I was just about to fall to, when I noticed a slip of paper sticking up in the tumbler. It was a note, and though the most of it fell in with my wishes, the last sentence came near spoiling my whole dinner.

Dear Cousin Gerard:

Please don't go away till I see you. If you stay to-night, I think I can smuggle you into the house. You won't mind sleeping on the sofa downstairs, will you? But we must be careful. I think it best for me to keep away from the summer-house till evening. I'm afraid William smells a rat. He caught me with the tray—wanted to take it out there for me. I'll be in the summer-house between eight and nine—how deliciously thrilling!

I don't understand what you said about Mr. C and Dan Mitchell. Did Dan come out here? What was the matter between him and Mr. C? You must tell me.

You heard all my shameless talk about Mr. C. What must you think of me? That I am setting my cap at him? But what would you say if I told you I was actually going to wed him?

Lovingly,

Domini.

P. S.—I hope there's enough iced tea.

Well, there was enough iced tea all right, but too much altogether of Mr. Gordon Crowninshield. Had my cousin, after all, agreed to marry him? Or was she only joking? Sure, when she and her father left the pavilion, she was hedged with a pretty safe proviso. True, she had yielded more than was to my fancy, but at that she had not committed herself. To my way of thinking no girl with a mind of her own would commit herself, no matter how much she might love her father. Domini loved my uncle, but I made sure she didn't love him to the extent of throwing herself at Crowninshield's head. That was too much.

And yet, here was the letter.

The prospect of Crowninshield's marrying my cousin was all but sickening, so that for a little my appetite clean left me. But pretty soon I got hot; something in my chest began to smoulder and smoke and burn, and finally flared up strong (an angry heart if ever there was one); and I swore a big oath that by George, before ever I saw my dear kinswoman made unhappy, I would break that match to flinders! And thereupon my hunger came back, and I made an excellent meal, drank all the iced tea, and sucked the lemons afterwards.

But it was all very fine to swear round oaths— even such a mouthful as 'by George': I must be up and doing. And right away I see my main chance of thwarting Crowninshield lay in rescuing Dan Mitchell and making him acquainted with the whole particulars of this underhand business. Unlike me, he would have open access to Jack's House, and might go straight to my cousin and tell her his story—how he had been overpowered in the lane and held captive through Crowninshield's orders. For, though the details were obscure, I made sure Crowninshield had employed that gang of roughs simply to give himself a free hand in his wooing of Domini. But, in this supposition, it was clear that Crowninshield feared Mitchell as a rival: no matter, sooner Mitchell a thousand times than that beast of a Crowninshield: and besides, she had said she didn't care for Dan Mitchell any more than she did for me. Anyhow, once Mitchell made my cousin see the low-down, mean, contemptible trick— or rather, once he proved to her the trick was Crowninshield's (she could put a name to it, I imagined)—then good-night to Mr. Gordon Crowninshield's hopes, Catholic or no Catholic. My cousin might be the most obedient daughter in the world, but when it came to countenancing evil-doing and yoking herself with a man who was no more nor less than an outright villain, she would have spunk enough, I made sure, to draw the line.

I had done all this weighty thinking as I once more flew my perch and stealthily made for the woods.

Of the general location both of the bungalow and of what had been the cabin of the three kidnappers I thought I had some notion. With respect to

Jack's House, the bungalow would be south and east, between a quarter and a half of a mile; while the log shack (if anything were left of it) would be almost due east of me.

Well, I did a great deal of pushing about, but all to no purpose. For an hour, maybe, I continued the search, but spied not a soul nor, for that matter, any vestige of the burnt cabin or of a bivouac or a hiding-place.

At length, being on the summit of a knobby eminenee, I decided, as a kind of last expedient, to climb up into a nearby maple of giant bigness, whose spired top raked the surrounding hills and hollows. The trunk was of so huge a circumference that I couldn't begin to get a purchase on it, but had to shin up a neighboring ash, scramble out on a limb, and so drop into the crotch of the maple.

Up I went—up, up, as high as I could make it. For I had a difficulty, and it was this: the leaves of the great vegetable were so close-packed that for the first fifty or sixty feet I could see only masses of foliage and nothing at all beyond: above and below and on all sides round I seemed to be held in a tower of greenery.

But by and by a rift, like a window or porthole, opened out riverward; and I tell you I caught my breath—I was suddenly looking clean across the Mississippi to the Wisconsin bluffs, and felt a mile in the air. I hadn't thought myself near the river at all, and here it was, smack at my feet, crisping and sparkling in the wind and sun.   Edging out a little further on the limb, I saw all the woods beneath me, curving up and down like what I imagine sea-swells are: very regular and very graceful, with all the roughnesses mitigated by the distance.   Over somewhat to my right, in a deep trough amid these waves, lay Crowninshield's bungalow: I could descry the patch of bright lawn among the trees, with the house in the midst of it, and smoke curling upward from a single chimney—the whole like some toy plantation on a nursery carpet.

And then, apparently plumb below me—but indeed on the next hill—the figure of a man suddenly appears in a kind of oblong glade.   He halts and seems to give ear, and in a twinkle I guessed him for one of the three kidnappers: but whether Blue Island, Bill Short or Fiddles I was unable to discern owing to the distance and the perpendicularity of my vision.

Which of them it was, however, I didn't waste time in trying to make out, but dropped down through that tree hand over fist, every nerve upon the stretch for the hazardous game now before me. Plump into the crotch of the trunk I slid, and in the same breath got such a backset as near unmanned me.   Forth from the circle of underwoods that ringed the maple stepped my uncle and Crowninshield, in spirited talk, and made across the grass directly towards me.   I tell you, but I glued back against that limb! And when they came to a halt, only fancy! their heads were a scant two yards below my feet!

"But surely, Gordon," my uncle was saying, "it's all one to you. Besides, you would be willing to satisfy her scruple, wouldn't you?"

You can imagine I pricked up my ears; I knew what was toward; sure as sunrise my uncle was urging Crowninshield to become a Catholic. But the strange part of it lay in this: Why was he so eager to have Crowninshield marry Domini? The answer I was to learn ere ever I got out of that tree.

"Well, now, I'll tell you what, Blythe," said Crowninshield; and to me the coarseness and even the brutishness of the man were somehow revealed in his omission of the "Mr." "I'm heartily sick and tired of this whole damned business. I'm sick and tired of shilly-shallying, of beating about the bush. I love Domini, I want her, and by the Lord God I mean to have her! Talk's not my long'suit, but action is: understand me?"

My uncle's voice shook: it should have been with anger, but it was only with fear. "Of course, of course, Gordon, my boy. Of course. And you shall have her, too. But, good God, let's have no scandal. Be reasonable, my dear fellow. A scandal would disgrace me forever. Think of my position."

Crowninshield barked a gruff laugh, evil to hear.

"Think of your position! That's good, that is. Your position! Better call it your fix. Why, man, suppose I suddenly lost my fancy for Domini, what would happen to you to-morrow?"

There was a positive quaver in my uncle's reply.

"Don't! Don't, Gordon! For the love of God, don't! I'm an old man, and that would kill me!"

But Crowninshield, cruel as coarse, relished the baiting. He gave another unpleasant laugh.

"Do you suppose now," said he, with the detached air of one putting an abstract case, "she has any idea in whose house she's living and whose food it is she's eating?" Then he chuckled. "Jove! If she knew who supplied all her pretty frills and flounces!"

My uncle groaned; I'll say that much for him— he groaned: I hope for his daughter; it would have been something at least to his credit. As for me, I didn't groan; I could only stare down through the leaves, my mouth agape. Even into my thick head the truth was beginning to leak: and a kind of pity came plucking at my heart for this degenerate old man; and toward my cousin Domini, not a pity altogether, but a wild desire, too, to fight to the last ditch in defense of her honor and her happiness.

"But, Gordon, Gordon," protested my uncle, "say you'll come to-night. I have her word that she'll be your wife if you promise to become a Catholic. You'll assume no obligation—no real obligation, ànyhow. You won't mind—"

"Oh, as to that," flung out Crowninshield, "all religions are the same to me; they're all equally good—or bad, whichever you like. I don't object to play-acting once in a way—for a good cause. Anyhow, once the birdie's mine, my religious costume goes to the moth-balls. That's not the point. The point is: are you *sure* of her? I have no wish to play the fool again. To be rejected once goes hard enough with a proud man."

"Sure!" echoed my uncle. "Am I sure! My dear fellow, nothing could be surer. Come," he went on, in more cheerful tones, "when shall I look for you? Say half-past seven or eight. We must cinch everything to-night, you know."

"True enough," says Crowninshield. Then, after a little, "Well," he continued, "if you think this plan will work, I'm game for it." He laughed sourly. "I'm afraid if she knew I would as cheerfully turn Hindu or Holy Roller to get her, she might have a different mind—what!" This last word he rapped out so suddenly and withal so menacingly that (as I could see) my uncle jumped and lifted haggard eyes.

" 'Pon my word, Gordon, you—I—I am a trifle nervous to-day, and your abrupt remarks are just a little—a little disturbing."

Crowninshield lit a cigar before replying.

"Too bad," says he, "your nervousness. It must be the weather. Come, let's find some place to sit down. There are one or two other points I want to remind you of in case of Domini's not—well, not acquiescing in your wishes."

I heard my uncle's timorous "yes?"; and when Crowninshield spoke again, the pair were too far away for me to make out what was said.

But, as it was, I had heard a plenty; the brutal fact being that my kinswoman was sold—just as you sell live stock, for money. It was plain now why that poltroon, her father, desired the match: he would convert his daughter into flesh-and-blood specie to pay off his debts.

And yet, had Domini actually consented to accept Crowninshield? I could hardly believe it. Notwithstanding her own words in that note and in spite of what her father had said just now, the thing looked fishy. My uncle might be lying to Crowninshield. He was in desperate deep water and would grasp at anything to save his skin for a while longer. If a lie could serve the turn, lie he would: I knew that. If a lie could but feed Crowninshield's hopes, he would trust to luck to patch things up later.

On the other hand, what if it were true? What if Domini really had yielded to her father's importuning? There was no telling what had happened in the house after the pair left the pavilion. Strongminded as she was, her father might yet have wrested her consent: it was certainly conceivable.

Which was I to believe—that Domini had knuckled under or that my uncle had lied? All things considered, it was safer to go on the assumption that the poor girl had been tricked into the match. It was my part now to undeceive her. And for this I didn't need Mitchell.

Indeed, I had news here to steel my cousin's heart such as no other thing could steel it. But would Domini believe the story? She had only my word for it; for all his wickedness, she would still be loyal to her father; and when it came to a showdown, and she taxed him with his baseness or questioned him about it (which was the most I could hope for), he would deny outright the whole charge. And then I should be up a stump. . . . Mitchell, if not absolutely necessary, would be highly useful after all.

But it was my job now to follow Crowninshield and my uncle, and to continue my eavesdropping. In any event, even if I made no further discovery, I would disclose the whole story to Domini before eight o'clock that night.

Now, I was just within an ace of sliding to the ground, when a sudden passing uneasiness restrained me. What caused it, I know not: it wasn't luck (though my luck had turned, too)—I know luck when I see it, I hope; nor was it any natural warning I had received, for neither eye nor ear had detected aught. To tell you the truth, I like to think it was my guardian angel, there in the tree with me, laying his protecting hand upon my shoulder.

Whatever it was, it stayed me from landing plop on the head of Carver!

Noiselessly stepping from behind the tree-trunk, "By Jove!" murmurs he (as I hung over him with loosened knees and a goneness in the pit of my stomach), "so that's the trick, is it? Well, well, the old boy *is* up against it, all right."

Then, instead of spying further on my uncle and Crowninshield, as I thought he would do, he slips back behind the tree and sets out, warily and quickly, down the opposite slope of the hill. In two shakes I had decided to shadow him. He was my man, I saw at once: for he, not Crowninshield, knew where the kidnappers kept Mitchell.

Dropping cautiously to the ground, I began what at first I feared would be a risky business. But you are to consider Carver suspected nothing (as indeed, why should he?) and once, therefore, out of earshot of Crowninshield and my uncle, he proceeded with a careless lookout, or none at all, and even became so remiss as to whistle.

Pretty soon, though, he seems to advance a bit more guardedly, stopping now and then and lending ear. This put me up sharp, as you may suppose, so that I got mighty particular just where I set my feet. Surely, thinks I, he must be nearing the kidnapper's camp; and yet, as surely, he wasn't acting as if he were going among his own. And then, a few yards further on, peeping round a thick-bellied sycamore, I see Carver crouching, and beyond him the obvious explanation of all his stealth.

For beyond him, to my no little surprise (for I had lost track of my whereabouts) was Crowninshield's bungalow: plainly he had come to try his hand again at burglary!

XVI

I BECOME AN IMAGINARY BURGLAR: AND
THE SECRET OF THE BUNGALOW
IS REVEALED

FOR a long while now, Carver lay low, so that I wondered whatever he was boggling at. I even got a little out of patience with the man! Then, at last, occurred what he was waiting for. The front door swung open, and a bulky person in a brown straw hat and black alpaca coat came out. You may fancy the shock I got: his right hand was white with bandage! After slamming to the door and then giving it a tug, he passed on down the flags to the woods and so disappeared from sight.

But Carver didn't budge. I was beginning to think he had some other object in his eye than thievery, when at length out upon the lawn he springs and is up on the veranda in a twink. But he wasted no time at the door; up goes the identical window he had formerly used, and' into the house he vanished!

You may take my word for it I wasn't out for a Carnegie medal a second time! Carver might gut that bungalow from top to bottom—more power to him: I would sit here in the shade and watch. Only when he got through would my interest in him come alive again. Take it all around, it was rather a matter to chuckle over—one of my enemies double-crossing the other.

But my chuckling was short-lived. Chancing to cast a glance toward the spot where the flagstone path enters the wood, whom do I see but Crowninshield himself standing at the rim of the lawn with his eyes fixed on the bungalow. My chuckle, as I say, melted out the wrong side of my mouth; for right off I suspected I had been lured into a trap. But upon a second thought, and especially when I see Crowninshield steal back and squat behind an elder bush, his gaze still riveted on the house, I know I am safe and that this skit is to be staged without any cue of mine.

Evidently it was the open window that had aroused Crowninshield's suspicion; and I wondered if he could see Carver in the room. But whether he could or not, he didn't take long to come to a decision. The next thing I knew, there he was out on the open lawn, striding swiftly toward the bungalow. But his was just hop-scotch compared to Carver's stratagem. Talk about your clever tricks: listen to this.

Crowninshield hadn't covered ten yards, I imagine, when Carver pops half out the window, like a jack-in-the-box, and, frantically beckoning Crowninshield,

"Quick!" he cries. "Quick, Mr. Crowninshield!

To the back of the house! It's the boy again. I've got him trapped this time. Hurry round to the kitchen! Quick!" And with that, he springs out and runs up and down the veranda, peering round the corners of the house, for all the world as if he were bent on thwarting my escape.

Well, sir, you can imagine how I grinned! I was supposed to be in the bungalow, and here I lay kicking my heels. It was a cute dodge, and no mistake: Crowninshield at any rate was thick enough to be taken in. For without a moment's hesitation (I am certain that upon the spur of the alert, whatever his later suspicions may have been, it never crossed him to doubt Carver) he ups and tears to the back of the bungalow. His speed amazed me; he certainly made that hulking carcass of his chase over the ground.

"All right!" yelled Carver. "Now I'll run him out. Watch for him!" And thereupon he climbs in again at the window; and for some minutes all is silence.

Meantime, fearing to lose Carver and being pretty much in a sweat, too, to see the upshot of the farce, I skulked along the border of the grass, keeping behind the underwoods, till I reached a kind of outhouse. About thirty feet off, just halfway between the outhouse and the kitchen door, stood Crowninshield; gripping his knobby cane, his purple-jowled mug thrust out, and his bull body, like a wrestler's, all hunched and set, as though he expected to en-

counter, not one, (and him imaginary, mind you,)
but a perfect stampede of boys!

And then, all of a sudden, the kitchen door falls
open, and out walks Carver, cool as a cucumber.

"We were too late, I'm afraid, sir," says he,
drawing out a handkerchief and mopping his brow.
"He must have got out the back way when I called
you.   I thought this door was locked, but I guess
Jonas must have left it open."

Crowninshield thereupon cursed Jonas (who, I
took it, was the servant I had bitten).   "But did
the kid take anything?" he asks.   "I can't understand it.   Last time there was a twenty-dollar bill
under a paper-weight on my table, and the little brat
never touched it.   I can't understand what he's
after."

Says Carver: "It's a mystery to me, too, sir.   So
far as I can tell, he's touched nothing this time,
either."

Fell a silence in which I, too, shared Crowninshield's puzzlement.

Then, in tones plainly tinged with suspicion,

"Look here, Carver," says Crowninshield, "I
thought you said this morning the boy was gone?"

Carver's was a cool nerve.   Says he,

. "Yes, sir.   That's what I told you, because that's
what I thought.   But he fooled me.   I give him
credit for that.   He's slippery, he is."

But Crowninshield kept a dark and doubting eye
on his accomplice.

"And come to think of it," says he, slowly, "how the devil did you happen along here just at this time?" He let out a swear. "This boy business may be a gag for all I know. Has it struck you that the only one I've seen in my house was yourself?"

Carver was in a close squeeze; but upon my soul I was hoping he would get out of it—and he did.

He laughed. It was amazing cheek.

"That's because you didn't get here when I did," he replies off-hand. "I spotted the kid back in the woods and shadowed him here. I guessed what he was up to. You should have seen the little devil snicker when he saw Jonas' hand. I'm not a soft-hearted man, Mr. Crowninshield, but I tell you it made my flesh creep. He's a bad egg, he is, clear through. And if my guess is right, he's bent on upsetting your plans."

(Wrong and right, thinks I.)

"My plans!" exclaimed Crowninshield.

"Oh, well, sir," says Carver, "I beg your pardon; but I guess you've got plans all right, whatever they are, because, surely, you're not just playing a joke on Mitchell."

"Look here, Carver," says Crowninshield, with sudden earnestness, his suspicion clean dissipated, "you get this Linton kid, understand? Keep him close, like Mitchell." Here he cursed me—all the good it did him. "He'll spoil everything yet. Get him, Carver, and it'll be double pay for all hands. And when you've got.him, let me know."

"Yes, sir," says Carver. "Leave it to me. I'll have him before nightfall. [Which made me smile—not if I knew it!] But—but there's one thing I'd like to know. I'd like to know what that kid was after."

Crowninshield made no answer; only tapped on the stone path with his cane.

"I wonder now," continued Carver hesitatingly, "I wonder—if—if he could have got wind of the old yarn up in McGregor?"

"Old yarn?" echoes Crowninshield.

"Well, it's this way, sir," explains Carver, as though in a burst of confidence. "How much truth there's in it, I don't know; but here it is. People say there's treasure of some kind buried in these hills, and some even say on your property. Now this kid might have figured that you had a chart indicating the whereabouts of that treasure. That would explain why he left your money alone. He was only after the chart."

Carver might be hoodwinking Crowninshield; but he would have bitten his tongue off had he known I heard him: at which I could scarce forbear a chuckle.

"True enough," says Crowninshield, "it would. But—but what's this nonsense about buried treasure? It's the first I've heard of it."

"Just what I've told you," says Carver. "I don't know any more about it than you do. And of course if you've never heard of it, it isn't likely you've got the chart."

"Yes," interrupted Crowninshield, "but if I did have the chart, don't you think I'd use it and unearth the treasure myself?"

"But the boy might have thought you had it without your knowing you had it. Anyhow," he broke off, "he's barking up the wrong tree, as I'll be pleased to tell him."

And thereupon the pair of them passed round to the front of the house, leaving me hurriedly thinking many thoughts and all on edge to enter the lists with Carver for the lifting of the treasure. For it was plain as popcorn Carver was seeking treasure: else, why had he mentioned it at all? Why had he refrained from stealing the money in the safe? And especially, why had he adopted, just now, so freakish a manner of escape, when all he had to do was to skip out the back door? Surely, he had spied Crowninshield from the window; surely, there had been no call to cast prudence to the winds and run the risk he did run: so that to me a method rose out of his madness, and I saw the stake he had been playing for—to find out, once and for all, if Crowninshield had the treasure chart.

Then, with a start, I came awake. Fearful lest Carver had slipped through my fingers after all, I stole swiftly along the skirt of the glade, around to

the front of the bungalow.   More luck than sense!
—Carver and Crowninshield were just parting company, the latter entering the bungalow, and Carver
putting off down the walk.   Keeping well hid, I
followed.

When he came out on the railroad track by the
boathouse, instead of striking northward for Mc-
Gregor, he started downriver.   The hired thugs,
then, had been burnt clean out, two nights ago, and
had removed their captive to a new lurking-place
down in this quarter.   But what a chance had been
mine, that night when I found the cabin empty, to
kill at one blow their whole design!   If I had only
climbed that ladder to the loft!   Beyond question,
while I was sleeping below, Mitchell lay bound
above.

Carver, unaware of course that I was tagging
him, strode on boldly down the track; and I, about
a stone's cast behind, slunk along the foot of the
bluff just within the border of the underbrush.

Only one circumstance caused me any misgiving.
Already the shadow of the high hills above me lay
stretched quite half way athwart the great river:
and this meant that the afternoon was on the wane.
I must be careful lest, in pursuing one part of my
plan, I made shipwreck of the other.   For by this,
I had convinced myself that my uncle had spoken the
truth to Crowninshield, and that Domini, for some
reason (worthy in her eyes, to be sure) had consented to the marriage.   So, whatever else I did,

whether I freed Mitchell or not, I must, before
eight o'clock that night, warn my cousin of the plot
against her.   Believe me or not, she had got to be
told.   But if I could only fetch Mitchell with me,
my dead words would have a living proof.

Still Carver stuck to the railroad track, pegging
along as if he had miles more to cover.   With the
distance from Jack's House growing at every step,
I began to feel more and more uneasy in my mind.
Already we were come nigh to the foot of that enormous buttress of cliff at the top of which beetled
Eagle's Nest.   But looking up through the leafy
branches, I could descry nothing of the ledge or the
cavern; only the crag, like some huge fist, bulging
out from the brow of the sheer wall of rock.

I dropped my eyes again to Carver.   He was
gone!   I sprang to the edge of the underbrush and
craned out: and spied him just stooping through the
wire fence: he was going up into the woods to the
kidnappers' new den!

I stole forward quickly, for I had needs now get
closer in order not to lose him.   When I reached
the point where he had left the railroad for the bluff,
I found a path; and giving ear a moment, sure
enough, detected his footsteps further up among the
trees.   He was following the path.

Five yards or so below the top of the bluff (I
could see the crest of it through the bushes and the
blue sky beyond), the path bent out along the pre-

cipitous ascent, toward the river; for at this point
was the great bulge that fell off plumb under Eagle's
Nest. And next moment I knew Carver's destination: it was Eagle's Nest itself.

He had disappeared through the trees at the end
of this level stretch of path; and sneaking forward,
I spied him already on a broad ledge of rock, nothing but the empty air beyond him and far below the
dark river moving in the shadow of the bluff. It
gave me a shock to see such a sudden vacancy all
about.

But I lost not a second in figuring what to do.
Above the ledge the rock rose ten or twelve straight
feet to the very summit of Eagle's Nest. Out upon
this summit (which was grassy and level as a table)
I nimbly crept and, lying behind a patch of buck-
thorn, peered over the brink upon the ledge.

Carver had come to a standstill again: but not
to look back this time, only to halt there facing the
great empty spaces before him. (For the cavern
was around in front of the cliff.)

And as he so stood, my thoughts leaped out to
Silly Sim, and I thought I saw his share in all this
nasty business. The old rogue wasn't so cracked
as they had made him out. Of his motive in prowling about Jack's House I now had some glimmer.
He was a tool of Crowninshield's. He had aided
Bill Short and his gang: he was one of them. They
were now skulking in his cavern. Nay, he was—

a wild surmise enough!—the very captain of the crooks himself, the man called Reed!

·But next second all my guesses got a jolt. Around the corner of the rock, plump into the astonished Carver, rolled the one-armed seaman of the Royal Windsor!

XVII

THE ENCOUNTER ON EAGLE'S NEST

BUT more than my guesses got a jolt. You should have seen how slap that old sailor pulled up, and the look on the big face of him. As to Carver, he didn't budge. There. had been no tryst between these two: that was plain.

Then the one-armed man, to get his plumb, ventured a fidgety kind of a laugh: but a terrible hardness came into his eyes.

"Well, come, mate," says he in his enormous voice, "here's a ͵pleasant head-on. Payin' your respecks to Silly Sim? Must be a sociable old party, this here Silly Sim. I reckon he does something in the fortune-tellin' line, eh?"

"I guess you know what his line is," says Carver, in a tone that made my scalp creep. And then, "Where did you drop from?" he added with a swear. "Who are you, anyway?"

"Me? Why, you might call me Absalom Iron. But I ain't no objections to plain Ab. Ab's more friendly like. And as to droppin' from anywheres, well, mate, that's only a manner o' speakin', to be

sure: but this I will say, I didn't drop from heaven."
Here his eye glanced away to the abyss below, then
shot, like a dagger, straight back to Carver. "And
talkin' of droppin'," he added, "it's consider'ble of
a drop from this p'int to them trees down yonder."

"Now I know you've got it, Mr. Iron," says Carver, and swift as thought has a pistol leveled at the
sailor.

But Iron didn't turn a hair.

"Come, you're a smart sort, you are," he booms
out. "Will you kindly oblige my curios'ty by statin'
what I have got?"

"The chart," says Carver, in a voice of steel.
"And out with it, quick, before I let the daylight
through that carcass of yours."

"Well, now, my son, you look here," returns Iron,
as coolly as if he were arguing the matter in a tap-
room (he was brave, you can bet on that). "I've
squinted down the hatch o' too many o' them things
to be throwed out o' my course by one single p'int.
But I've got sense, I have, and I know when I'm in
a clove-hitch. I know when a ship's scuttled, I do.
I seen too much o' that in my time. But I tell you
this, too, my son: I've sailed a main deal o' water
and rolled over a main deal o' dry ground to lay my
clapper on this scrap o' paper, and by thunder before
ever I hand it over you can send me to Davy Jones!"

He stopped, and his eyes were two gimlet bits
boring Carver. Whether he looked for Carver to
take him at his word, I can't say; but as for me, I

buried my head in the grass: I.hadn't the nerve to
stare murder in the face.

But Carver didn't pull the trigger.

"Is that all you have to say?" he asked; and I
raised my eyes.

"That's my song," replied Iron, not a jot daunted.
"Not but what I ain't ready to sign articles," he
added hastily and (as I thought) with a new gleam
in his eye. "Coz I am. But the condition is mine.
You have your ch'ice. Kill me, and dodge a noose
the rest o' your days; or spare me, and split the
blunt. But my condition is—I keep the chart."

To my great relief (and to Iron's, too, I fancy)
Carver lowered his revolver.

"Well," says he, "that's a different tune. That
sounds fair enough."

"A man can't say fairer, mate," answered Iron.
"Leastways a man in my sitiwation can't. Come,
you stow that weapon, and we shake on it."

And there on the dizzy ledge these two desperate
fellows, mortal enemies a moment since, clasped
hands, if not in friendship, at any rate upon the
bargain. It was a near touch for Carver, I was
thinking: Absalom Iron might have flung him down
the precipice. But Carver must have read his man
aright, for, to my seeing, the deal was struck in good
faith: the honor of thieves was verified again.

"Now, mate," says Iron, a bland smile grotesquely
shifting the wrinkles of his face, "you and me makes
this cruise together, like. But we ain't got the rig-

gin' shipshape yet—leastways not clear away shipshape. What's your handle?"

"Handle?" says Carver. "Oh, well, Dick's my
name. You can call me Dick. Dick will do,
won't it?"

"To a dot. And I like your taste, mate. Dick's
trim and tidy, Dick is.. I knowed many a good seaman by the name of Dick, and all on 'em lucky as
loot. But as for me, I never had no ch'ice, not I;
and it's been rough sailin' with this here Absalom.
The parson had the drop on me, you may say, and
runs up Absalom clean agin my wishes; and I ain't
never been able to haul her down. Howsomever,
them as was at the christ'nin' says I up and kicked
the book out of his hand: and that's a comfort.
Well now, Dick, you'd perhaps want a wink at this
here chart. But what I want to know is, can you
parley-voo?"

"Parley-voo?" echoes Carver.

Iron, during all his booming nonsense, had been
drawing at a cord that encircled his neck. He now
fetched up from his bosom a buckskin pouch, greasy
and black with age.

"Yes, parley-voo," he repeats. "Coz all these
here words ain't the ordinary kind you learn in
school: though the chart's drawed mighty pretty: I
ain't no kick agin the chart. It's the words as gives
me a black eye. They're wrote in French."

"French!" cries Carver. "Then I'm your man.
I can make my way through French—or could once."

Iron had the pouch held between his teeth, and was opening it with his thole-pin fingers. But suddenly he crams the thing back into his breast.

Carver's face fell—and mine, too. For look at the chance I missed. Had Carver translated it then and there, I should have sneaked the secret and had it in my power to beat them to the treasure!

"Come, Dick," says Iron, laying his paw on the other's shoulder, "let's you and me play this safe. I'm all for quick action, by natur' I am. That's my one besettin' sin, as the parson p'inted out. I'm all slap-dash-bang, I am. That's been my failin' from the cradle. Many a sweet chance I've hashed along o' my hurry and tear. So let's you and me go easy on this here prize. Let's—"

"But French," cuts in Carver. "How do you know it's French. Can you read *English?*"

"Like a dominie. But you look here, Dick. Nobody *except* a Frenchy has a name like Jackquees Curnott. And Jackquees were good enough to sign this here paper."

Carver cracked his hands together. (As for me, all my nerves went taut upon the name.)

"Jack's House!" he cried, with a blistering oath. "It's Jack's House, sure as sin! I guessed as much. Why, see here, Iron, I know where the treasure is! Come, let's have a slant at that paper."

But Carver's outburst roused no response in Iron; the old sailor's eyes had become dens of slyness.

"You're a lucky man, Dick, sure enough," says

he. "But I was remarkin' we'd better go easy, like. This here rock is mighty open—like settin' on the courthouse steps. It would jump kind of funny for me and you if somebody glimmed us up here, and Silly Sim cheepin' away his last notes back yonder in the cave."

I caught my breath. Had the monster slain the poor half-wit? But Carver gave my question tongue.

"You killed him, then?" says he.

Iron chuckled grimly.

"Come, Dick, I ain't no raw-head-and-bloody-bones. I don't set up to be no Sunday-school super-'nten'ant; but I don't go round lettin' of daylight through parties neither. I'm hot and quick on the uptake, I am; but when it comes to a ch'ice of words or weapons, I'm all for words. The tongue is mightier'n the sword, the parson said; and by gum, I learnt that lesson. Now you listen here, Dick. Here's what knocked Silly Sim galley-west. I lay aloft here like a true-blood gentleman, and find him a-mumblin' and a-mutterin' over a fishnet; and, says I, 'Howd'ye do, Mr. Simon Doumic,' I says. 'I've got a message, I have, from your friend ——' ah, well, I named the party, and Silly Sim, quick's he heard it, keels over in a fit. Water nor brandy warn't neither of 'em sovereign, so I offs with this here necklace o' his, and sails plumb into you, Dick, and, dash my buttons! not a bad jam-up neither."

"Well, come, then," rips out Carver, "don't stand

here wagging your tongue all day. Let's get out
of this. We've got to study through that paper,
and map out our plan."

"A lad to my fancy you are, mate Dick," says
Iron. "You and me'll cotton like born brothers on
this v'yage. Shove ahead." And thereupon the
pair of them started back for the bluff trail, Iron
already launched forth upon a fresh rigmarole.
They passed so close beneath me that I might have
dropped my arm and swiped off the sailor's hat. I
daresay it would have staggered them.

So soon as they were well on their way down the
bluff, I jumped up, ran back to the path, and stole
out on the ledge. Absalom Iron might have told
the truth; but I had my doubts. In any case, if
Silly Sim were still alive, I could help him.

The platform before the cavern mouth was somewhat wider than an ordinary room. Heaped in the
middle of it was a great pile of dead ashes fringed
with blackened fags of burnt logs. Not knowing in
what condition I should find Silly Sim—perhaps
gone clean crazed and violent—I tiptoed to the corner of the entrance and peered in. There on the
rock floor lay a pitiful wreck: a half-clothed skeleton
of a man, his hoary locks tumbled about his face,
gibbering through his beard, low, inarticulate sounds
like an animal.

No blow had been struck so far as I could see;
but what little intelligence poor Silly Sim had possessed was now extinguished for good and all.

I glanced around. Further within the cavern,
beyond the clutter of nets and old boxes and dingy
clothing, was what looked like a second chamber.
For there was a narrowing of the rock and leaning
against one of the walls, a board partition used, I
surmised, to stop up this neck during the winter:
and on the other side, a pallet of pine twigs and rags
of blanketing.

To this rude bed I dragged the poor wretch and
fixed him thereon as comfortably as I could; though,
mercifully, ease and distress, plenty and want, were
all one to him now. A battered vessel, half full of
water, I set beside him, in the hope that he might
regain strength enough to drink.

But that hope was vain. Already a glassiness
had overspread his eyes, and his jabbering had
dwindled to a mere gurgle, like a death rattle.
Death, indeed, was upon him, and in the immediate
nearness of it I went on my knees to his Maker and
mine for the mercy I, too, should look for at the
end.

But life clung on. Though the withered frame
was all but sped, it still breathed. And as I gazed
down on it, the strange wild life that was now at
the last ebb set me on a muse. Was he, I wondered,
the sole survivor of the massacre at Jack's House?
But that could hardly be. How, then, had he come
by the chart? And above all, having the chart,
why had he not years since lifted the treasure himself? Then I recalled one of the stories about him,

that he was biding the return of a partner: and, in a flash (my flashes took an unconscionable time a-coming, I admit, and still do), I saw how Absalom Iron fitted into the puzzle. He had known this partner—had he not been within a breath of naming him?—and through fair means or foul had won to his secret. I bottomed now Silly Sim's lurking and spying upon Jack's House: the treasure was there, and like a magnet it drew the poor witless creature. All these years he had kept his watch upon it, but had not sense enough to make it his own.

At this point a faint movement of the dying man's head fetched me out of my thoughts and glancing round, I noted with alarm the growing dimness of the cavern.

Running out to the platform, I was dismayed to find the evening already come. The whole wide river between me and the Wisconsin bluffs was mellowing toward twilight. I must hustle, else I should be too late to warn Domini. This, I knew, was going to be a ticklish task—ticklish in three ways: counting Jonas and Absalom Iron, my enemies were now seven, and I had the whole gang to give the slip to; Domini herself was still to be convinced in the face of her father's certain denial of my charge; and last, a bare hour remained to make Jack's House.

But you are not to imagine me lingering there on the ledge and conning my risks. Already I had made a start. But dusk came on ere I had covered half the distance; and then, upon the back of this, I lost my way; so that, when I reached the trestle-work of a water tank in the woods behind the house, it had fallen quite dark.   Was I in time?

Quickly I stole around the tower on the north end of the house.   The open windows of the post-room were all ablaze.   My heart sank.   Crowninshield, then, was here ahead of me?

I listened.   Not a sound.   The whole house was silent as the grave.   Gliding to the nearest window, I ˉpeered cautiously within.   Beyond the center-table my uncle was pacing the carpet.   I saw none else.

For a couple of minutes, maybe, I watched him. He seemed in a desperate fidget, for in that short while he lit and tossed aside two cigarettes, and flipped out his watch at least four times.   But one thing could cause his flutter—Crowninshield's delay. I was still in good time.

But where was Domini?

Dot to my question she appeared at the far end of the room: all in simple white she was, but ten-fold lovelier, if possible, than ever—surely, not more dear; and in her breast was one red rose.   I had thought her face would be sad, but nothing of the kind: a smile was on her lips when she kissed my uncle.

He, the blackguard, patted her cheek, telling her she was as beautiful as good.

"Domini, my dear," says he, "before I go to bed to-night I shall be the happiest man in the world."

"Not if I know it, old boy," vowed I, and darted to the porch. My uncle, then, had indeed wrung Domini's consent, but he had yet to deal with me. The way I jabbed **that** bell-button, **you** would think I looked **for a fight—as** indeed I did.

XVIII

MY UNCLE TAKES THE COUNT

INSTEAD of Mary, the maid, whom I expected, my uncle himself answered the bell. Mighty lucky for me I was standing to one side of the gush of light.

"Step in, Gordon, step in," he cried heartily, swinging out the screen door. "We've been waiting for you, man. A thousand welcomes! I had—"

The words died on his lips; his dandy old face fell all awry. Ere he could take up the recoil of the shock, I had entered, laid hold of the heavy house door, and banged it shut. Then, with my back against it, and my heart shaking me, I confronted him: but there was a cock to my chin.

"Good evening, uncle," said I. "May I speak to my cousin Domini?"

"Wha'—what—b-brass is this!" he spluttered. "You—didn't I order you to quit my premises?" He had taken the high hand: nothing could better have steeled me for my part.

"*Your* premises," I sneered, and fixed him with a look.

184

My shot hit home, I think, for a kind of daunted haggardness started from his eyes. But next moment he came about, and, thrusting forth a trembling hand,

"Leave at once!" he squalled, "or, by God, I'll have you pitched neck and crop through that door!"

It was Domini who answered him. Upon my uncle's clap of rage she had hurried into the hall. But one glance she flung me, all wonder and fear and pain: and then her arms were about her father, seeking to support and soothe him.

"Hush, papa!" cries she. "Think of your heart, dear! There's nothing so awful the matter. He doesn't mean any offense. I—I'm to blame. I invited him to stay."

Little the poor girl dreamed my errand; and there and then all my soul yearned out to her for the pang she must suffer.

"Cousin Domini," I blurted, "I'll leave this house gladly. You know how gladly. But first I must tell you something that will wring your heart. Your father is selling you to-night to Mr. Crowninshield. The bargain has been struck."

The thing was said, brutally said, like the blow of a bludgeon; but it was no time for mincing speech, and anyhow, upon the moment's spur, my tongue could do no better.

Domini only stared, uncomprehending. Not so my uncle. Stark terror, like a death print, stamped his brow; but this he quickly concealed in a desperate attempt to beat me down with sheer fury of words.

"It's a lie!" he screamed in a voice cracking with passion (sure, his anger was genuine enough). "I say it's a lie! Eat those words, you insolent whelp, before you budge! · Tell her it's a lie!"

"What's a lie, papa?" asked Domini, palely calm. "I don't understand."

"That I'm a ruined man. That only your marriage with Crowninshield will save me. That he's promised an allowance—" He checked himself, his face a-twitch, realizing, I suppose, that he had blabbed more of his infamy than I had charged him with. Doubly enraged, he turned upon me again.

"Tell her you lied!"—It was more like a frenzied bark than human speech.—"Quick! Now! Down on your knees, you sneaking beggar, and tell her you lied!"

But I only looked at Domini. A wide horror was dawning in her eyes: she knew the shame at last. But, to my dismay, I saw that a dread of me was on her: her spirit seemed visibly to cower back.

"No! Oh, no!" cries she in a low, pitifully broken voice, seeking the protection of my uncle's arms. "You—you tell me, papa! Your word is enough. But oh! oh, tell me quickly!"

I knew what he would say: I knew Domini would believe him. But I had come to save her, and the botch I was making of it fairly drove me to desperation. Ere he could make answer, I sprang quite up to him: and I think my look meant business.

"You dare not tell her!" I shouted, dashing the lie from his lips. "You dare not! I defy you to tell her!" Every roaring word I let him have full in the face. Sure, if mere rant was to carry the day, the lung power was on my side. But truth lay with me too, and for the next few minutes I poured it into him, broadside after broadside.

"No, but tell her this!" cried I, and a fierce joy seized me to see defeat already cringing in his blinking eyes. "Tell her you came out here, not for your heart's sake—though God knows your heart's bad enough—but for the sake of Crowninshield! That's why he alone knows your whereabouts. That's why you receive no visitors but him: tell her that! Tell her you *are* a ruined man, and Crowninshield has ruined you. Tell her you begged him to marry her—on your knees you did. And when she refused, because he was no Catholic, you implored him to become one. You said he had only to satisfy her scruple—that he assumed no obligation—that he had only to sham it out: that's what you said this very afternoon—tell her that! Tell her his answer: that he didn't 'object to play-acting once in a way, and anyhow, once he had the birdie safe, his religious costume went to the moth-balls!' That was his answer—tell her that! And tell her what he said before: that he was sick and tired of shilly-shallying, of being fed with empty promises; that he loved Domini, and wanted her, and by the

living God meant to have her—tell her that! **Oh,**
you know what kind of a love is his, and you welcomed it—nay, you begged for it: and you call yourself her father!"

I paused out of sheer breathlessness, for, I tell
you, I had never reeled off so many words at one
stretch in all my life. But I didn't take my eyes
from his—not for a single second. I saw I had
him cowed, and cowed I meant to keep him to the
end.

"You have called me a liar," I went on, a little
more calmly, but driving into him just the same.
"Is it a lie that Crowninshield hired a gang of thugs
to kidnap Dan Mitchell? Is it a lie that at this very
moment Dan Mitchell is held captive within a mile
of this house? Is it a lie that Crowninshield said
he would as soon turn Hindu or Holy Roller to get
Domini? And when you invited him here to receive Domini's promise, is it a lie that you said the
matter must be cinched to-night? Cinched! as if it
were a money-bargain—as it was, by thunder!—
and not your daughter's happiness and honor!
Answer me—is it a lie that Crowninshield owns
this house?—that the very food you eat is Crowninshield's? Didn't he say so? Didn't he say—and
chuckle over it too, by Heaven!—that he supplies
the very clothes your daughter wears? No wonder
you want this marriage!"

I was out of breath again; but I filled my lungs
and gave him a last shot.

"You bade me tell your daughter I lied. Now, look her in the face, and if there's any father left in you, confess I've told the truth!"

And here, for the first time, I turned to Domini. I won't describe her look, because I can't. But this I will say: it was fortunate for me—for her, too—that I had kept my eyes bayoneted into my uncle; for, had I but glanced at her anguish, I shouldn't have had the heart to maintain the attack.

As for my uncle, he made a pitiful effort to pull himself together.

"My dear," says he, clearing his throat, and trying to assume an air of dignity, "I hope you will not take too seriously what this fellow has said." Domini's heart, as I could read in her eyes, was fighting with her mind: but her mind was on my side. "He has misconstrued a few unfortunate facts, basely mis—"

"Facts! Oh, papa! you call them facts!" I leave to your fancy how she said it.

The old man coughed again, struggling for aplomb.

"Well, certainly, my dear, some of these—er, charges are—well, undeniable—"

"Undeniable!" She had shrunk from him as from a thing unclean; dead white she was, and her lips were quivering. But she didn't faint—not she. "Undeniable! Oh! . . . Oh!" And then the shame of her father's scheme made a poppy of her face. "Undeniable that—that man would buy me!

Undeniable that he is—is that kind of a man! Undeniable that he would pretend to be a Catholic! Undeniable that we are living in his house!—that he —oh!—that he pays for my *dresses!* All this undeniable!"

She seemed to tower before my uncle, her hands clenched, her bosom heaving, and in her eyes an edged scorn sparkling. I tell you, she was angry! Compared with her, I had offered but a mild protest.

"And you—you told this brute I had consented to be his wife!" she almost screamed. "You told him that! You asked him here to-night to receive my promise!"

I was well nigh staggered. Domini was safe after all: her father had been stuffing Crowninshield. God only knows how he had expected to tide over the clash; perhaps, with Crowninshield in the house, he had meant to take a new tack.

By this he had so far recovered his poise as to essay the rôle of the indignant parent. But his attempt was as futile as the puff of a man's breath in the teeth of a gale.

"Come, Domini," says he, trying to put some sternness into his look, "is this the proper language of a daughter? I am your father, girl! Where is your reverence, your duty? I—"

My cousin stamped her foot.

"Reverence! Duty!" cries she, unheeded tears upon her cheek (I thought women always broke down when the tears came, but she didn't). **"Do** you dare speak of reverence and duty! Both have been yours—you know it—yes, and love, too, the love of all my heart! And how have you paid me? Oh, see how you have paid me! Where is my reverence? You have killed it! You have killed my love—even my respect!"

This was one too many for my uncle: he saw his game was clean up at last, and in a breath fell all to pieces. The change in him was not pretty: small and slight before, he now became a mere manikin, trembling for his own mean self, contemptible in every word and gesture; his foppish clothes sorrily incongruous with the senile wreck of a face he lifted to my cousin.

"Domini! Domini!" he quavered, the tears slavering down his sunken cheeks, and his shaking hands outstretched. "It's true, all true, my girl. But you must save me—O child, save me! It's gone—all gone. Every dollar. I'm a pauper! O God, a pauper! But Domini, you've been a good girl. Marry him—oh, marry him! Nobody will find me out then. Not a soul. He's promised it. Think of my club! Think of my friends! Think of the hundred things your old father needs. O Domini, marry him, and give me back my life! Just one little word, and all my happiness again!"

Although he spoke the truth, this playing of his last card was more disgusting than all his lies clubbed together; for the selfishness of a lifetime was distilled into his words.

Domini made him no answer: only stared with fear and loathing in her eyes.

And then, all in a moment, ere he could utter another word, my uncle made a horrible grimace, tottered, caught at a chair, and tumbled asprawl.

I sprang forward. But Domini was before me. Scarce had he struck the floor, when she had his head in her lap and was covering his face with sobs and kisses. But, my God, the face she kissed! Only half of it was human; the rest was a gargoyle's: the mouth, in a hideous grin, twisted to the ear, a curl of the upper lip baring the teeth; for an eye, a bulging yellowish whiteness.

"Papa! Father! . . ." But no, I must draw the curtain here. I cannot tell you this. Even to me her agony of self-reproach, her passionate protestation of love, was something too sacredly intimate to hear, much less to gaze upon. So I turned my back and—and—wiped my sleeve across my eyes.

And then on my ears fell the tinkle of the doorbell: but in my heart it was like a peal. One leap, and I had shot the bolt.

"It's he!" I whispered over my shoulder. "But he shan't come in! I—"

She raised her hand, pointing to the door.

"Cousin, he shall come in. Open it."

I stared at her, half fearful lest grief had unhinged her mind. But the light of her eyes, shining steady through the tears, reassured me.

"Cousin Gerard, open the door." Her voice was low and even, quite passionless.

This move of Domini's was entirely beyond me; and I hesitated. It was all very well to let him in, but there would be the devil to pay to get him out: the house was his. Then, my eye lighting on a cane rack in one corner, I whipped out a knotty stick, more like a cudgel, stepped to the door, swung it back, and stood by for trouble.

Maybe you have seen astonished faces in your time, but I am ready to lay a bet that Crowninshield's out-astonished any of them. He was just clean flabbergasted, knocked so plumb about that he looked silly. He simply couldn't bottom what he saw. But, with all his surprise, he had an instinctive hunch, I fancy, that his plan was ditched. He wasn't long in learning how badly it was ditched— or who had ditched it.

"I understand, Mr. Crowninshield," says Domini, "that this is your house. I cannot say that my father and I are thankful for your hospitality." So quietly she spoke as fairly to startle me: I did not see the bridle in her voice. "My father—look at him. I—I think you have killed him. But to-morrow, please God, we will vacate this place, he and I. You will find nothing taken. These clothes your money bought I will send to you. Do you know they are an envelope of flame around me? But my fingers shall bleed to earn me honest ones."

Not if there's blood in mine, I vowed, and gripped my club. "That—that is all, I think. Except that I never promised to be your wife. I would sooner die. Now leave me."

Crowninshield, shifting on his feet, opened his mouth to reply. But Domini cut him short.

"Go! Oh, go!" she cried, her voice thrilling deeply. "Go quickly! Can't you see? Oh, *can't* you see? There's that in my heart, woman as I am, would have your life for the wrong you have done. Go, you devil! the sight of you is choking me! Go!"

He was already backing toward the door, awed into silence by the vehemence, not so much of her words, as of her spirit. But I watched him like a lynx: over his great brutal face passed wave after wave of darkening passion, so that, when his heel struck the threshold and he stopped, he was glowering like a thundercloud. In that short interval, it seemed to me, his love had run to hate.

I stepped forward, the door-knob in my hand, to shut him out. Then it was he first noticed me. Up flew his shaggy brows.

"Ah!" he said. "You?" and bent on me such a deadly countenance as quite appalled me. My doughty club dwindled suddenly to a toothpick— or felt so: and my knees were like a rag-doll's.

But next moment, without further word or menace, he span on his heel and went off into the night. In one shake I had clapped to the door and sent the bolt home. My midriff quivered for very joy of the relief. It was a near touch, I tell you.

Yet, it's funny how courage comes and goes: one black look had been enough to shatter mine; another look—how different!—was enough to repair it wholly.

"Cousin Gerard," said Domini, lifting her eyes to me, "you will not leave me now?"

A thousand gallant things were in my heart but my lips said, "Well, I guess not."

And then I took my uncle in my arms and carried him upstairs to his room. Already the frightful paralytic havoc in his face was somewhat mended; and, as Domini knelt beside him, his left arm came groping out for her.

"My little girl," he whispered.

I stole out.

Below in the post-room I tried to think things over. But somehow I couldn't make my thoughts be still. All I did was to drop into a chair by the table and fidget. I knew it was up to me to help Domini out, for I had gumption enough to see, however dimly, that we weren't yet quit of Crowninshield. And there was my uncle, like enough on his last legs. . . . But, as I say, my thinking was all at sixes and sevens.

And then, as I sat there, the deathly silence of the house made me more nervous still. Bar the chirruping of insects in the woods without, all was creepy quiet. Against the night the open windows before me were oblongs black as ink; and through them a drifting air stirred in the curtains, noiselessly, like an unseen hand.

A book was lying on the table at my elbow. I picked it up. It was the Bible, of all books! bound in leather and printed on fine gilt-edged pages. Was my uncle a Bible-reader? I smiled at the thought; and turning to the fly-leaf, found, sure enough, my cousin's name. She wrote a pretty hand.

Idly the thin pages slipped under my thumb, smooth as silk, stopping at the Psalms. Idly my eye fell on a verse—and glued there: three times I read it.

"For many dogs have encompassed me: the council of the malignant hath besieged me. And they have looked and stared upon me."

I wasn't a bright boy, but the pertinence of that text struck home like a knife thrust. I raised my eyes—the book thumped to the floor—and all my hair stood up!

Absalom Iron was peering through the window!

XIX

THE next I knew I was erect on my two feet, quivering like a plucked string, and gazing crab-eyed at the blackness of an empty window!

Was it possible that my fears of a beleaguered house, of our being hedged in by enemies, had played me this trick? Yet my thoughts had not been on Absalom Iron and the treasure: Crowninshield had been the heart of my anxiety. But now, with a shock that made me tight about the ribs, it came home to me that that gigantic sailor was to be reckoned with, and the desperate stake of treasure. Here was an enemy of another stripe, an enemy likely to prove more formidable than Crowninshield's crew. Nor did the fact that Carver had a hand in both designs lessen our peril one jot; rather, was it heightened—for his snaky dexterity would be guiding both flanks of the attack, and victory meant for him the spoil of buried gold.

But don't suppose for a minute I just stood there quaking in the middle of the room. Already I had switched off the light, had the windows closed and made fast, and was on the point of going upstairs and acquainting Domini with the whole particulars of this new source of danger. But should I leave the room unguarded? That the treasure was located somewhere in this old wing of the house was past doubt; so much at least the chart must have told Iron and Carver; so that either the tower or this post-room contained the cache.

I gazed around on the walls. Only fancy, the treasure might be but a few yards from my hands! I might reach out and seize it, if I only knew which way to reach.

A step sounded in the front hall. I skipped to the portière and looked out. A middle-aged person of very grave and even solemn aspect was standing at the foot of the staircase. On seeing me,

"Beg pardon, sir," says he, "I was just taking a look around before going to bed."

"You're William," I blurted; a recognition which he acknowledged with a dignified nod. "Now look here, William, there's been the devil and all going on here to-night."

"Yes, sir," says he, as though I had asked him to hand me my hat. His serenity surprised me, but of course both he and Mary had probably witnessed the whole fracas from safe coigns.

"Mr. Blythe's had a stroke," I continued, "and there's no telling how serious his condition is."

"Beg pardon, sir," interrupted William, "but

Miss Domini just informed me he was resting easy. I'm on the job, sir, if I may use the expression."

"It's a bigger job than you think, William," said I, stepping up to him. "Are there any guns in the house?"

A flash of alarm passed over his composed features. But next moment he calmly said he would fetch what weapons he could find.

Then, after telling him we were defending Miss Domini, and that he should stand guard in the post-room till I returned, I skipped upstairs.

Just as I was about to knock at my uncle's chamber, the door fell open and Domini with a lighted candle stood on the threshold.

"What's the matter?" I whispered. "Is he worse?"

"No," said she. "About the same. But he wants to see you. He asked me to get you. Oh, Cousin Gerard," she added, with a kind of awe in her eyes, "he's changed—changed! God has been good to him. You will be good, too?"

I looked into her dear face. "Have no fear, Cousin," said I. "I have been to Communion this morning." And then, over her shoulder, I saw the bed and the drawn face upon the pillow.

I crossed the room and sat down at the bedside.

"Uncle," said I, "you wanted to see me?"

He turned his head slowly, and regarded me with sad, still eyes. For a long time he so looked, and no word came. I heard Domini set the candlestick on the dresser, and then leave the room. At last, "The light," he murmured; "I want to see Jim Linton's boy."

I arose and fetched the candle. He blinked sharply into the orange flame, shading his eyes with a weak hand.

"Enough," said he; "set it down. . . . Jim, Jim, it's been a long time and a bad time. Were you kind to little Kitty? Ah, you were kinder than I. . . . Can you hear me, Jim?"

I knew he was not confusing me with my father, but that in some strange way he felt that my father was close by.

"Uncle," I said, "I am sure both he and my mother hear you."

The candle sputtered through still seconds.

"Yes," he resumed, "I think they do . . . and does God? O God Almighty, will you hear me, too?"

"Yes, yes, Uncle," said I hastily; "God is Infinite Mercy. You must know that."

"Infinite Mercy." He sighed, and groped out with his sound arm till he found my knee.

"Listen, child. I cannot say it all, I haven't strength. It was business—crooked business. I got Jim in—in deep. He thought it straight. But he found out and—and denounced me publicly. And Kitty stood by him."

He closed his eyes, fatigued with the effort. The bedclothes rose and fell over his labored breathing.

"Uncle," said I, "say no more. My father and mother have long since forgiven you; in Heaven there is no grudge nor hatred. Don't think of them. Think of God. Him you have offended. Oh, think of Him!" I spoke warmly, with tears in my eyes; but of tears I wasn't ashamed: the business was worthy of tears.

"And you, child," said he at length. "I—"

"Oh, me," I broke in. "That's all right. Forget it. Uncle, can you say the Act of Contrition?"

He took his hand from my knee, and fumbled on the bedclothes. I saw what he was after: Domini had been before me in the matter: a crucifix lay upon the counterpane.

I put it in his hand.

"Say the words for me," he whispered.

I said the act, a little at a time, he following; and at the end he sagged down on the pillow, his respiration, I thought, doubly difficult.

I went to the door and found Domini and Mary in the hallway.

"Cousin Domini," said I, "you have telephoned the doctor?"

"Telephoned!" says she. "There's no telephone. And it's the priest we want, Gerard, above. all."

"Well," said I, "we'll want the sheriff, too, pretty badly."

"The sheriff!" she echoed.

"Yes, the sheriff, and a whole posse. Now, listen, Domini," said I. (It was nice to drop 'cousin';

and besides, she herself had given me the lead.)
"I don't want to frighten you"—this I said for
Mary's sake; the poor girl was as white as her
apron—"but Crowninshield hasn't played his last
card yet. You told him to-night that you were going to leave to-morrow. But your father can't stir
from here. . If my guess is right, Crowninshield has
a watch on this house; but that's only a guess.
What's certain—two men are trying to break in
here." And there and then I related as briefly as
I could the whole business of Absalom Iron and the
treasure. "So you see," I wound up, "we've got
to defend ourselves. William is on guard now."

"And yet," Domini reiterated, "we must get the
priest. Can't we send William?"

"No," said I, "I'm going. Soon as it gets light
enough William can defend the whole house from
the top of the tower. To-night he and I will watch
downstairs."

She looked at me with glistening eyes.

"God bless you, Gerard," said she.

Below I found William in his stocking-soles
prowling about the post-room, a great ten-gauge
shotgun in his hands. He led me to an elbow of
the wall, beneath the staircase, where we might
safely light a candle. Sure, our munitions of defense made a varied lot. Besides the shotgun there
was a .32 Winchester rifle; three Indian tomahawks;
an old long-barreled horsepistol that wouldn't work;
an ivory-handled dagger, like a stiletto, with a fili-

gree in the blade of inlaid silver; and a Colt's revolver.

"Well," said I, "this is a pretty fair layout. I only wish we had Dan Mitchell though."

Then I fixed on our plan of defense: I would guard the tower, the post-room and the room adjoining, while William was to sentinel the remainder of the floor.

Fortunately, between the post-room and the other apartment was a door, so that, sitting square in this opening, I could keep my eyes and ears upon the windows of either room. This put the open tower door immediately at my back; thus the least noise from that quarter, too, could be detected.

But of course I didn't stay seated long at any one time; I was afraid of sleep. Instead, I kept up a stealthy sentry-go from room to room, with my Winchester at full cock, ready to blaze away. But I don't believe I ever put in a stiller night: when you can hear your own heart beat, things are pretty quiet.

The tower, as you may suppose, I was eager to explore, but this of course was out of the question: I durst not turn on the light. But in the darkness I discerned what looked like a settee around the wall, and a staircase winding upward; and just over my head, through one of the narrow loopholes, three stars shaking in the black night.

By and by, however, after what seemed an interminable period (it must have been close on to daybreak now), I grew so sleepy I could hardly hold the rifle in my hands. Indeed, I never realized before how heavy a gun could get. Accordingly, thinking (like a ninny) that I might just as safely put in the rest of my watch sitting down, I dropped into a chair, and dropped plumb to sleep in the same act.

When I awoke I jumped clean into the middle of the room. Someone had touched me on the shoulder. I whipped around, the rifle in my hands, ready to fire. In the gray twilight of the dawn Domini stood before me.

"Gerard," says she, "you must let William go for the priest."

I had played the sluggard; I wasn't going to play the coward too.

"Not on your life!" I declared. "It's time now I was off."

She stepped closer and put her hand on my arm: in her eyes was sudden fear—fear for me.

"But I saw a man down in the pines, Gerard. They're watching the house."

"Of course they're watching the house," said I jauntily; (but my heart jumped: my job was to be no cinch.) "I've counted on that. But, great guns, Domini, don't you think I can give those fellows the slip!"

Whether she thought so or not, I didn't give her chance to say, but stampeded her anxiety with a rush of whispered words and cautious bustling; and within ten minutes stood ready for the hazard; all the while with my heart buoyed up because she feared for me.

We were in the kitchen, Domini and I: for my plan was to go through a window here to the back porch where were shielding vines, thence drop behind the privet hedge which girdled the house, crawl to the front, dart across the drive to the rose bushes and, once among these, to snake my way down to the belt of pines.

"Good-by, Domini," said I. "I'd better be off. It's getting lighter every second."

She looked at me without uttering a word, her face pale and her lips quivering.   Then,

"O Gerard," she said, and raised her hand.

Then I made a strange gesture, though sincere. Explain if you can how I, a graceless country lad, came to achieve so gallant a leave-taking.   Perhaps I just wanted to end her dear protest; perhaps the riotous devotion of my heart found expression at last.   Anyhow, all in a breath I doffed my cap, dropped on one knee, seized her outstretched hand and pressed it to my lips.   The next moment, red as a tomato, I was through the window and down on all fours behind the curtain of vines.

XX

I RUN AN ERRAND PERILOUS

THE dawn had not yet completed its work, for a star here and there in the blue-tinted sky glimmered palely; and out yonder the dark pinewood still hugged the twilight.

Safely I reached the front lawn, and had already wormed it over half the distance to the pines. My next screen was a crescent of gaudy colias. I made the upper horn of the crescent and began to work my way under the outer rim. Then, almost in my ear, a hoarse voice whispered,

"This way, Blue. Under these colored ones."

I think my heart quit beating; I know I didn't breathe. On the other side of the bed lay one of our enemies. They were adopting the same method of attack as I of escape: and, what sent a shiver up my back, they were succeeding! Was William blind?

Still as a mouse, I heard the first man pull himself over the grass and pass me; then came the second: a brushing, sliding noise, punctuated with muffled grunts. And all the while my mind was in an agony of indecision. If I let them go, they might take the house; if I tried to stop them it was good-night not only to my safe get-away but likely to the success of my errand to boot: nay, it was something nearer still, for these desperadoes would certainly know that my escape meant the sheriff and tables turned. And yet, if I let them go, there was only William. . . .

The second man had already reached the tip of the colias.

I sprang to my feet.

"William! William!" I shouted, and bolted for the woods.

I didn't pause to glance around; I was certain they would pursue me: and sure enough, ere I had got fairly started,

"Look!" cries a voice. "The kid! Get him, by God! Get him!"

Then a shot rang out; and, as I plunged into the pines, with the tail of my eye I saw the two men bring up short and look back. They stuck for a moment only, but my handicap lengthened by yards; and I blessed William in my heart, not for being such a poor shot, but for having fired at all.

Away I sped, up hill and down, straight for the bluff and the railroad beneath. It was no time for thinking, but I had the sense to see that on the railroad track was my main chance of meeting somebody; and in my present stress anybody—anybody at all—would be a friend.

All the while my enemies hung close upon my tail.

Now and again they let fly at me, but the bullets whined harmlessly overhead: the brush was a good screen.

At length, just as I lurched out of a thicket of hazels, I saw before me a breakneck descent and beyond, through the leafage, gray glimpses of the river: I had gained the bluff-line at last.

But here was a poser: on either hand the declivity, though studded with tree-stems, was almost totally devoid of bushes. Bar a clump of milkweed immediately below me and scattered patches of grasses, there was no concealment: and up the slope behind my pursuers were pressing. Though my own chest was pumping like a bellows, I could hear their whistling gasps—they were that hard upon my heels.

But you may suppose I didn't hang there long. Decisions come quick in fixes like that. Swift as a gopher, I scooted down for the milkweed—"scoot" is the word, for the whole bluffside here was steep as a flight of stairs, and the ground all crumbly with loose soil, like a raked garden-bed, and pebbles.

Scarce had I reached the covert when my enemies burst into view on the crest above me. Though the sweat was smarting in my eyes, I could see them plain enough: Blue Island and Bill Short it was, and both gripped pistols.

"Got away!" gasped one.

"Doubled—back!" cried the other. "The—little—!"

But his epithet, vile enough no doubt, was

drowned in the scream of a freight engine, whistling down the track. Like all freight whistles, the
piercing blast continued for seconds, so that I lost
my pursuers' words: but I saw what they did. They
parted: one this way, the other that, scouring the
brow of the bluff.

And then my luck broke against me. To get
better set for a start, I made a shift in my position;
but the ground slipped beneath me, and I shot out
into the open.

"There he goes!" came a shout from above.
"Whang it into him!"

The quarry was up again, and the hunters raging
after it. A pistol roared behind me, and I saw the
bark spit out from the tree-trunk I was flying past.
I don't think I ran down that hill; I just fell. There
was no keeping my feet; all I tried to do was to
avoid the trees that went whizzing by. Earth was
in my eyes and nose and mouth and down my back
and in my shoes: I was a human landslide.

Only twice I glimpsed my pursuers: the first time
I saw why just one shot was fired—they couldn't
aim; next, to my downright glee, the man on my
right—Blue Island, I think—executed a sudden,
complete somersault, his revolver escaping from his
grasp in a wide arc. He at least would "whang
it" no more that trip.

And then with stunning abruptness I hit the bottom and crashed like a boulder through a tangle of
bushes. A shattering noise smote upon my ears,

and I wondered what that meant. I tried to pick
myself up, but something invisible held me down.
I turned my head and looked: I was lying beneath
a barbed-wire fence. I rolled under it, and sat up.
Before me red box-cars were clashing and clanking
by: perhaps a dozen or more filed past ere wit
enough returned to seize my chance.

Crawling down the embankment, I made ready to
swing on. The train was not going fast—perhaps
ten miles an hour—and I knew I could board it.
Then thirty yards or so to my right I saw Bill Short
come out on the bank. I made a leap at one of
the iron rungs, missed my foothold, my shins striking cruelly, and dangled.

A sudden grasp fell on my right foot. I kicked
out viciously with my left. The grasp relaxed, and
glancing down I saw Blue Island rolling on the ballast. But, ere I had mounted the ladder, he was
up again and running with the train. He, too, was
going to jump it.

As I pulled myself up on the roof, I think I nearly
gave up in despair: some ten cars back Bill Short
was coming on the run. I scrambled to my feet and
staggered forward. My sole hope now was to
reach the cab and the engine crew.

Those few desperate minutes on the top of that
freight train have always seemed like a nightmare.
How I kept my feet is more than I can say. Once,
indeed, I thought I was a goner. I was crossing the
gap between cars; I stumbled, and one leg dropped

into the opening; but I clutched out wildly for the brake-wheel and saved myself.   It was then that I cast my second look to the rear.

What I first saw deepened my dismay: Blue Island was in the chase too; only three cars separated us. But further back, behind Bill Short, I spied over the crawling red roofs something that nerved my heart and muscles: out of the caboose tower one of the train hands was clambering.

I pushed ahead, reeling like a drunken man, the coal-tender but two cars forward.   I reached the edge of the front car.   I saw the engineer with his head out the window and his left hand on the throttle; I saw the open furnace door, and the blazing fire within.   Below me was the rocking hill of coal. I leaped!

I landed.   A cry rings out above me.   Blue Island, his legs apart and his long arms spread, towers in menacing silhouette, like some monstrous black goblin, against the morning sky.   But he didn't jump; he hesitates a breath too long.   With all the power of my soul and body I let fly a chunk of coal pointblank at his chest.   It took him squarely.   He staggered, toppled for an awful second, his face white and his eyeballs rolling—and then disappeared.

· I turned to scramble up the coal.   Safe at last! Then, above the clanking din of the wheels and the hiss of steam, sounds a second cry.   From over the brim of coal a savage sooty face—to my terrified eyes it was like the face of the devil—was glowering upon me. It was the fireman, I made sure, and,

"Help!" I shouted. "They're after me!"

But my voice was lost in a deafening shriek of the engine whistle; and next moment the man heaves up and strikes at me fiercely with an iron rod. I sprang back, the coal sliddering under my feet. A sudden yaw of the car, and I was teetering over the embankment! Gravel and weeds were sliding under my eyes, and my belly quivered. But I had no choice; my balance was gone.

I jumped.

Sure, my guardian angel picked out the spot: I lit, feet foremost, in a pile of sand, rolled thrice over and sat up uninjured.

The cars were thundering past. I looked up and my eyes almost popped out of my head. Swaying on the brink of a car-top, two men were locked in mortal struggle. While you might count five slowly I followed them. Then the car swept from sight round a bend, and I got dazedly to my feet.

Once again I tried to board the train, but either it had picked up speed or I was too weak: my attempt ended in a jarring fall. There was nothing for it now but to take to the woods. And here for the first time—just as the caboose went banging by—I realized where I had landed. I was in a rock cut.

I glanced swiftly round. On the bluff side the scarp was high and sheer; and riverward, though

it was low and jagged, I had no mind to go.   That
bank was far too open.   Luckily, here, as I say,
was a sharp curve in the track.   I was standing at
its salient point and could be seen for only a short
distance on either hand.

I started forward round the bend, scanning the
rock for footholds to the bluff above.   For thirty
yards, perhaps, I walked, and then stopped dead.
Yonder, sitting on a rail, was Bill Short with his
head in his hands.   But ere he spied me, you bet I
had skipped out of sight.

Back I chased, hoping to find an ascent at the
lower end of the cut; but remembering, too, that
Blue Island, dead or alive, was down this way.   And
sure enough, that happened which I feared: suddenly I saw him, unscathed and striding up the
track.   But I was a wink too late in dodging to
cover.   A hoarse cry told me I was spotted.

Back I darted again; but my nerve was clean
gone.   I was trapped in the cut!

And then, all at once, a brightness gleamed on
the rock overhead: 'twas sunrise over the Wisconsin
bluffs.

XXI

THAT first flash of sunlight showed the way that saved me, for so crushed was I with the certainty of capture that I hadn't thought to try the river bank. But now, glancing out yonder at the sun, almost in the same act I had leaped upon the lower flank of the cut and gained the crest. To right and left I looked: neither Blue Island nor Short was yet in sight. Below me, a levee of creeper-covered rocks fell away for perhaps thirty feet to a line of willows along the water's edge. I must reach those willows: they were my only protection.

Back in the cut, Blue Island shouted for Short and presently after came Short's answer. But already I had made the willows and was crouching behind them, my eyes searching through the leaves the top of the levee. The cries continued. A moment more and they must smoke my dodge: and then it was all over with me.

But one chance remained. Smoothly as a snake I slipped into the water. My nose only above the

214

surface, I glided with the current. No sound reached my submerged ears. All was quiet save my pounding heart. Softly, with no movement but a gentle paddling with my hands, I floated on down. By and by I raised my head. I was still hugging the shore, but the cut was a long stone's throw behind. Then I began to swim in earnest: and I knew how to swim. Two minutes more, and I had made good my escape. But, though I had escaped, I had foozled my job; McGregor and Father McGiffert were as far away as ever.

As I lifted my eyes to the immense green bluffs above me, I remembered Domini. She was back there in those hills. She was in hourly peril of a man the depth of whose villainy neither she nor I had yet begun to plumb. A great sorrow was at her door (though, boy-like, I didn't make much of her father's imminent death). Perhaps she was even now, imagining me in McGregor; perhaps she had bid William watch from the tower for the first sign of help: and here was I (who had kissed her hand) fleeing away from my errand—fleeing to save my own mean skin.

It was these thoughts that nerved me to my next decision, a decision I took ere I had swum ten yards further. For at this point, rounding a head of willows, I drifted into view of Crowninshield's boat-house shining in the morning sun. And quick as a flash a picture of that bungalow room was before me. I saw the walls and the desk and the safe, and then something on the desk that sent all my body's blood to my heart: I remembered the telephone!

To you it may sound simply foolhardy, if not ridiculous; I gasp when I think of it now; but that morning in the river I clicked my jaws on a perfectly plain, though risky, duty: I must telephone Father McGiffert.

On with the current I floated till within thirty yards or so of the boathouse. Then I made for shore and climbed out dripping on the rocks. The first thing I did was to peel off my clothes and wring out the water. Thus lightened, I crawled up to the brow of the embankment and scanned the track. Both ways it was empty. I lay low and listened. Only the bark of a squirrel came out of the woods.

Following the method of that master of stealth, like Carver I tiptoed up the bungalow path. Every few yards I halted for a listen. Not a leaf stirred; the air was dead; the chattering of that single squirrel was the only sound in the whole glen. No movement. anywhere; except where the sunlight, piercing through the leafage, struck and quivered on the dew. At last, around the path's elbow, my eager eyes beheld the goal.

What monstrous luck! Behind the screen, the door stood an arm's length ajar!

But was it luck?

Five minutes I waited, every sense tight for the faintest hint of Crowninshield or Jonas. And each passing second I saw the telephone yonder on the desk and my mission accomplished.

Then I moved. I moved swiftly. With my heart in my mouth I streaked it straight for the veranda; I was up the steps and through the door and standing breathless in the little hall. You might have heard a pin drop in that bungalow.

The door to the room on my right was shut. Gently my fingers closed on the knob; gently my wrist turned; gently the door swung inward: there was the telephone, and the room was empty.

But there was something else. At the edge of the desk lay a pistol. Sure, my luck was outdoing itself. With infinite caution I closed the door. Next breath I had darted to the desk, caught up the receiver in one hand and the pistol in the other.

A small voice spoke distinctly in my ear, so that I started. "Number, please?"

I glanced at the door, fearfully.

"Father McGiffert's," I whispered.

"Louder, please," said the voice.

Louder! If that young lady only knew! I shifted to the other knee, so that I commanded the door. Then I put my lips quite up to the mouthpiece.

"Give me Father McGiffert's," said I, biting off the consonants. My voice seemed to reverberate through the bungalow. But central must have caught me this time, for there was a sudden buzzing at my ear, and then silence. Another buzzing, some queer clucking noises, then a big voice said:

"This is Father McGiffert."

A tap sounded on the door. My heart jumped into my throat. But only Jonas would knock. It wasn't his master. I leveled my shaking pistol one foot above the knob.

("Hello, hello," said Father McGiffert.)

";Come in," I called, simulating Crowninshield's heavy voice.

("What?" said Father McGiffert.)

The door fell open and there was Jonas looking at me stupidly: his right hand was still in bandage.

"Come in, quick!" I snapped. "And close the door."

He obeyed; but I honestly believe the inside of his thick skull hadn't yet registered what his eyes reported.

("I can't make out a word you're saying," complained Father McGiffert.)

"One moment, Father," I flung into the mouthpiece; and then addressed myself to Jonas.

"Just come around here, Jonas, and take a seat in that chair. Good. Now, see this pistol? It's pointing straight at your gizzard, isn't it? Well, a single word from you and it'll do more than point, understand?" Here was a threat I knew I wouldn't carry out: fancy, killing a man for uttering a word! Had he given the alarm, like as not I should have dived through the nearest window. Anyhow, tall talk goes with the upper hand; generally, not without effect. I swung a leg upon the desk and faced him with a chuckle. "I just dropped in to do a little telephoning, Jonas, and don't you dare interrupt."

"Hello," said I, stooping to the instrument, but with my eyes along the barrel that covered Jonas.

"Hello! What's the matter?" replies Father McGiffert, a little testily. "Are you talking to me?"

"Listen, Father," said I. "This is Gerard Linton. Remember me?"

"Well, of course," says he. "What on earth happened to you? Did you find your uncle?"

"I've had rather an exciting time, Father, since I left you," I answered, grinning away at Jonas' doltish mug. "I'm still somewhat in the thick of it too, though right now I'm feeling pretty comfortable." And I positively winked at Jonas, so hugely was I tickled. "But I'll tell you about that in a second. First, my uncle is dying and wants to see a priest. Can you come out right away?"

"Sure," says he. "I'll be right out."

"Wait a minute, Father," said I. "There's something else." Conceited as a cock, I was smiling in triumph at Jonas, as who should say, "now your game's up." But he wasn't looking at me at all. A sudden creepiness went up my back: I knew what had happened. Next moment, ere I could turn, the pistol was knocked clean from my grasp, and a strong hand had plucked me off the desk.

I looked up into Crowninshield's blazing eyes. I thought he was going to slay me on the spot, but he only said, "You've meddled enough, boy. You won't meddle any more." Then to Jonas, "Get some rope."

Jonas took one step, and then hung before us, regarding me with an odd look; his heavy, oafish face working queerly.

"Mr. Gordon," says he, "may I ask a favor, sir?" He held up his bandaged hand. "He gave me that. I should like to pay him back."

"Certainly, Jonas," said his master, and chuckled deeply.

I gasped. The sweat started on my forehead. Was the man going to bite me in cold blood? I looked at Jonas. A shudder took me at sight of his cruel face. The gluttony of revenge was in his eyes; it twisted his mouth in horrid lines. His side-whiskers lifted with the leer, like some great grinning cat's. His tongue slid out, and licked his lips.

I stood up straight and waited.

He stepped close, gloating, and drew back his fist for a blow. But the blow never fell. With might and main I kicked out, my toe gouging deep into his belly. Doubled up, he fell sideways to the floor.

"Damn you!" cries a voice at my ear, and next

breath what might have been a sledgehammer knocked me cold.

I awoke in pain and darkness. To me it is surprising that I awoke at all. I was parched with thirst and all but suffocated; and piercing twinges racked my jaws and neck. Between my teeth was fixed a savage gag; my hands and feet were triced tight, so that both utterance and movement were impossible; and in my eyes naught but stifling blackness.

How long I lay thus mewed up, I was at a loss to determine. (Later I computed it roughly as five hours; so that the wonder was I didn't die of the sheer torture.) Often I swooned; and stood by cool streams in wide green pastures: only to wake in the midst of what seemed like black fire, and many horses pounding my temples with iron hoofs.

In one of these fainting fits I must have been dragged from my prison, for quite suddenly I found myself in the light. Delicious water was gurgling in my throat.

"He's all right now," some one said. "See, his eyes are open."

I sat up and looked around. I was on the floor, and Carver and Crowninshield were standing over me.

"Water!" I murmured.

"Water, eh?" says Crowninshield. "Well, give him some more. He's got to move out of here."

For all his wickedness, as I gulped down that

cooling cup, I had a moment's friendly feeling toward Crowninshield. But he himself destroyed it. He kicked me, brutally.

"Get up!"

I struggled to my feet, my legs wavering. At once a blinder was clapped about my eyes. "Now the arms!" Again the biting cord, like a thousand needle-pricks, stung into my galled wrists. Then a coil of rope was passed about my middle.

"Come," said Carver's voice; and there was a pluck at the rope that nearly fetched me off my feet.

"No, wait," says Crowninshield. "We're forgetting this decoration. Open your mouth, boy, or I'll knock it open."

It was the gag again!

"No, no!" I cried. "O dear God, not that!" From one to the other I looked with desperate, unseeing eyes. "I won't open my mouth," I panted. "You can shoot me dead if I do!"

Fierce fingers dug suddenly into my cheeks; my jaws popped open; and a stick of wood almost tore apart the corners of my mouth.

"Now," said Crowninshield, "take him away."

Another tug at the rope, and I lurched forward on a *via crucis* the bare memory of whose anguish is little short of a torment. Let me pass over it swiftly. The savage wrenches of the rope, the malignant curses launched at me, my heaving chest all but splitting, the awful sense of suffocation, the cruel falls, and, when I failed to rise, the blows I writhed under—these things I suffered: but above them all a dear face shone, and I looked up at it bravely.   And then, at last, a voice spoke somewhere, "Here he is;" and I dropped into a blank.

XXII

IN THE KIDNAPPER'S DEN: AND AFTER

WHEN consciousness returned, I found my head lying in a puddle of water (O welcome puddle!); both gag and blinder were gone; ten inches or so before my eyes rose a rock wall, tufted with moss; beyond my feet, through leafy bushes, the sweet sunshine filtered; and for a foolish space I hugged the dear delusion that friends were by. Then I heard voices behind me, and I knew better.

"What kick have *you* got, I'd like to know?"— It was Carver that spoke.—"You've queered this job right from the jump. And now you want to stick your tail between your legs and sneak back to Chicago. You've got enough of it, eh? Well, Mr. Blue Island, you can go just as soon as you damn please, but you don't get one red cent from me."

"Don't I get nothin' for what I done a'ready?" whined Blue Island. "Is that your way, Mr. Reed?"

Reed! Of course it was Reed!

"That's my way—for quitters: not a beggar's penny. Why, I never saw such a bunch of bunglers! First, that shack burnt down through your own fool carelessness. It's my guess the whole crowd of you were soused to the gills."

"Well, maybe we did have a drop too much. I ain't sayin' we didn't, am I? But I want to tell you this, Mr. Reed, I 'most got burnt to a cinder gettin' Mitchell outa that cabin. That's somethin' for you anyhow, even if we was drunk. Supposin' he was burnt up in that fire?"

"Why, that would have been your own lookout, my man," replies Carver coolly. "But that fire isn't my only count against you. You let that kid get out of Jack's House. You laid down cold and let him get away for help."

"Laid down cold!" cried Blue Island. "He knocked me offen that train, didn't he?" Then, in a sudden gust of fury, "By God!" he blurted, "I'm gonna kill him for that!"

"Pity he didn't kill you," sneered Carver. "It wouldn't have been much of a loss."

"Well, anyhow," grumbled Blue Island, "we didn't sign up to capture no forts. And that there house is a regular fort. If I want to capture forts, I'll join the army."

Carver laughed acidly.

"You join the army!" he fleered. "You couldn't join Coxie's army. You're brave, aren't you? You're spunky—I don't think. There's about as much spunk in the three of you as there is in a rubber hose. You were bluffed cold by one man, and him

a priest. That capped the climax! And after I'd
warned you, too. What have you got to say to
that, eh?"

Here was glad news! Had Father McGiffert,
then, got into Jack's House? Half dead as I was,
my heart began to beat for joy; the peril I lay under
looked not so fell. I had done my errand. There
was another hand for the defense of Jack's House.

"Well," said Blue Island . . . "Well. . . ."

"Well, what?" raps out Carver. "What have
you got to say?"

"Well, I guess I ain't got nothin' to say," replies
Blue Island in sheepish tones. "Only, he just got
out of that rig like he was ten men, and told us to
stand back. He said he had God with him—said
we dassent touch him."

"Pooh!" says Carver.

"That's what I thought, too," agreed Blue Island
readily. "But it didn't help none. He just went
on by. But, looky here, Mr. Reed, I was the first
one to chase after him. I chased him to the open,
and then somebody cuts loose at me from the house,
and I ducked."

"And you call yourself a man!" was Carver's sole
comment; and for a little there was silence.

It was all as plain as a picture now. Not Father
McGiffert had struck those murderers stark, but He
whom Father McGiffert bore: His enemies had gone
backward, as once, in a Garden long ago, they went
backward and fell to the ground. And an awe crept

over me, even there in that den of cut-throats, at the nearness of Christ's power; so that my heart, in the midst of the paths of evil, grew strangely light.

"So then, old jailbird," resumed Carver, "you admit you've made a pretty poor job of it. Well, now, just to show you what kind of a sport I am, I'll let bygones be bygones and double your pay if you break into that house. And what's more, I'll come across with a part of the jack this very night. Is that fair enough? Or do you still want to run away?"

"Oh, I knowed *you* was all right, Mr. Reed," says Blue Island. "I never had no kick against you. It's this here Short that got my goat."

"Never you mind Short," says Carver. "From now on I'm your boss—personally. You take your orders from me. Now listen: to-night we're going to turn the trick. We have three new men to help —never mind who they are. Counting myself, we'll be seven." He paused. "But you lost your shooting-iron, didn't you? Well, don't worry, you'll be heeled to-night. See here now, you come with me to Jack's House right this minute, and I'll show you and the other two what's to be done."

"And leave this kid alone?" says Blue Island.

"Why not? He's about done for. He hasn't even come to yet. Besides, he's tied, hands and feet. Unless you want him gagged again. But I guess he won't yell any. Who's to hear him but us? Come on."

"Well, you're right, I guess, Mr. Reed," says Blue Island slowly. "But one thing I asts—and no offense to you—I asts to handle that there little devil all by myself. I want to take and tie him up against a tree and mash him with rocks. He knocked me offen that train."

"Just as you please," says Carver. "That's your own fun. But you've got to attend to business now. Come on."

They went away. I heard them moving through the brush; fainter and fainter became the sounds: the pair was gone. Now was my only chance! But such a shaking seized my body, such a fluttering my wits, that I could neither act nor think: I could only sit up and gaze around.

It was a rock cavern or cave that I was in. Immediately before me was the mouth, choked with sassafras and elder; about me on the ground were rags of scorched blanketing, a pine box, a coffee-pot, the inevitable jug, and a pail half full of water. I rolled over, stuck my face into that bucket, and drank and drank and drank.

And with the water I found my head. How soon Blue Island would be back I didn't know. But this I knew: once back, he would never leave me again till he left me dead. Between me and that terrible prospect how many minutes were to run? Lurching to my fettered feet, I stood swaying, wild-eyed.

Then, suddenly, I saw hope. I saw one corner of the cavern's mouth: the rock came to an edge.

Against that edge I flung myself.   How I sawed!
how th'e salt sweat blinded! how my heart, pounding
in my throat, almost choked me!

But the cord dangled at last from my bleeding
wrists.

Freeing my feet was but the work of seconds: I
leaped up, ready to bolt.   Then my eye fell on the
pine box and, inside, a loaf of bread.   I seized it,
turned, and was stopped dead in my tracks.

Out of the black throat of the cave came a stifled
groan.

Dan Mitchell!   It was Dan Mitchell of course!
In the extremity of my own danger I had clean
forgotten him.   But sure, here he was; that groan
could come from no one else.

I rushed into the interior of the cave. Beyond
a narrowing of the walls was a bend; and here, lying
on his back, stretched the figure of a man.   By the
dim light I saw the piece of paleness that was his
face, and in the midst of it two eyes darkly burning, and athwart it a severing straightness that I
knew.

I dropped to my knees, tearing at his gag.

"No time to lose!" I whispered fiercely.   "They'll
be back any second!   I'm Domini's cousin—the boy
that tried to help you in that fight.   Domini's in
danger—now—at Jack's House.   It's surrounded,
but you've got to get there.   Crowninshield's the
man. . . .   There.   Can you talk?"

But I didn't wait for his effort.   Dashing out, I

grabbed the bucket of water and was back in a breath.

"My hands—feet!" he gasped between gulps.

I set the bucket down, bowled him over, and plucked at the hardened knot. A bitter tight one it was.

"Does it hurt?" I asked, pausing.

"Go on, for God's sake!" cries he. "I feel nothing."

Loose it came at last; and as I fell to work on his feet, he wrung his hands. "They're no good now," he whispered. "Good God, I hope my legs are better!"

I whipped the rope from his ankles.

"Now stand!" said I, springing back.

He struggled upright, staggered, then canted against the rock.

"Oh, weak!" he breathed. "Weak as a kitten! You—you go. I'm no good."

Then I had a positive inspiration. I snatched up my loaf of bread, tore it asunder, and, setting an end to his mouth, "Eat!" cried I.

He tore off a mouthful, his breath, as he chewed, whistling through his nostrils.

Then, upon the back of my first inspiration, flashed a second. Sure, in that desperate pass, my guardian angel must have been busy at my ear. Cramming the half loaf into Mitchell's pocket, out to the cavern's mouth I darted again, plucked the stopper from the jug, and smelt. It was whisky,

sure enough.   Long and hard was the pull I took:
then near gave up the ghost.   Spasms shot through
my throat and chest; my breath came in gasps; my
insides burnt with liquid fire.   But a moment later
I was primed for come what might.

I tilted the jug to Mitchell's lips.   "It's strength,"
I urged.   "Drink!"

For full five seconds the liquor guggled in his
throat.   Then, "Oh!" cries he: and, "oh!"   But
his next words fell incisive and strong: "Come on!
We'll beat these damned rascals yet!"

But the whisky had lent more vigor to his spirit
than to his body: he could only wabble beside me,
leaning on my shoulder.   At that, I thought we
were safe, for we hadn't used many of my precious
minutes.   But at the end of the cave, as we paused
to hearken, came the dreaded sound: to our left, a
man's footsteps amid the snapping brush!   I peered
out.   Blue Island it was, and scarce thirty yards
off.

"Crawl out that way," whisper I.   "Keep in the
bushes.   I'll handle him."

He looks at me, shaking his head.

My patience goes.   "Darn it!   *I* don't need you;
it's *Domini!*"

That tumbles him.   He presses my arm with
weak fingers, and then, on all fours, is swallowed in
the greenery.

The broken loaf in my left hand and a fist-size
stone in my right, I crouch at the corner of the cave.

Blue Island is in for another jolt, if rock throws as true as coal.

Nearer comes the rustle of the foliage.

Then, in a twinkle, falls the unexpected.

A cry goes up; Mitchell is spotted. Blue Island must be stopped. Stooping, I dart into the elder bushes; and, as the ruffian tears by, hurl myself bodily at his knees.

Down he crashes. Ere he can gain his feet I am bending over him.

"Look!" cry I; and as he lifted his startled face, I smashed it with my stone.

Back I leaped, but lingered still: me he must chase!

Up he staggered, spitting blood and teeth and curses. A second longer I looked into that face, black with fury and dripping crimson. Then I turned tail and ran as I never ran before: for death was at my heels.

The course of my flight was not hard to choose. Behind and on either hand were hills; straight ahead down the valley I dashed. But if fear lent me wings, rage and revenge spurred Blue Island on. I could hear him behind me, tearing through the brush in deadly silence; and all my soul shriveled at the thought of capture.

Then, almost before I knew it, the valley deflected to my right, narrowing inward like a woody defile. I turned with it. Fifty yards further it wound riverward again, the sides drawing closer and steeper; so that a dread fell on me lest I had fled into a trap.

But suddenly through the leafage I spied the end of the gulch: a sharp breast of ground clear as a stubble field. Blue Island, I knew, had no gun; so up this open ascent I charged. At the top I found a bushy declivity falling sharply away. Headlong down the slope I sped. And all at once the bushes disappeared, the mealy soil dropped almost plumb, and my heart died within me: below, spread like a lurking terror at my feet, lay a shining black surface.

It was the bog!

I dug my heels into the sliding ground. Wildly I clawed at the sparse grasses. No use: down I shot straight for the heart of the quag. Then I did the only thing that was left me: I jumped. Desperately, with every last ounce of my energy, I jumped. On my two feet I landed, lurched out, and fell prone; a jutting root catching my midriff, and knocking me breathless. But I had cleared the bog.

Up I struggled and fell again, fighting for my breath. If you have ever had the wind knocked out of you, you will understand my condition. Madly as I wanted to rush on, I couldn't. I was scarce able to budge; my legs were as good as paralyzed. All I could do was to roll about in the weeds, gasping for air.

In this fix I heard a sudden cry; and turning my

head, saw Blue Island scoot out of the belt of bushes
and down the crumbly incline.   He had spied me.
Next moment he was in the air; but either he had
fouled at the take-off or simply hadn't enough spring
in his legs.   Plump into the center of the bog he
squashed!

I rolled over and sat up.   There he was, up to
his middle in the black mire, lurching this way and
that and plunging his great fists into the ooze for
a purchase.   Fiery crimson was his sweating face;
but when he saw me sitting in the weeds scarce five
yards away, baffled rage made it positively purple,
and curses bubbled from his bleeding mouth.

But to the curses I paid no heed, nor to the nearness of my enemy.   He was near, but he was far off
too.   I was out of danger.   By this I had fairly regained my breath; and as I sat there looking at him,
a calmness and a security came over me—even a
movement of pity for that raging beast of a man.

Something of this he must have sensed, for upon
a sudden his face went white as paper (the red blood
against that whiteness made me shudder).   He
flung up his hands, all sticky with mire as with black
cobwebs; lunged out desperately, squirming his trunk
and shoulders.   Revenge left his eyes, and a sickened horror filled them.   But all his huge effort, as
I could have told him, was unavailing: the bog
gripped him like a vise.

Then I did, perhaps, a foolish thing.

"Catch hold of this," said I, reaching out a spar of wood: "maybe I can save you yet."

He grabbed it, frantically.   I tugged and strained. Facing around, I got a hold with my feet, and bent my back.   For a full minute, maybe, I heaved against the clutch of the bog.   Then I looked over my shoulder: the man was up to his armpits.

"No use," I gasped.

"No use!" cries he.   "Oh, don't you say that, buddy!   We're making it.   You come a little closer. Ketch her fu'ther out.   There.   Take her tight. Tight, I say!   Tight as you can!"

Suddenly, just as I had got a firm grasp on the limb, but no sound footing, he jerked.   I reeled, toppling over the brink of the bog.   To save my-self, I must take one step toward him, and plop my left foot into the quag.   He clutched at it, his finger-tips brushing the calf of my leg.   That touch and horror at his unspeakable treachery, more than my strength, snatched my foot from that awful suck.

I looked at him, panting.

"You deserve to die," I said.

Then the man changed again.   To him I was no longer present.   In a trice sheer terror made him mad.   His lips frothed.   He howled like a dog. The veins on his forehead were a purple net-work. There in the clear sunlight he waved his upstretched arms, the miry fingers clawing as in a spasm; and from his mouth, a lather of blood and foam, spouted between howls the language of the damned. Up into the face of God, Whom he was to meet so soon, he flung the rage of his black soul; and sank to his death blaspheming.

From that picture of hell I stumbled dizzily away.

XXIII

THE CONVERSATION BELOW THE WATER TANK

HOW far I fled I did not then know, so addled was my brain; (as it proved, I was just over the hill in the next ravine) but at last my legs refused to bear me further. On a grassy slope I fell, rolled with the tilt of the ground till I struck some bushes, and had just strength and sense enough to drag myself under their cool protection. Ere I had fully recovered my breath I think I was asleep.

Like dead I slept; and when I awoke, putting aside the leafage of my covert, I looked up into a sky of stars.

I rose to my knees, but with the movement hunger seemed to skewer my very vitals. All else vanished before that appetite. I was ravenous. The leaves, the very turf, I could have devoured. Then my groping hand grasped something like a smooth oval stone; but it was much too light for a stone. I felt of it again, and it cracked under my touch. I put it to my mouth, positively trembling; sure enough, it was the half loaf I had filched from the kidnappers' cave!

By what mighty instinct I had clung to it through

all the fearful hazards of my escape I did not pause to consider; but tore it with my teeth like a starving dog. Doubtless it was inground with clay; doubtless blood was on it; but neither blood nor clay withheld me. Bread I was eating—I thought of nothing else! And when I had finished it, I picked at the ground for fallen crumbs.

A half dozen loaves I could have eaten; yet it was wonderful how strongly and how quickly that battered half-loaf set me up. What with sleep and the bread in my belly, I crawled out of my hiding-place and stood up, as fresh and sound as when I first hit the road for Jack's House—ages ago!

How far into the night I had slept was a matter of mere guesswork. Yet I had something to go on, too: about me on the hillside hung a misty kind of light; I could make out the dark masses of trees, edged whitenesses that were rocks, and clumps of bushes: and I knew that the moon must be somewhere in the sky. And if it was the moon, it was a new moon dropping behind me into the west; and the night was still young.

Had the attack on Jack's House started yet?

I sat down on a boulder to size up the situation. Of course I was now free to hustle on to McGregor and fetch the sheriff; but McGregor was more than four miles away, and it seemed to me that before I could get there, rouse up a rescuing party, and return, Jack's House must be taken. Father McGiffert and William were its only defenders; like enough, poor Dan Mitchell was captured, or else wandering useless in the hills. True, to offset this handicap, Blue Island was done for. Nevertheless, as the sides stood, it was two against six. I made up my mind then and there to hasten single-handed to the succor of the besieged. In your ears this may sound like an unwise resolve; and indeed, as you shall hear presently, it pitched me headlong into a stream of perils whose swirling currents bore me far from Jack's House.

Well, when I reached the crest of the hill above the ravine, sure enough, through the trees, low down in the west, shone a delicate young moon. Like a thin burnished crescent it hung among the leaves; but it was faery bright, and its radiance, like a silver mist, sifted over the whole hilltop. In another half hour it would be gone, and I knew I must make Jack's House ere the blackness fell: after moonset the attacking party was sure to begin operations.

But I must proceed cautiously; if the light aided Father McGiffert and William in holding off their assailants, by the same token it would aid those assailants in taking a clean pot-shot at me. For all that, the moonshine advantaged me too; for had it been outright dark, I should have been hours getting to Jack's House, if, indeed, I had got there at all. But, as it was, I went forward pretty rapidly. And by and by, on the far side of a valley which lay at my feet like a pool of ink, I saw the pine-tops like a fish's fin and above them the fretted crest of the tower with one tip of the clean-sliced moon sticking in it.

On I stole down the hillside, feeling my way carefully through the yielding brush. Knowing I was now to the front of Jack's House, I aimed to fetch around and come at it in the back. That part of the lawn was quite clear of shrubbery and flowers, so that our enemies would hardly launch their attack from that quarter. Once there I might safely crawl to the fringe of the pines; and after that, if Father McGiffert or William didn't shoot me, I should be in a fair way to win into the house.

Having groped across the thick gloom of the valley, I crept along the opposite slope among the pines. At length, though the moon was now down, I judged I was abreast of the southern end of the house. The tower-top bulked darkly against the northern stars. I listened: not a sound in that sea of blackness.

On I went, stepping as nicely as a cat after rain. But for all my caution, now and again a twig would pop underfoot, or a feather of low-hanging needles stroke my cheek like a caress; and each time a little tightness would dart across my chest. By this, I guessed I must be come pretty well to the back of the house. I halted. The same deathly silence filled my ears. To the right I turned. One, two, three, four, five steps I took; then my hands touched the bole of a pine; a bit of the bark cracked under my fingers.

"That you, mate Dick?" said a voice from the other side of the tree. The tone, in reality, was a rough whisper, but a screech couldn't have shocked me more. I stiffened like a standing corpse.

"Well, shiver my sides," growled Iron under his breath—it was he, I knew right off—"somebody's by. I'd take my davy I catched a sound. There now, I'll just cock my other ear."

You bet I wanted to get out of there; but you bet, too, I didn't stir a peg—I didn't even breathe. After a little,

"Well, now, that's funny, that is," mused Iron. "If I was Tom Donkin now, I'd say they was spooks about. Howsomever, Dick won't be long a-coming 'less he loses his bearings in all this night. But he sighted this here shed mighty sweet and tidy, and I reckon he can steer his way back."

He lapsed into silence, and I, fearing lest I had wandered abroad (owing to his mention of a shed), craned around the tree-trunk and could just make out an oblong shadow; and lifting my eyes, thought I saw a kind of frame-work. And higher up, sure enough, perched amongst the treetops, was the water tank, dead black against the starry night. I had reached the right spot; but there were others here before me.

Softly I withdrew one step, so softly even I couldn't hear it. But next moment the darkness in front was stabbed by a ray of light, like a sword. I glimpsed the ground vividly, as by a lightning flash, and one black shoulder of the squatting sailor. Ere I could find my head,

"What the blazes!" cries Iron, springing up.

"Psss-t!" hissed a voice.

"Oh, it's you, Dick," whispers Iron, relieved. "But what in thunderation were that there light? That warn't the signal."

Why I didn't slip away in that little gust of excitement is more than I can say; I could have done so, and neither of them the wiser. But Carver's next words set me on a quivering listen.

"Look here, Iron," says he, in swift low tones. "I've got a better plan. Let's clear out of here till all this fracas blows over. You and I don't get anything out of this job to-night—you don't, anyhow; and I'm willing to sacrifice my end of it. It's nothing compared with what we've as good as got. There's going to be hell and all a-popping to-night, and I have my doubts whether we can take the house at that. One of our men's got yellow already— beat it to Chicago."—That was Blue Island, but he wasn't in Chicago—"Two of their outfit are loose in the woods, and one of them, I know, has gone for the sheriff. Cro—the boss of our gang knows that, but he's stark, raving mad. Now, listen. You and I can light out for the river, take a motor-boat I know of, cross to the Burlington tracks and catch a freight straight in to Chicago. We'll lay low there for a week or so—a month, if necessary—and then come back to a deserted house and easy pickings. That's plain common sense, that is. What's your word?"

Iron was slow to answer, and in the interval I did some tall thinking. One thing was certain: I must somehow filch that chart. Without it, we should have to gut the house—perhaps even tear it down altogether: and this was impossible. A day or so longer, if we weren't all murdered in the meantime, and we must quit Jack's House for good. Our peril tallied exactly with our hope of lifting the treasure. And the treasure Domini must have—wasn't she now harder up than I? And Lord knows I wasn't any Rockefeller. On the other hand, if I followed Carver and Iron for the chart (and small chance of getting it, but that didn't dash me), wouldn't it look like leaving Domini in the lurch? Yet, with Carver and Iron deserting, and Blue Island dead in the bog, Father McGiffert and William would have but four to deal with. And above all, didn't Carver just now say that Mitchell had made good his escape and was gone for the sheriff?

". . . But what about my chest back in that hotel?" Iron was urging. "I ain't in half a mind to lose my chest. I love that chest, same's you love your own wedded wife. Have I shipped this many a year with her, ever since I climbed the sides of the *Susan B.*, a blessed landlubber, on'y to be a-leaving of her now high and dry in that dirty fo'c'sle of a hotel? And every swab that sets his deadlights on her, he'll up and say, 'That chest were Absalom

Iron's, but he's left her, he has—run off and left her.' 'A. Iron, mate,' is printed mighty pretty and mighty clear, pretty and clear as ever was, right on the topsides of her."

Whether the old sailor meant sense to be at the back of his prattle and was showing Carver, in his own queer way, the danger of their being traced through the chest, I, in that ticklish pass, didn't even suspect. Nor did Carver, either, at first jump; for he lets off an impatient swear. But then,

"Ah, I see," says he. "But don't you fear. You'll wire to have it sent to a certain address in Buffalo. I have friends there. And when we've finished our scoop, you'll have your chest all O. K. Come, if that's all that's on your mind, let's be off."

"Stand by to go about," says Iron; and immediately there fell another dart of light through the trees. "But what's that, mate? What devil of a machine you got there?"

"Not so loud," warns Carver. "It's only an electric torch. But we're lucky to have it. We'd never get through these woods without it. Come easy now. We've got to give these other birds the slip."

XXIV

IN THE BOATHOUSE

THEY started off; and, had I not been all but on top of them to begin with, I must have lost the pair at once, for the night swallowed them completely, and Carver didn't use his flashlight again till he reached the bottom of the hill. Indeed, as it was, my heart sank more than once for fear they had escaped me. But always some little sign—a stumble, a muttered oath, a hissed warning, the swishing recoil of a spray of brush—pointed out their path. And when Carver began to spear the pitchy air with that torch of his (as he did pretty regularly, now that they were off the hill), following them was easy as tracking rabbits in the snow.

Of course, I had more than a guess what motorboat they were after: perhaps you have, too: Crowninshield's it was, sure as shooting. And the only plan I had in my head so far was to beat them to it and put it out of commission. For once they were out on that river, it was good-night to my hopes of getting the chart. Yet, how was I to make the boathouse before them? I couldn't strike out on my own hook in this solid block of gloom.   There was nothing for it but to hang tight on their rear, and trust to luck.

By and by, after covering a prodigious deal of ground, the two of them came to a stop and I saw Carver's light squirt the darkness this way and that.

"Ah, there's the house, right there," said he. "Come on.   I think I can find the key.   We won't waste any time then forcing that lock."

They went forward.   So did I.   And a moment later, out of the ring of trees, I saw them moving darkly across the lawn for Crowninshield's bungalow.   Now was my chance!

Quickly I found the path, quickly I threaded it; and, while Carver was still searching for the key (as I hoped), I had skipped down the steps to the door of the boathouse.   Though I knew it wasn't open, I gave the padlock a jerk anyhow; and then stood back, all in a flutter what to do.

But I didn't stand there long.   If the back of the boathouse was closed, perhaps I might be able to get in by the front; and I darted out on the dock. But the sliding door over the water was also shut; and locked to boot (I guessed), for it only shook under my hand but gave not an inch.   There was but one thing to do and without an instant's stick I did it: I dived, clothes and all, under the boathouse door.

I came up by the stern of the launch; I could feel her screw and then one smooth side standing higher than I could reach. On my right was a two-by-four running underwater, and above it the edge of the dock. Another three seconds and I stood dripping on the boards.

There was not a moment ·to lose. I groped toward the wall, but my shoulder struck something that gave. Raising my hand, I touched the gun-wale of a canoe. A canoe it was I could tell by its smooth canvas sides and its close-ribbed interior. I ducked under it and went feeling along the wall for an axe or a crow or some such tool. A yard or so beyond the end of the canoe I came on a sort of all-round store closet. There were oars standing, and a pile of oilskin cushions, and rubber coats—and then my fingers closed on the handle of an axe! I snatched it up and fished out with it for the gunwale of the launch. I leaped aboard.

A moment's groping, and I found the engine—a mechanism that I knew no more about than I did about differential calculus. But knowledge of a thing is not necessary to destroy it. I just up with my axe and whanged into her—five crashing blows. Bits of iron tinkled to the bottom of the boat. The job was done. If that engine ever ran again, there was no virtue in axes.

Now to hide somewhere close by and await de-velopments. Even now I had no definite plan how to come by the chart: I must crib it some way, that was certain; a lucky stroke perhaps would yet befall; but for the present I must stick as close as possible to Iron and Carver—so close as would enable me even to eavesdrop.

To this end, after slipping the axe into the water, I tiptoed to the closet and hid behind a sheaf of oars standing against the outer wall. On my right, toward the door, hung a rubber coat, so that on three sides at least my blind was complete. And there, in the intense dark, with my back against the closet wall and my heart going like sixty, I waited.

Five minutes passed. Then came footsteps on the stairway without, and the sound of fumbling with the padlock. The door opened, and Carver said:

"Here we are. Careful now: don't step off the boards. . . . First, we'll slide up the door. Grab that rope, Iron."

"Heave ho!" rumbles Iron, and the door rattles up its grooves.

"Now tumble 'm," says Carver briskly.

I could hear the launch souse down under their weight. My knees shook at what the next breath would bring.

"What the hell!" cries Carver.

"What's up, mate?" asks Iron anxiously. "No gear fouled, I hope?"

"Fouled! Well, I guess it *is* fouled. Spark plugs smashed to flinders. Let's see. Yep, all four of 'em. And by thunder, look at the crack in this cylinder case! How the devil could that have happened?"

"Maybe," suggested Iron slowly, "maybe somebody knowed our dodge."

I held my breath for Carver's reply.

"Could they?" he wondered. Then flatly, "Nonsense!" he declared. "Impossible, man! We didn't know it ourselves till fifty minutes ago. No. I can't explain it but I know we don't cross the river in this launch."

I breathed again.

"Well, by gum," says Iron. "That's a hitch, that is, sure enough. But ain't there no other craft in this here shed? Shoot that lightning around. . . . A skiff, mate, bust my bulwarks! Look at her! trim and tidy as ever I see."

I thought they had spied the canoe: but not so. Iron was scrambling out the other side of the launch.

"Come, mate Dick. This ain't not only half bad, but a far sight better. I feel at home in a skiff. When the *Snowbird* went down off the Great Nantuna, I floated clear to the Malay Islands in a skiff. She rode them seas sweeter'n a gull, and warn't an inch bigger'n this one, neither."

"Any oars in it?" says Carver.

(You may fancy how I took this mention of oars, with a stack of them before my nose!)

"Nary a one that I can feel," replies Iron. "Come up here with that glim."

"Nup, not a one," says Carver. "Well, there's some here, I know. There, go round to that closet. They must be in there."

I could hear Iron's footfalls coming round the stern of the launch. Then the door fell open, and the hafts of oars, like black bars, popped before my eyes. Beyond them the stream of light gleamed upon the wall. Then a shadow interposed. Iron was standing in the doorway.

"Nothing here, either," says he, almost in my ear.

There was a rustle of the coat at my right shoulder. Then the silhouette of a hand appeared, not four inches from my eyes: the big fingers touched an oar.

"Aye, aye, here they be. How many, matey? Just two, I reckon. I ain't got but one flapper."

"One pair," says Carver. "It's single-locked anyway."

Iron made to draw them out, but bungled it, and the whole lot slid sideways, half of them clattering loudly to the floor. The blade of one rested on my head.

"Not so damned much racket!" warns Carver.

"Right you are, Dicky," says Iron, fumbling in the mess. (I could hear his grunting breath as he stooped.) "Now let's see. Here's one. And here's the mate to it. . . . Nope. Lemme see again."—His hand reached in and took the oar off my head.—"Ah, here she is. Good."

"Well, get a wiggle on now," says Carver. "We've got to launch this skiff."

Imagine my relief when Iron withdrew! That was a tight squeeze, I tell you. My knees still shook, or rather began to shake in earnest now that the nearness of it was over, so that they had launched the skiff and were off ere I had quite recovered.

I peeped out. Through the raised door of the boathouse I could see the starlit sky and the wide blackness of the river, and out yonder on its surface a darker object moving. They had got away, and all my efforts had been useless. No treasure for Domini now; the key to 'the treasure was fading further from my grasp with every stroke of those oars. I tell you, I felt bad.

Then I remembered something. But the dare of this sudden idea almost took me breathless. And yet, why not? I had survived worse dangers. And there was still a fighting chance.

It was but the work of seconds to ease the canoe off its supports and slip it into the water. Then, groping about, I found a heavy coil of steel cable which I loaded into the prow for ballast.

Out there in the starlight the skiff was easily discernible, making across on a long downstream slant.

But could they spot me? I didn't think so, for the boathouse lay in the shadow of the bluffs. And if I hugged the shore-line for a mile or so, I could not only keep them in view but cross the river without raising their suspicions.

Then, every nerve keyed to the chase, I dug my paddle into the water and shot down with the current.

XXV

THE CHASE FOR THE CHART

IT was a tremendous big river here—over a mile wide. Further down it broadened still more and then, beyond a great spit of black-clumped timber projecting from the Iowa shore, narrowed and disappeared. On the other side the Wisconsin bluffs loomed immense against the starry sky and swallowed in their somber shadow the entire left bank and the river for a hundred yards out.

Yonder in midstream still moved the steadily plodding skiff; but by this I was almost abreast of her.

Then, all at once, I found myself pulling through dead water: the current had sheered off toward the middle. While I was yet in two minds to leave the shelter of the bluff, a deep-toned hoot, that seemed to shake the million stars above me, came rolling and echoing up the river. Then, dimly at first but momently waxing louder, sounded the hard hollow panting of a steamboat; and as I still hung in the dead water, with my paddle raised in air, far down the river, around the dark cape of woods, swam into view a fairy sight.

Over that great reach of inky water it resembled a drifting cloud of splendor, a blazing glory in the night, like some huge and shining jewel moving lustrously upon the black river.   I had heard tell, of course, of steamboat excursions and made sure this was such.   Music and dancing were probably in full swing, although, owing to the distance, I could as yet neither hear the one nor make out the other.   The boat was still but a tower of glowing light.

But one thing was certain: I must tax my wits to take advantage, in the pursuit, of this excursion boat.   I glanced across at the skiff.   To my surprise it had shifted its course from slant to straight. Though slipping somewhat with the current, it was making dead for the Wisconsin side.   At once I saw the reason: the channel hugged that shore; the steamboat would keep to the channel; and Carver and Iron aimed at crossing the steamboat's bows and passing her on the starboard beam.

This left me but one course.   Swinging the nose of my canoe around, I buckled down hard and drove her clean out into the starshine and headed for the steamboat's stern.   My plan was to cross well below her, gain the shadow of the opposite shore, and lurk there in the darkness for the skiff.

The steamboat, larger now and more distinct, panted steadily upstream.   From a mere mass of incandescence, like a luminous solid, she began to resemble an immense bubble of golden light, with black bars and flitting specks inside of it.   A little further and I descried her triple deck and the wide glare of her upon the shiny floor of water.

And now she began to tower high and big: so high I must lift my eyes, and so big that my canoe looked like a cockle-shell; and a bit of a quiver pounced upon my heart at the hugeness of everything but myself.

The skiff, far up on my left and at the very fringe of the bank's shadow, had put about with the current and was headed for the steamboat's bows.

I took a fresh grip on my paddle and spurted. Although a good two hundred yards off, the steamboat was now almost abreast of me. I could see her crowded decks, and even discern the faces of people leaning against the rail. On the middle deck, by the regular movement of the throng, I judged a dance was in progress; and sure enough, a little after, between the mighty coughs of the smokestacks, I caught the sound of music creeping tinklingly across the water. Laughter mingled with the music now, and a rippling babble of voices. Little those merrymakers knew what was afoot upon the dark river to either side; little they would have cared, had they known.

Well without the large radius of her lights I passed her. Ten more lunges with my paddle, and I reckoned I was close to five hundred yards ahead of the skiff. At that, I thought to play it safer, and repeated the strokes. And then I turned.

And not a moment too soon, either. The prow

of the canoe seemed to rise straight into the air, the stern, to my dismay, dropping beneath me.   I had clean forgotten the furrowed wake of the great boat. And my heart stood still.

But, luckily, I had changed my course in time, and could take the waves stem on.   Had that first roller hit my beam, I should have turned turtle like a saucepan.   Even as it was, I had a tough ado to save my little craft from capsizing, and more than once, as I hovered on the feathery top of a white-cap and heard it bristling beneath me, and saw the black plunge imminent, my breath clean left me and a helplessness bound my muscles.   And yards ahead in the swart night I could see the water crisping palely over the crest of the long washes and the starlight glinting in it like sparks of fire.

But the canoe swam like a duck, and ere long, though the back flow of the wake jounced me pretty roughly, I had weathered the worst of it and was come to within a stone's toss of the Wisconsin shore. The shadow of the bank sheltered me now, and for the first time since encountering the steamboat's wash, I looked up river for the skiff.   Not a trace of her on the starlit surface; only, away up yonder, that stately hill of light plying now in midstream.

The skiff couldn't have passed me; she must have grounded further up; and I bent to my paddle desperately: Carver and Iron were not to be lost after all this trouble.

But the gloom near the shore was almost im-

penetrable, so that I could distinguish but a little beyond the canoe's prow.   I knew I was in the current; and, putting out my hand, got a start as I felt
the strength of it.   How much progress I was making I could only guess, until, upon the dark shore-
line, a yellow eye popped out and stared at me.
What this lantern signal meant was more than I
could tell (I knew next to nothing about river navi-
gation and channel signs); but anyhow I saw it
slowly dropping behind and realized that I was making headway..

Now it was well that my eyes and ears were on
the alert, for suddenly, out of the darkness ahead,
an oarlock creaked.   I backed water hard, then
glided toward the bank.   Presently came another
creak.   And a moment after a black object slid into
view.   It was the skiff; and as I floated breathless
with the current it passed me scarce six paddle-
lengths off.   I made out the dim figures of two men,
one at the oars and one seated in the stern.   Just as
I was wondering how far to let them go, Iron's voice
spoke up.

"No, mate, it's easy seen you're a landlubber.
We got enough bilge in this boat to do a first-class
schooner."

Carver swore.

"Oh, that water isn't going to kill you," says he.
"At any rate we're safe now."

"Yes, we're safe now," agreed Iron, "if that's
any comfort to you.   But I'm 'most drowned, I am,

and this here chart wet as a barnacle.   I sang out 'sta'b'ard' in plenty o' time, too."

"Damn your 'sta'b'ards' and your 'la'b'ards.' Why didn't you speak English?"

"Well," said Iron, "they ain't no use comin' to cutlasses about it.   It's done now.   You just keep a sharp lookout for your cove."

All this while I had kept well back and followed them by their voices. · But now the voices left off, and I must creep closer.   It was mighty ticklish work, I tell you; for, though the canoe was noiseless as a floating leaf, there was always the danger of the skiff's sighting me if I sighted the skiff, and Carver, manning the oars, would be facing my way.

· But I didn't have to sight them.   Suddenly Carver said:

"She ought to be along here somewhere."   And as he said it, a long arrow of light shot across the water toward the bank, showing me what looked like the mouth of a creek, and above it a rock embankment.

"That's it," says Carver; and I backed water gently, and hung out, waiting for the next gleam of the torch.

It wasn't long in coming.   But the skiff had already entered the creek, and I was below it, still in the river channel.   The night was so black and direction so uncertain, that, had it not been for that flashlight, I should have lost them right here at the river bank.   But I aimed at the point where I had last seen the skiff, and took two or three stout pulls as softly as I could. And then the bright ray streamed up the embankment, and a moment later the skiff grounded on the rocks. And now I felt no current, and knew this new water was no creek but a slough.

From now on Carver used his torch pretty constantly. And I, being out of the current, just stood off in the shelter of the dark and watched them disembark and scale the embankment, the whitish beam darting on ahead and revealing, away up there, the sheer gray side of a cliff or railroad cut. Here, I supposed, was the Burlington track.

"All right," says Iron, breathing hard with the toil of his ascent. "We're aloft at last. Shiver my timbers! I never seen such a night—blacker'n a ship's belly. Now which way?"

"Up the track. But don't talk so loud, man! Don't talk at all. The night has ears. You can't tell who might hear us."

"Hear us!" echoed Iron, a note of alarm in his voice. "You ain't meaning sperrits, mate Dick? I never took no stock in sperrits. But Tom Donkin, he did and says he, 'Absalom,' says he, 'you can laugh now and you can poke your fun now and you can ballyrag now, but you can't insult sperrits forever,' says he. 'You'll be sorry,' says he, 'some day!' But I was on'y skylarkin' with him, so to say, an' never meant—"

"Cut it!" snaps Carver.

I lingered till their footsteps almost died away up the track. Then, gliding to shore, I stepped out and cautiously climbed the embankment.

I listened. Out of the darkness ahead came the sound of men walking. I tiptoed up the ties. Soon the rock cliff on my right gave way to a high wooded slope, almost vertical, like an immense sable curtain; and on my left, below the embankment, slept the still water of the slough and beyond it, the silent wilderness of bottom forest.

For a half hour or more, perhaps, Carver and Iron kept up the hike, I slinking along behind them. At intervals the flashlight would cleave the darkness dead ahead, showing the gleaming rails and the two trudging figures in silhouette.

But my chance of getting the chart seemed more hopeless now than ever. Once the excitement of crossing the river was over and I had time to look at the matter calmly, what I had thought to be a daring venture appeared in its true colors—a wild-goose chase. Did I imagine I could cope with two desperadoes and them armed? (Certainly, Carver carried a pistol.) If ever I had done a foolhardy thing in my life I was doing it now. Nay, it **was** worse than foolhardy, it was mad.

Besides common sense, what brought me to a sane view of the business was, I think, my wet clothes. The night air felt ten times chillier now so that as I stole along, I shivered at every fresh touch of my damp garments.

I halted. It was folly to go on. I was beaten, that's all there was to it. The wisest I could do was to go back, find my canoe, and hit for Jack's House.

And then, up the track ahead of me, something **happened.**

XXVI

TOM DONKIN'S PROPHECY COMES TRUE

CARVER and Iron had come to a standstill, the flashlight flickering here and there as though they were examining their whereabouts. I skipped down the offside of the roadbed, crouched behind some bushes, and watched. Talking followed, but the voices were so low I couldn't catch a word.

Presently both men left the track, and as I stole forward along the drain ditch I saw them swing out a wooden gate and enter the woods.

Quickly I crept nearer. Again I spied them. They were moving about under the trees, fetching windfalls, it seemed, to one spot. Then I understood—they were about to build a fire. Were they going to camp here for the night? I sneaked along a wire fence, almost to the gate, lay low in the tall grass, and pricked up my ears for their talk.

By this, they had got the fire started. The ruddy blaze, leaping up, illuminated the surroundings very clearly. The place was a level valley, lying between the great hill we had just passed and one which lifted its dark crest against the stars a hundred yards or so up the track. But it was something more than a mere valley; for, as I craned out of the grasses, I saw there was little or no underbrush in there, but a smoothness like a cropped lawn. There were plenty of trees, though, their straight stems black against the red glare of the fire. And then my eyes fell on the traces of a road, and old buckets and tin cans and bottles strewn about. It was a picnic grounds, or looked mighty like it.

Just as I was about to roll under the fence and worm closer,

"I tell you what," says Carver, in tones clearly audible, "I'm leary of this fire, Iron. We're not as safe as you think. That little wetting isn't going to hurt you."

"Oh, come, mate," says Iron. "Who the devil's going to sight us, I should like to know? No *humans*, anyhow. Besides drying my duds, this here blaze is cheering, mate; and I ain't in no mind to wait for you in the dark. I'm uneasy, mate Dick, a little shaky in the middle, like. But Tom Donkin, he says sperrits can't abide the light. Well, I hope not. Now you look sharp and be brisk."

"Oh, I'll be back in thirty minutes," replies Carver. "The bridge can't be more than a quarter of a mile further, and the switch-tower is on this side. Let's see: it's half-past one now. There ought to be a freight along here before daybreak. But the switchy will know for sure, if I can pump him right. This little flask will see to that. And in case she

don't slow up I'll just borrow a lantern to flag her.
You sit tight now, and forget Tom Donkin and his
'sperrits.' "

He came out toward the gate and as I hugged
the grass still as a snake, passed through it and put
off up the track.   With only one to contend with,
now was the time to make a try for the chart.   But
how was I to set about it?   I cudgeled my fat brains:
no result—all I could contrive was to creep closer
and trust to my rabbit's-foot.

Now the fire was thirty or forty yards back in the
woods; between the black boles of the trees I could
see the dancing flames and, beyond them, old Iron
hanging his coat on a couple of stakes.   I rolled
under the fence, intending to crawl to the very rim
of the firelight.   I knew he couldn't see me.   Besides the shelter of the tree-trunks, I had the shelter
of that glare; to one sitting by a campfire it's nothing
but solid night outside the reach of the blaze.

I had covered perhaps ten feet, when something
white on the ground to my left caught my eye.   It
was nothing but an old raggedy table-cloth, likely left
here by some picnickers.   I let it go and crawled
ahead; but, as you shall hear in a moment, that cast-
off linen was to do me yeoman's service.

Between me and Iron I had put a shielding trunk.
·When I reached it, though still some twenty yards
from the bivouac, I peered out.   The old sailor was
squatted hatless by the fireside, the red flames playing bright and ruddy on his big face and shiny poll.

Then, as I yet looked, he cast his eyes furtively about—even glancing over his shoulder—and drew from his bosom the pouch I had seen on Eagle's Nest. Holding it between his knees, with two of his club fingers he fished out the precious bit of paper, unfolded it, and spread it on his thigh.

Came to me then a hare-brained idea: to rush in, make a snatch at the paper, and dart away. Seeing that chart, so near and yet so far, all but overthrew my balance.

But this madcap impulse I mastered, and scrooched tight, my heart thumping for the closeness of my quest, and my eyes devouring Iron.

He was reading the chart, or attempting to do so, his great sconce bent sidewise to the light; and every now and again he would start and look around, with the queerest mixture of cunning and guilt palpable upon his face.

What could he be afraid of? Brave he was, I knew. Had he not dared instant death on Eagle's Nest? And certainly no man, with his shrewd sense, would be daunted by the bogey fears of darkness. And yet he had been babbling of ghosts. . . .

Then, all of a sudden, an unearthly sound boomed out: from the black wall of gloom beyond Iron, came quavering deeply and almost with the loudness of a roar, the weird cry of a hoot-owl.

You should have seen Iron! Up he jumps, as if he had been shot at; leaps across the flames, hugging pouch and chart, and stares into the dark.

I took the owl's cue, and answered. (I used to be a pretty good hand at most bird calls, and could do an owl's to a nicety.) At my first hoot Iron whipped around and positively backed into the flames. I saw his face now, white as a clock-dial; a scared man he was, and no mistake.

Scarce five seconds elapsed after my imitation, when old Mr. Owl strikes up his tune again; and just in the midst of it I remembered the table-cloth and scooted back among the trees. I was going to play this ghost game for all it was worth.

Draping the cloth over two sticks, I held it high before me and, gently waving it, advanced. Through a rent I could see Iron's gigantic figure cowering by the fire, evidently distilled to a jelly by the last cry of the ghost.

I let out a hoot. Iron snaps about, and spying the awful table-cloth, gives one tremendous scream, like the neigh of a horse, plumps down on his knees, and holds up chart and pouch.

"No fu'ther, George!" he pleaded. (Such a voice!) "Don't come no fu'ther! You wouldn't hurt your old mate, George, your old mate what bunked and messed with you this many a year!"—I tried a groan.—"Ah, George, I knowed you would come back for it. I knowed you would. But you was as good as dead anyhow when I hooked it. I tell you true, George, you led me into temptation yourself. You told me about it so often, and where to go and all."—I groaned again, waved the cloth,

and took a few steps forward.—"George!" he
yelped. "Don't harm me, George! Ah, don't!
Warn't I always true to you? When you first
shipped with us, and they begun naming you 'Frog'
and 'Methus'lum,' didn't I stop their blasted mouths?
Didn't I call Watkins down and fight him? Didn't
I now?"

All this Iron had rattled off in a very paroxysm
of fright; but now he paused, panting and sweating
—the sweat was cold, I fancy. As for me, my next
cue was plain: it was no trick at all, seeing what I
already knew, to put two and two together.

"Leave it there," said I in sepulchral tones.

He dropped both pouch and chart like live
embers.

"Go—go—go—go!" I chanted dismally. At my
second "go" up he springs, and without stopping to
seize coat or hat, dashes off like mad into the
woods.

I lost not a moment. Tossing aside my spook, I
darted in to the fire. With one swipe of my hand
I had the pouch; but the chart, in falling, had flut-
tered nearer to the flames and lay within two inches
of the glowing coals. My breath left me to see
how close my luck was breaking. Stooping, I laid
trembling fingers on the slip of paper.

At that instant a stunning detonation rocked the
night: the fire flew up into my face, spouting sparks;
and a voice behind me cried, "Stop him, Iron!"

A second shot followed, and a shout from Iron,

I think.   But I was away like the wind, with pouch
and chart clutched tight.   As I vaulted the fence
Carver's revolver roared again; the wire snapped
asunder between my hands; and falling heavily to
the ground, I rolled down the bank into the drain
ditch of the roadbed.

But I was on my feet in a finger's fillip, and going
at top speed up the track.   Behind I could hear Iron
bellowing nautical phrases, and, as I took my only
backward glance, the flashlight leaped my way accompanied by a loud oath that told me the chase
was in full cry.

On I raced up the glimmering ballast, aiming for
the shelter of the switch-tower.   And as I ran I
stuck the chart into the pouch, slipped the leather
string about my neck and thrust the whole of it into
my shirt.

For a quarter of a minute maybe I pelted on in
the dark.   But suddenly the bright ray quivered
along the rails; a shot rang out, and two feet before
me the white pebbles flew up in a spray.

And now the track began to curve.   It curved
sharply, leaving the bluffs for the bottom-land.   No
more shots were fired.   I was gaining.   On ahead,
beyond a green dot, I could make out a switch and,
at the far end of it, a square black tower with a light
in an upper window.

The last fifty yards I made in a desperate spurt,
reached the door, and flung my weight against it.
It was locked.   I banged and yelled.   No answer.

I pounded with both fists on the creaking wood. Again I pounded. Above me a head pops out.

"What's the racket? What do you want?"

But it was too late. Already, out of the gloom, Carver was rushing toward me.

Once more I took to my heels. Straight up the track I tore. And then, ere I quite knew what to make of it, the ballast was gone, and I was stumbling over the open ties of a bridge. But there was no turning back. I must go on. But oh, how my heart choked me when I thought of the depth below!

Then, as I strained my pulsing eyes along that dark reach ahead, an engine whistle screamed on the night; and next moment, away yonder in the blackness, the piercing ray of a headlight streamed down the track. My legs wavered and my insides seemed to shrivel up: I was caught between Carver and the train!

But the headlight served a turn, too. By its vivid glare I could see the straight stretch before me: there was no trestlework, but on the left-hand side a runway of three planks without a railing, and every fifty yards (or thereabout) a platform holding a water-barrel. A little more, and I should reach the first of these barrel-stands.

Then Carver fired. A pain, like a sudden burn, shot through the calf of my right leg. I sprang forward, threw myself upon the platform, and crouched gasping behind the far side of the barrel.

At the same instant the bridge began to quiver and hum. I looked up. The tall headlight, like the burning eye of a giant, was bearing down upon me. Louder and yet louder grew the thunderous din; the platform shook and swayed beneath me. I shut my eyes and huddled close to the barrel. With a rush and a roar the great engine swept by; and then began the long stream of cars, pounding and booming and clanking.

Though it took all the nerve I had left to put my head so near those hideously grinding wheels, I peered round the barrel. And at the sight I went all giddy. Along that fearsome footway Carver was approaching with the swiftness and sureness of a monkey.

I stood up, grasping the rim of the barrel, and cried to God. No boy, nor man, either, ever made a prayer more sincere. Then, with a sob (I remember that sob), I got on all fours, and began to crawl along those planks. I seemed to be crawling under the very train, so close it was, so stunned was I with its roar. Perhaps thirty feet I pushed ahead, feeling the pull of the train on one side, and shuddering at the awful void on the other.

Then, I think, my prayer was answered. Thus only can I account for my looking back. Carver was but a few arm's lengths behind, his thin face straining palely through the gloom. Why he didn't shoot me, is more than I can say: perhaps he thought it unnecessary; perhaps he thought he as good as had me.

But he was mistaken. Jerking the pouch from my bosom, I popped it into my mouth; stood up on the brink of the dark gulf—stood and swayed— then jumped.

XXVII

MY FLIGHT DOWN THE RIVER

WITH a shock like dynamite—a shock that seemed to rend me apart—I soused into the water; and sank, sank, sank, sank. Gently my feet touched the bottom, but a force like compressing steel was squeezing my body. My ears sung. My lungs felt crushed. But not for long; faster than I had submerged I was shooting to the surface. Clean to my middle I bounced up; the pouch spouted from my mouth; I caught it in my left hand, and gasping for air, floated on my back.

High above me loomed the dark bridge, the narrow plank-way and the barrel-stands etched against the twinkling stars. The train was gone; I could hear its echoing rumble along the Wisconsin bluffs. Of Carver there wasn't a trace. What had become of him, and whether he had followed me in that tremendous leap, I little cared. I knew I was safe at last.

I recognized my whereabouts. That bridge was the one I had descried the morning the kidnappers' cabin burnt down. I knew the river it spanned— the Wisconsin; and I knew that the Mississippi was but a mile away—certainly not much more; and across the Mississippi, Jack's House. If it had lain in my choice, I couldn't have pitched upon a more direct route; with the current it would be dead easy. The water, besides, was warm and comfortable. I decided to stick to the river and swim to the Iowa shore.

But just then my planning was rudely interrupted. From the left bank of the river came a cry; and looking thither I saw, away yonder across the water and just below the end of the bridge, a streak of light I knew only too well. Along the black shoreline it flitted, and presently leaped out and rested on the margin of the river. A faint figure appeared, stooping. Across the dim distance sounded the rattle of a chain; then the words, "Steady now!" guardedly spoken but wonderfully distinct in that stillness: and I knew that Carver and Iron had again taken up the chase.

I turned over and began to swim. Down yonder was an island. Once there I would crawl up into the underbrush and let them pass.

This was all very fine till I chanced to look around. Already they had caught up half their handicap; but what was worse, that deadly white beam was sweeping in a wide arc over the surface and reaching clear to either bank. I glimpsed a black snag sawing up and down; and then, as I yet looked, pegging away on my side, something on that floor of water gave me heart. In the streaming glare I saw little gray wisps, like curlycues or ghostly pigtails, floating on the river; and knew the mist of dawn was gathering. Another half hour and not that flashlight nor even the break of day would spy me out.

Well, the first thing I knew, I struck shallow water: when I stood up I was scarce knee-deep. Fifty yards dead below was the nose of the island, wooded to the water's edge. Like a fool, I began to wade. Carver's gun made a monstrous noise over the river, like the roar of a cannon. I don't know where the bullet struck, whether near or far: but I know I lit out for that island as if I were running on granitoid.

Breathless I crashed up into the brush (it was black as your hat under the trees), halted, and gave ear. Sure enough, came the dip of oars. They were heading straight for the island.

Gingerly I stepped through the bushes toward the right-hand channel: that had looked the narrower of the two, and thus would be deeper.

Deep it was and with a vengeance! I didn't think I was anywhere near the water, when suddenly the ground caves underfoot and squdge I go into the river over head and hands. Of course, I popped up like a bladder, but the harm had been done. No, I don't mean Iron and Carver—I didn't give them a thought: the pouch was full of water and the chart soaked.

But it was lucky I retained it at all. Had it

slipped from my neck I must have lost it at once
in that darkness. . Anyhow, soaked or not, it was
mine still; and the words on it would have to be
mighty badly blurred before I gave up trying to
decipher them.

Meanwhile what was I doing?   To hear me telling this you would think I had climbed out again
and was sitting on the bank bemoaning my drowned
chart.   Nothing of the kind.   I was scooting down
under that bank like a log in a rapids.   The water,
though deep, was swifter than any I had yet struck.
Times I would hit a projecting root and be turned
clean about; times the hanging boughs would brush
my head; times again I would run slap into a tree
lying out on the surface: but always I hugged the
bank, for it was in my eye to make dry land at the
foot of the island.

But the foot of the island was an unconscionable
time a-coming.   I must have been manhandled by
that ugly bank for upwards of a quarter mile.   I
began to be played out.   It wouldn't have been so
bad had I been able to use my eyes: but you couldn't
see your hand before you.   At last I decided I had
got enough of it (besides my leg was beginning to
pain me sore); grasped some viny vegetation,
dragged myself out of the water, and sat dripping
on a log.

And as I sat there I listened sharply: not the
faintest sound of my pursuers.   Then, deciding to
wait for daybreak, I stript off my clinging clothes,

and felt for the wound in my leg. It was but the merest flesh scrape, but the touch of that ploughed skin made me creep. A wetness I felt, but whether it was blood or water I couldn't tell: my shriveled finger-tips were too benumbed. Anyhow, I ripped a bandage from my shirt and bound my leg tight. Then, rolling up my clothes, I secured them with my suspenders, and wished for the day.

But, instead of the day's coming, the night seemed to have grown darker—darker and ten times colder. I made up my mind to take to the river without daylight: the river, at any rate, would be warmer than this numbing air.

I made to get up, but in the act, my hands touching the log, for the first time I remarked its shape. I felt of it again; the sides were four and rather evenly cut: sure enough, it was a railroad tie, washed up here by the high water. If I could only launch it now, I should have the next thing to a boat.

Well, launch her I did; and then set my bundle of clothes on one end, grasped the pouch (which I kept hung about my neck), and slipped in. You can bet I was glad to feel that water once more; it was almost as good as sitting by a fire!

By and by—I can't say exactly when, but it was after my tie had grounded on a mid-river sand-bar— I found myself surrounded by the ghostliest grayness you ever laid eyes on. You couldn't call it light, because it lighted nothing. Seeing **was** im-

possible.   I was just as bad off as if it had been the
dead of night.   And yet I knew the night was gone
and the dawn come.

Shortly after this something brushed along the
tie, and I felt wet leaves stroke my face.   I reached
out for my clothes (I couldn't see them); they were
still aboard.   I guessed I was passing another island, and steered my tie to the right—and rammed
her plump into my enemies' skiff.

"Hard to la'b'ard!" sang out Iron.   "You've
fouled a log!   Easy, easy now!   Dod rot this dod-
rotted fog!"

"Hold on," says Carver.   "That log hit us.   We
didn't hit it."

I held my breath, scared almost to death.

"Stand by!   Stand by!" orders Iron, and I heard
something—an oar, perhaps—strike the water.
"No good.   We've lost her, I reckon."   But a second later something dark thrust out of the envelop-
ing grayness, and pushed my bundle of clothes into
the river.   "Hard about!   Sta'b'ard!" yells Iron.
"Here's a queer feel!".

"Where?" cries Carver.   "Damn it, man, I can't
see! Which way?"

A close shave it was for me, as quick steering was
impossible with my clumsy craft.   But luckily Carver had pulled the wrong oar, swinging the boat
clean about so that (as I judged) it headed upstream.   Both of them were swearing and singing
out contrary directions and by their clamor I knew

I had already slipped yards below them.   It tickled me to hear them floundering thus uselessly about; so much so that (except I knew it was safe), "Catch me if you can!" I cried, and shoved mv tie athwart the current.

"By God!" shouts Carver.   "Listen to that!" I heard his oars dig savagely into the water and the boat rush downstream with quick, spanking strokes.

But, as I say, I knew they could never find me in that fog: it was by the merest chance that they had already brushed me—a chance in a thousand. And sure enough, they went on past, further abroad than ever. And after a while—direction gets so mixed up in a fog—their voices seemed to be straight ahead at one time, then dead behind the very next moment, to my right now, and then away over on my left.   What they said was plain enough—an interchange of advice mostly, larded thick with curses —but where they were I could not rightly make out. Indeed, all I knew for certain about my surroundings was the set of the current.

Gradually, then, the grayness waxed whiter, though the fog rolled more heavily, if anything, than before.   Did you ever look at a fog closely?   I did that morning: sure, I had opportunity a-plenty.   A fog is not like thin smoke, as I had thought; but millions and millions of tiny whitish particles to the square foot drift up and down and in and out, twisting and turning, always on the go.

Well, by this, the voices of my enemies had died

away altogether. On down the stream I floated, the wash of the tie murmuring and swirling under my chest, and this monstrous hood of whiteness ever shrouding me. Presently I ran into some shallows, but when I tried to stand up the current almost took me off my feet. The real cause was my weakness, though as yet I didn't realize this; I thought it only an uncommonly swift river. A little further, and I began to hit more shallows, one after the other, with pockets of deep water lying between.

A half hour perhaps I floundered through this gantlet of deeps and shallows, and then suddenly found myself in a bottomless hole (I could tell by the feel of it), the current gone but the fog more impenetrable than ever. I wondered if it could be the Mississippi at last; but the Mississippi would have live water, and this was dead, just like the water of a lake.

How long I floated about here I cannot tell. Not only was direction confused but time, too. Often I would strike out for what I imagined was the nearest shore, but as often I would give over: for aught I knew, I might be heading the wrong way.

Shoving the tie around began at last to tell on me. I was not only tuckered out, I was sick,—in the pit of my stomach I felt a strange lightness. Flashed upon me then the awful fear of not being able to cling to the tie; and at once I strove to board it.

No go: I hadn't strength enough to put it beneath me; and when my bundle fell off, it was all I could do to lift it out of the water and set it back on.

Then, to my infinite relief, I heard the dip of oars. A cry rose to my lips. But fear—a different fear—stifled it. Drowning was preferable to falling into the hands of my enemies.

"Well, I guess it'll be a coon's age before you see another ghost, eh, old-timer?" says Carver, as clearly as if he were holding to the tie beside me.

"Tom Donkin's a lying swab, is all I got to say," replies Iron surlily. "If ever I get aboard the *Sarah* again, I'll make pork of him."

Carver left off rowing (it was well he did—they were almost atop of me), and laughed one of his creepy laughs.

"But what did your spook look like?" says he. "You know, I'd give anything to see a genuine spook, like the kind you saw."

Iron thundered out an oath.

"Belay there, Mr. Smart-Aleck! Belay that hazing! I won't stand for it. You just batten down your hatches and pull for shore."

"Pull for shore!" exclaims Carver. "Well, I like that! How do you expect me to pull for shore when I can't even see the water? Iron," he broke off in anxious tones, "we're in a devil of a pickle. Suppose we ram a log or something? Can you swim?"

"Not a stroke. I never seen a true seaman yet

what could. But this water's ca'm as a teacup. All
we got to do is sit tight and wait'll this dod-gasted
fog lifts."

"True enough," says Carver. Then the oars
dipped and a sudden, jerking sound followed.
"There it goes again!" he cried with an oath. "Oh,
damn this boat and the fog and everything! We'll
never get to shore at this rate."

"Easy, mate," says Iron. "What's wrong now?"

"This oar-lock's out of commission. Come here.
You know more about these things than I do. See
if you can fix it."

"Abaft, then," says Iron. "Steady! Steady
now! Trim her to port—to port, I say! Where's
your hand? Stead—"

Came a swift noise, a shrieking curse from Iron,
and a prodigious splash. Then, as he took to
rowing,

"I'm sorry you can't swim, matey," Carver called.
"I can't either, but this boat swims good enough for
me. Good-by. That treasure isn't enough for
two, anyhow."

No sound from Iron except the thrashing of his
frantic struggle. In ten seconds this subsided, and
the marrow of my bones went cold at the brutal
treacherous murder. I was paralyzed, or as good
as paralyzed; for, in the face of prompt impulse, I
had been unable to push my tie to Iron's rescue.
And now it was too late: the poor old rascal (whom
after all, I had somehow liked) had gone to his ac-

count. On the spot I put up a prayer for him—and for myself, too! How soon might I follow after!

Then a kind of stupor settled on me. I no longer felt the water, or even the wood under my arms. The fog seemed to creep into my mind, and all things became a haze.

A half hour, perhaps (I make but a guess), this fit of exhaustion endured. But all the while my arms clung to the tie. Then, my senses brightening, I rallied my strength and,

"Help!" I shouted. "Help! He—!"

A violent oath exploded behind me. My heart stopped dead, and then cried, "Carver!"

XXVIII

JACK'S HOUSE AGAIN

"WHAT'S up? Who's there?" yelled a voice: not Carver's.

"Here!" cried I. "Oh, quick! quick!"

The black prow of a skiff nosed out of the fog. I flung one arm over the gunwale.

"Well, I be tarnation jiggered!" said the voice, and looking up, I saw a pair of eyes fairly popping out of a perfect jungle of whiskers.

"Oh, thank God!" I sobbed. And then, pulling myself together, "Take this bundle," I directed.

Without a word, but his gaze still fixed on me in stark amaze, the stranger reached out and lifted my clothes off the tie.

"You'll have to pull me aboard," said I. "I can't make it."

"Get around in back then," says he. "This boat tips like a bucket, and I don't want to lose them fish."

Hand over hand I crept to the stern. He grasped me under the arms, and, "One—two—up you come!" cries he.

Panting with the effort, I sprawled on the seat.

282

The fearful stench of rotten clams assailed my nostrils; but this, you may be sure, didn't disgust me: the perfume of roses couldn't have been sweeter.

My rescuer squatted before me amid a welter of fine channel cats (it did my heart good even then to see them).

One of the fish bounced up. The old man swore. "You bee-have!" Then, "Why, by cricky," says he, staring at me again, "I never looked to ketch sech a kind of fish."

"Neither did the fish," said I, with a ghost of a grin.

He sent a squirt of tobacco juice plop into the water. Having wiped his mouth,

"Here's what you want now er I don't know nothin'," says he; and he proffered me a leather-covered flask.

The liquor tingled to my finger tips, and in the flirt of a whip my strength returned. "Thanks," I gasped. "Now if you'll land me on the Iowa side— will you?"

"Shore," says he at once. "Shore I will."

He manned the oars and began to row; and as he rowed I put on my clothes. By this, the fog had lifted somewhat, so that I could make out a boat's length all around. Still, this was no great help. To me it was a positive miracle how he sensed direction.

"Aren't you afraid of being lost in this fog?" I asked.

"Lost?" says he, and spat with relish. "Why, no. Fogs ain't nothin'. You wouldn't get lost in your own house, would you? Well, this here ol' Miss'ipp', she's my house. But how come, bo, you went a-swimmin' so early?"

I had thought he would ask the question—you couldn't blame him. But already I had made up my mind what to answer. Had I not been so certain that Dan Mitchell had gone for the sheriff and that, as a consequence, the siege of Jack's House must now be raised and its defenders rescued, I would have told him all and would myself have hurried to McGregor.

"Well," I replied, "I was out on the river last night, and fell in, and—

He threw back his head and guffawed.

"Got tight and pitched over, eh?" said he. "Well, thet's a good one, that is. You got to be keerful on them excursion boats. One drunk overboard don't bother them fellers. They don't mind. But say, bo," he added with an oath, "you must 'a' been driftin' around a mighty long spell. How come I never heerd you holler?"

I let my own story go: his had it beat all to pieces.

"Well, I should say it was a mighty long spell— since 'way last night. You see, I fell off up the river [I didn't say which river], and luckily found that tie; but by the time I got this far, and nobody came to pick me up, I sort of lost hope. The yell you heard was about my last, I guess."

He said nothing more and buckled to his oars. As for me, though my clothes were soaking wet, that whisky warmed the cockles of my heart and made me glow all over.   Besides, my wild attempt to gain the chart had been crowned with success.   The chart was mine—mine!   I pressed it against my breast. Already, I was as good as come to Jack's House: I would go to Domini, give her the chart, and tell her the treasure was hers—every last cent of it.   And if I had had but a small share in defending her, and in fetching the rescue party, at least I had made this possible by freeing Dan Mitchell.

"Well, here we are," announced my ferryman at last.

But, looking out, I saw nothing save solid fog. "Where?" said I.

"Right yonder," says he.   "But it's quite a step up to McGregor."   A moment later, dark clumps loomed out of the whiteness, and I knew they were the willows that lined the foot of the railroad embankment.

When I had stepped out,

"Wait a second," said I.   "Is this anywhere near Eagle's Nest?"

He hesitated, holding his chin and looking narrowly at the shore.

"Le's see, le's see.   Nup, s'fur's I kin make out, this is the *p'int* right here.   Eagle's Nest is a sight fu'ther down—'bout a mile, I guess.   Well, s'long, bo.   You be keerful how you carry your likker next time you go on the 'scursion boat." Even as he spoke, his boat slipped out into the fog.

On shore! Well, the next thing to do was to get out of the fog; and the only way to do that was to gain the top of the bluff. I had nothing now to fear from my enemies; by this, if they weren't all under arrest, at least they were scattered and hiding. And if we heard each other's footsteps, not I, but they, would slink under cover.

On the crest of the bluff (which I reached after a mortal tough climb), I found the fog all broken. It drifted over the grass in detached vertical fragments, trailing at the bottom like long white garments. Creepy it was to see a column of it fifteen or twenty feet tall, trembling and floating, like some monstrous ghost, among the dark still trees. I thought of old Iron. Ghosts would frighten him no more. Poor man, he was now a ghost himself.

While I was still looking about, trying to identify my surroundings, the light on every hand seemed suddenly to grow broader, and turning my head I saw an orange disc, big as a cart-wheel, sticking away out yonder in the fog. It was the sun, I knew; but it looked for all the world like an immense Japanese lantern.

Well, going up a little to my right to see if I could pierce at all down into the vast white gulf, it struck me that I had been here before. You remember when I spied Crowninshield's motor-boat the morning I bit Jonas' hand? That was the time.

Unless I was mighty badly mistaken this was the very spot. At any rate, I would give it a try.

Straight back into the woods I hustled (though I had to limp a little on account of my wounded leg), turned to my right, crossed a couple of ravines—as I had done that morning, you remember—and then, figuring I was come to the ravine at the top of which I had seen my uncle and Crowninshield, struck back to the top of the hill. If I failed to hit the automobile tracks, I could at least sight Jack's House, as I had done before, by climbing a tree.

But it wasn't necessary to climb a tree. Almost immediately I spied the markings—and in that exact identical gopher mound, I do believe. But following the trail was not so easy a matter. My leg began to pain me now in earnest; every touch of my foot to the ground was like a knife thrust in my calf. And not this only, but the fog, drifting heavily around, obscured the way and confused me to a degree. But I remembered that the trail had led me neither up hill nor down; and this knowledge together with two or three reappearances of the tire tracks, plus great good luck, brought me at last among pine-trees, and I knew I had reached my goal.

So happy was I, despite exhaustion and my racking leg, I could have shouted for very joy. And when, a few minutes later, I came in sight of the house, sitting tranquil and secure in the hush of the morning, my heart swelled with gladness that our perils were past and Domini safe at last—safe and rich with treasure.

On I limped, filled with joyous, wondering thoughts as to how they would welcome me—she would welcome me; and I had all but reached the lawn when,

"That you, Short?" came a guarded voice from the trees.

Fancy what an overturn I got! And all because I had idiotically supposed Carver meant Mitchell, and not I, had gone for the sheriff!

But I recovered my wits, sized up the situation at a glance, and dropped to the ground behind a low trailer of fog.

"Yes," whispered I; but shook to my toes.

"What you doin' over here?"

What was I supposed to be doing? I had no answer. What would come next?

"Is the boss ready on the other side?"

"Yes." But should I have said no?

" 'Bout time to blaze away then, eh?"

Out of blankness was born an idea. I looked toward the house. To the front door it was a dash of sixty or seventy yards. Over the lawn and flowers drifted wisps of fog; but these were low— scarce three feet from the ground: my friends could see me all the way.

"All right," I whispered. "Let her go. Empty your gun."

He did. The discharge of artillery couldn't have

been more·deafening. Bang! Bang! Bang! Bang! Bang! Bang!

At the last bang, I shot out into the open, game leg and all, and raced for the house. A cry went up behind me; but my eyes and soul were riveted on that front door. Half the distance covered, and still it remained closed—desperately closed! Did they see? Would they never open it? Up the porch steps I flew. A report roared out behind, the bullet shattering the bell-button on the doorpost: I heard the tinkle inside. Then, as if in answer to that ring, the door swung back, and I dashed headlong into the hall.

The whole defense seemed gathered at the door. I glimpsed Domini's shining eyes, and Mary palely cowering, and William with his arm in a sling, and Father McGiffert holding the ten-gauge shotgun. But I didn't stop. Snatching the firearm from his hands, "To the back!" I cried, and tore through the post-room to the windows looking upon the lawn in the rear.

The shades were down. I twitched one up. Crowninshield was coming hotfoot for the kitchen. Without waiting to open the window, I up with the gun and let off both barrels. All I remember is a horrible loud explosion, and a kick that sent me spinning like a top. Then, like a girl, I swooned.

XXIX

I CAME to my senses and looked up into eyes that were looking down on mine. I wondered, listlessly, whose eyes they were and what I was doing stretched out on such a comfortable bed.

"Gerard?" said a voice.

I knew that voice: it was Domini's! I sat bolt up and looked at her, and then around on the dainty, pink-and-gold room, and quick as a bat's dart everything came back to me.

"Did I hit him?" I cried.

She smiled, her eyes brimming, as she pressed me gently back upon the pillow.

"No," says she; "but you hit the window—gloriously."

My fingers flew to my neck. The pouch was gone!

I sprang straight up again.

"The chart, Domini! Did you see a leather—"

"Is this the thing?" She crossed the room and returned with the precious object dangling gingerly from her fingers.

"Keep it," said I. "I've had the deuce of a time

290

getting it, but it's yours, Cousin Domini, and the treasure too."

She had turned to the light, to open it, I thought.

"The paper's all wet," I continued. "You better dry it, and then try to make out the French."

She faced me again, and stooping suddenly, kissed me on the forehead.

"Hush," she murmured; and when next she spoke her voice was strangely choked. "You dear, dear boy! . . . But you must try and sleep now. You will be sick if—"

"But there's so much to tell you, Domini," I urged. "Besides, I've got to help defend the house."

Already she was at the door.

"There are plenty to defend the house," said she; "at least till nightfall. Dan Mitchell is with us now, you know."

"Dan Mitchell! Then he— And your father?"

"He's dead, Cousin Gerard. He died just after Father McGiffert gave him the last sacraments."

The door closed softly. Poor Cousin Domini! Anyhow, she had the treasure. . . . I turned over, and saw against the wall a white dressing-table and upon it, near the mirror, a framed photograph on a stand—one of that rich, brown-tinted kind. Some people, I supposed, would have said Dan Mitchell was handsome.

The next twelve hours I slept like a tree. From six to six I pounded my ear in sweet oblivion to rivers and charts and Carvers and everything else; and woke only then because some one had shaken my shoulder. But I woke in famous spirits, sound as hickory, and hungry as a calf.

But I wasn't hungry long.

"I'm sorry to have to wake you," said Domini, and set a steaming tray on the bedside. "But you'll want this more than sleep."

"O-oh!" cried I at sight of all that good food.

"Fall to!" ordered she, with a smile and a flourish of a napkin, as if she were starting a race. "And remember, you don't have to impress me with your good manners."

And indeed, for the nonce, I'm afraid manners went by the board. I didn't even break my bread. But then Domini, sitting by my side, buttered the slices whole.

"Do you think you'll be able to stand on your leg, Gerard?" she asked.

"My leg!" I exclaimed, almost choking on a mouthful. Indeed, I had forgotten all about my leg. "Oh, that's right." My hand shot under the covers and felt a neat bandage. "You fixed it?"

She nodded. "Does it hurt now?"

"I don't feel a thing," I replied: and no fib either. "I'll try her out soon as I finish. But I want to tell you my story now. There won't be time later. You want to hear it, don't you?"

"*Do* I!" She gave me a shining look; and then

smiled.   "It will do you good, too, telling it; you're eating too fast anyhow."

Well, I told her everything, from beginning to end: but of course telling her and telling you are quite different cases; I toned it down for her ears and didn't toot my own horn so much, either.   You see, I'm not facing you.

"And now," I wound up, "after all that, if the water spoiled the chart—"

"Oh, but it didn't," says she, drawing the thing from her bosom.   "See, it's not what you thought, Gerard.   It isn't paper, it's the finest kind of dried skin—just like parchment.   The ink is a little faded, but you can make it out easily.   See?"

We bent our heads together over the sheet, Domini reading off the words in English.

Just then a knock fell on the door: and on our hearts.

"Come in," said Domini.

Mary entered, visibly in a fluster, but visibly, too, making a brave effort at composure.

"Miss Domini, they want you downstairs.   Mr. Mitchell says there's a flag of truce."

"A flag of truce!" cried I.   "We've got 'em beat, by George!   But don't decide anything till I come down, Domini."

I sprang out of bed plump on my game leg: it didn't even make me wince.   There was my suit laid out on a chair, cleaned and pressed; it was fit for church; and my other clothes all washed and ironed. I knew whose dear hands had done it.

Below I found all my comrades in the post-room, standing about the table, a regular council of war. At my footfall, they turned as one man, and Mr. Mitchell (how different from the fellow I had found in the cave!) stepped forward.

"Here's our hero!" cries he, smiling and grasping my hand. "Here's Jim Hawkins back at last. Courageous comrades all, I give you Jim Hawkins with nine rahs and a tiger!"

Of course, I knew who Jim Hawkins was, and accordingly blushed to my ears.

Father McGiffert shook my hand, too, saying little, but his blue Irish eyes speaking much.

Then Mr. Mitchell, who appeared to be in top feather, started again; but Domini broke in.

"Oh, Dan, you're such a boy," says she. "One would think this whole thing's a lark."

"Why, it *is* a lark!" he cried, taking us all in with his merry glance. "Who could have imagined such a lark! Why, Domini, you'd have to go back to story-books to find its equal. Isn't it so, Father? Just fancy, right here in prosy old Iowa, surrounded by enemies and fighting for your life—fighting for the best girl in the world, if I do say it publicly. And—"

Domini put her hand over his mouth. "*Will* you keep still?"

"Well," said I, "this is all very fine. But is anybody keeping guard?   I wouldn't give two cents for their flag of truce."

"Practical Jim!" exclaims Dan (I was calling him Dan within five minutes.)   "You keep your feet on the ground, eh, Gerry?   Well, I'm not such a fool, for all my foolishness: good old William is up in the tower with a pistol long as your arm.   He'll checkmate any treachery."

"Well, to business," says Father McGiffert. "What are we to say to their flag of truce?"

"First," said I, "did you all locate the treasure? We've got to get the treasure before we leave this house."

"Ah, treasure!" cries Dan with gusto.   (There was no repressing him.) . "I had clean forgotten that!   Didn't I say it was a lark, Domini?   Lord, what more could you want!   The dream of my youth's come true!   If this house was only a ship now—a rakish brig, with all sail cracked on, the treasure in the hold of her, and our twelve-pounders abaft barking at the black pirate.   Father, you'd be captain, and I'd be mate, and Gerry, you'd be cabin boy—they're always heroes anyway.   And Domini you'd be—what *would* you be?   No, you wouldn't be along.   We couldn't have any women on board. T'wouldn't do at all.   You and Mary must be pac- ·ing the high headland at home, daily scanning the empty sea with anxious eyes."

Domini laughed in spite of herself.

"Dan Mitchell, you're a perfect goose!   I'm beginning to think you have no more idea of our danger than the man in the moon."

He stuck his hands into his pockets and grinned.

"Less," said he. "Frankly, Domini, this is what I'd call a pleasantly exciting house-party. Isn't it, Father?"

Father McGiffert was smiling, too.

"To be sure," says he. "Only, emphasize the exciting, please." Then, turning to me, "We hit the stone, Gerard," he added. "But we didn't have anything to pry it up with. Besides, we couldn't spare the time from our lookouts. But now you're here, you can finish the job."

"No fair," says Dan. "I want to be in on the finish too. You must call me when you strike the doubloons, Gerry."

But his flippant nonsense seemed to me ill-timed.

"Well, if you think it's all a joke, all right," said I. "When you're ready for business, call me. I'm going to take a look at their flag." And I crossed in a huff to the nearest window, put the shade aside one inch, and peered out.

"Cabin boy properly rebukes mate," I heard Dan say. "Mate, properly humbled, touches his forelock."

At that moment Carver stepped from the rim of the woods, carrying a pole with a white handkerchief attached, and advanced toward the house.

"Look!" said I and I held the shade aside.

They craned together.

"He trusts us, at any rate," said Dan.

"But we won't trust him," I declared. "Not on your life we won't!" I grabbed the Winchester off the table. "Put up the window, Dan. Stand aside, everybody."

Carver was already half way to the house.

I poked the muzzle of my gun through the screen.

"Stop where you are," I yelled. "You're covered."

He brought up short, like a soldier halting, and grounded the pole like a musket.

"This isn't very decent," he called. "We ask for a truce and you point a gun at me."

"It's decent enough for you," I replied. "What have you got to say? Out with it—quick."

He hesitated a moment, looking about. Then, "May I come as far as the drive?" he asks. "I don't want to shout my proposal."

"Let him come," suggested Father McGiffert. "I don't see any harm in it."

"All right," calls Dan. "Step up and talk."

Carver, not one whit abashed at sight of the rifle, strode alertly forward and planted his pole on the drive.

"I have come, gentlemen," says he, speaking in low, rapid tones, "to offer you favorable terms. I suppose you are aware that we have the upper hand. You must acknowledge that fact."

"Nonsense!" Dan interrupted loudly, and with a laugh that grated on my nerves. (I knew they did have the upper hand.)

"Well, we won't argue that point," pursued Carver. "Only, if you admitted it, my task would be easier. Mr. Gordon Crowninshield, for reasons both you and I may guess, wants to take this house and its inmates—one of its inmates at least. He wants to kill her, and kill her with his own hands. That's brutal, but it's plain. All the men with him are in his pay—I'm in his pay. And I may tell you he will balk at nothing to accomplish his design. Now here's my offer: I will double-cross him; I will make his men desert him; I will have him bound hand and foot, and I will let you all go scot-free, the lady included—upon one condition."

He paused to let this sink in. And Dan Mitchell, to improve the interval, foolishly thought fit to let out another guffaw. "You're pretty high and mighty about it, I must say," he remarked.

"Not so loud, please," warned Carver, in tones more guarded still; "unless you want to spoil your chances. I am delivering a different message from the one I was entrusted with.

"There's no use making two bites of a cherry," he went on. "We both know of the treasure. I know exactly where it is. You do, too. It is now a quarter of seven. At nine o'clock I shall be at the front door alone; and if I am convinced that the tower floor has not been tampered with, you will be free to go.   But you must leave unarmed, and you must foot it to McGregor.   To-morrow you may return with as many as you like and get your effects. The house, I know, is Crowninshield's.   That is my proposal."

"And it sounds reasonable enough," whispers Father McGiffert at my shoulder.

I flung him a glance of astonishment.   Were we going to surrender the gold that easily!   Was Domini to be thrown on the world with a dead father and an empty pocketbook!   On the spot I inwardly vowed never to give up the treasure.

"You go back to the woods again," called Dan. "When we're ready with our answer, we'll give you the white flag out the window."

Without a word Carver faced about and retired.

XXX

THE PARLEY: I CALL THE TUNE

NOW," said Dan, with emphasis, "that's square enough. I'm all for accepting his terms. What do you say?"

I looked at him, simply amazed. Then,

"What do I say!" I cried hotly. "I say you're a quitter, that's what! Why, what's the matter with you? I thought you said this was just a house-party! Are you going to let that man break up the party? A moment ago, there wasn't a bit of danger; now you're snatching at a coward's chance to save your hide!"

He only smiled good-naturedly, and shrugged his shoulders.

"Now, now, Gerard," interposes Father Mc-Giffert, "we can't afford to come to words about it. A house divided against itself hasn't much of a chance, y'know. See here, my boy, I think you'll admit we're in a precious bad fix. Well, why not take this opportunity to get out of it? I see nothing cowardly in that."

I looked at my cousin. "May I tell them, Domini?" I asked.

"Tell them what, Gerard?" says she.

"About—about your not having any money."

She smiled—a brave, sad little smile that pierced my heart. "Oh, they know that," says she. "I've told them everything."

I faced the two men, faced them pretty warmly, too.

"Well, I'm surprised at you," said I. "You know she hasn't a penny to her name. You know what that means. And yet you advise running away and leaving behind the treasure that's as good as hers already. It's her property. I gave it to her. And yet you want to beggar her just to save yourselves a little danger. Domini," said I, "don't you give up your treasure."

"We must do what's best, Gerard," says she.

I turned to appeal to the men again. But I could scarce believe my eyes: both were grinning broadly! It was the first and last time I lost patience with a Catholic priest.

"Well, what in Heaven's name are you grinning at!" I cried. "Where's the joke?"

"There now, Gerard," says the Father kindly. "We didn't mean any offense. But, look here, my lad, I'm afraid you're setting too great a store by that treasure. Don't you think your cousin's life is a greater treasure still?"

I saw their drift now.

"Oh," said I, yet more indignant (for I had suffered something to come at that treasure), "you don't take any stock in buried gold. That's it, is it? You think it's all a fake. You don't think there *is* any treasure. It's a dream, you think—that's the size of it! All right. What about Carver, then? Is he a dream? Is Absalom Iron a dream? Carver murdered Iron for this treasure. Is murder a dream?" I whipped the chart from my pocket. "Is this a dream? I've gone through fire and water for this chart—to get the gold for Domini; and by George, the gold she shall have!"

"Gerard," says Father McGiffert, "I admire your spirit, my lad. And if we were here by ourselves, I'd say—defy 'em to the finish. But see, lad, we haven't ourselves alone to consider. We must consider Domini and Mary."

"Well, leave it to Domini, then," I flung back. "Domini, what do *you* say?"

"Enough!" cut in a new voice; and turning, I saw a new face. It was Dan Mitchell's face, but it was set and grim and commanding. "Come," said he, "this talk must end. There's only one way about it. We must be ready to leave here by nine o'clock."

I could have struck the man, right then and there. It was all very well for him to say, leave; he was rich; the treasure meant nothing to him. I stared at him; nay, I glared. But there was something about him—his will, I suppose—that forced me to knuckle under. There was no gainsaying his hard resolve.

But, ere a soul spoke, a new light broke upon me. I took a fresh tack.

"All right," said I. "I yield. Accept his terms if you like. Only, let me warn you. Let me tell you what kind of a man you're dealing with. Carver is a professional crook. He was hired by Crowninshield to kidnap you, Dan Mitchell: which he did to the queen's taste, as you'll allow. He's hired now to capture this house and everybody in it. But he's not only a crook: he's crooked—false to the core. He double-crossed Crowninshield last night. He double-crossed Iron this morning; he murdered him in cold blood. I wasn't five yards off. He murdered him just on the chance of getting the treasure all for himself. You must admit he isn't very long on keeping faith. All right. Now he comes to you with a proposition—his own make, mind you." Father McGiffert was nodding to my points, and even in Mitchell's eyes gleamed a doubt—which encouraged me. "A murderer and a liar comes to you and says that if you'll put yourselves into his power, he'll let you go free." I looked slowly around on all four faces. "Do you believe that? Do you believe that Carver is going to keep his word? Remember, he's paid by Crowninshield— and paid big—to get you. Do you believe he's going to ditch that pay for an *uncertain* treasure?"—I rolled the "uncertain" on my tongue—"sure money for stuff that may not exist? Why, good heavens!"

I ended in a burst, "what's to prevent him from be-ing as false to his enemies as he was to his friends!"

"Right!" cried Dan. "Father, pardon me, you and I are a couple of ninnies. Gerry, you set us right every time: you're the rightest chap I know. This little house-party goes merrily on."

Without giving the Father chance to say aye, yes, or no (for which I was glad),

"We're ready for you now," he bawls out the win-dow and thrust his handkerchief through the hole in the screen.

Carver came quickly up the lawn, halting as be-fore on the drive.

"Well?" says he.

"Our answer is this," replies Dan, "we reject your offer absolutely. That is all."

Carver raised his eyebrows. He imagined, I sup-pose, we should be marks as easy as Crowninshield and Iron.

"Very good," says he, biting his words. "You have called the tune: now you shall pay the piper. What I did, I did out of kindness to the lady. I see I had my pity for my pains. But understand this: I mean to have that treasure. You may unearth it, and you may conceal it again; but if torture can make men speak, the treasure shall be mine. I guess you know me. That boy there does at any rate; and—"

I could hold my tongue no longer.

"Know you!" I cried. "You bet I know you! I

know you're a liar! God's truth can't live in your soul. But worse than that—I know you're a murderer! You drowned Iron in the middle of the Mississippi: I am witness to it. And when you stand up before the jury to lie your way out of it, I will swear you to the gallows if it's the last word my tongue can utter!"

Carver was a cool hand and a brave but I got under his skin that trip. In the deepening shadow of the house his face whitened like starch: but his eyes were blazing.

"You will regret you ever blabbed that evidence to me then," says he, quite evenly. And indeed, ere many hours had run, I was to regret it with a vengeance.

"That'll about do for you," Dan spoke up. "I'll give you just fifteen seconds to make cover."

Carver didn't linger to argue the matter. He wheeled and bolted. It was really ludicrous, after all his big talk, to see him flying headlong for the pines. The indignity, I fancy, didn't serve to sweeten his temper. But I couldn't help a laugh— none of us could—even Mary; a little gale of merriment rose from our hearts.

"There," said Dan, securing the window and pulling the shade, "that's what they amount to—a bunch of bluffers. Why, it's a joke, I tell you, a positive joke. They couldn't take this house in a month of Sundays—not that crowd, anyhow. We might as well stand guard, though. They may try to get their fingers burnt." And with that he steps briskly to the table where the firearms lay.

I wondered at him. He was beyond my plumb altogether. At first, our peril was only a lark; then, upon Carver's making his shifty proposal, he veered to the gloom of a raven, croaking direst evil; and now, again, comedy returned—no lark this time, but a downright joke. These weathercock changes were past my bottoming.

"Gerry," says he gayly, "you take this shotgun to the billiard room where you stopped that fool Crowninshield. You removed the window nicely, so there's nothing to interfere with your peppering him hot next time. Father, shooting at folks isn't in your line, is it? Maybe you won't object, though, to using one of these tomahawks. Here, you watch in the dining-room. I'll stay in here with the rifle. Hey, you, William! Come down out of there! Now, Domini, you and Mary serve out the rations to the old guard, and then turn in. You two need some sleep. You've had a tough day."

William appeared, solemn as an owl, and as unruffled. Seeing me, he didn't bat an eye: a servant he was to the marrow, whether the order was to kill men, or to have the eggs boiled three and a half minutes.

"Ah, there you are, old-timer," says Dan. "You just unlimber that field gun of yours in the kitchen, and look sharp out there. To your posts now, everybody!"

In the billiard-room were three windows; one on the north end, next the tower, and two looking west. Of these two that opposite the post-room door I had blown to smithereens. I crossed to it softly and peeked behind the blind. Sure enough, the whole lower pane was shattered; but the jagged glass, sticking from the sash, would make a man think twice before trying to climb through.

The sun was down, but the western sky was full of pink and purple clouds, like puffs of dyed cotton; and lower the horizon ran with golden light as with a liquid, and against the fierceness of it the pine-tops were printed sharply. No air stirred. We were in for a hot night, it seemed, especially with the house all locked and bolted. I was half glad now I had blown a hole in that window.

But besides defending the house, I had other business afoot. Beyond discovering the stone over the tower vault, Father McGiffert and Dan had done nothing else toward lifting the treasure. They claimed they hadn't the time and the tools to pry up the stone. Maybe so, but their real reason was different: they simply didn't believe in the treasure. Hadn't they as good as told me they didn't? Hadn't they grinned at me as if I were another Wolfert Webber? Well, I would show them!

I set my shotgun against the wall, and looked around. Between the west windows was a great brick fire-place, with heavy andirons and a very crow-bar of a poker. I had found my tools!

Gradually then the room gloomed. Gradually the slits of light at either edge of the blinds softened and faded. No voice, not a whisper, in the still house; only, now and then, the dim sound of a foot-fall.

The more the light failed the stuffier became the room. I stole to the broken window and peered out. Away yonder in the west still hung a kind of glimmer but above, the sky was dark with rolls of sullen cloud. All the stars were hid, and the only thing that hinted at a moon was a vague grayness in the heavens. It was going to be one of those nights when everything is at a standstill, soaked in black ink: the sky full of clouds that don't move, and the woods full of air that doesn't move, either, but gets warmer and warmer till you think you're going to choke.

"Gerry!" came a whisper. I started. A black form was standing in the post-room doorway.

"Dan?" I whispered back.

"Yes. Come here."

I tiptoed across the room. "What is it?"

He bent his head close. His face seemed whiter and somewhat drawn; but that may have been in contrast to the dark.

"Gerry," says he, "after midnight Father McGiffert is going to make a try for McGregor. He says he knows these hills like the back of his hand. God help him to win through. We're in a tight place, Gerry."

"Why," I exclaimed, "I thought you said there was no danger at all!"

"S-s-sh!" His strong fingers grasped my wrist. "Not so loud! . . . Gerry, did you believe all that chatter of mine? Don't you think I realize what we're up against? I know Crowninshield. He's a savage."

"But why the lark, then? What—"

"Would it have heartened her to see our anxiety, Gerry? Do you think she would have slept a wink if she had known how much we really feared?"

"Oh!" My eyes were opened. I saw his gallant gayety and myself insulting him. I began to feel pretty small.

"Gerry," he said with sudden solemness. "Whatever happens to-night, you will stand by Domini to the finish?"

"Will I!"

He squeezed my arm.

"And, Dan," I stammered. "I—I'm sorry for the things I said."

"Go 'long," says he, and chuckled. "I expected you to pitch into me worse than you did."

"But," said I, "I'm going to show you there's treasure in that tower after all. Can you keep watch on both these rooms while I go after that floor ·in there?"

"Why, I reckon so," says he, "at least till Father McGiffert goes. S-s-st! . . . What was that?"

We listened. But it's hard to listen when your

heart is beating like a drum. My heart, in that black silence, was all I heard.

"It's nothing, I guess," he whispered. "I thought I heard a scraping at that window."

"Then I'll get to work," said I, and tiptoed to the fire-place for my tools. Depositing them softly on the tower floor, I returned and got my gun and a candlestick.

The door giving into the stronghold was a thick one; the edge of it filled my hand. But it swung on noiseless hinges and closed with a click scarcely audible.

I struck a match, lit my candle and, holding the clear orange flame aloft, gazed around on the tower chamber. Often in dreams I have seen that chamber since and have waked in a sweat and cried aloud.

XXXI

THE candle-shine, gleaming on the high wall of rough stone, revealed a large circular room, almost barbaric in its furniture. Hanging from the masonry on every hand was a quantity of outlandish redskin gear: wampum belts, and beaded moccasins, and tomahawks, and flint-tipped arrows, and great long calumets, or peace-pipes, gaudy with dyed feathers. Even the staircase, winding upward against the wall to the room above, was decorated with these relics.

But you may guess I didn't waste any time gawping about. There was only one feature of the whole place I was interested in—the floor. It was of irregular flags running two feet square, you might say, and tolerably smooth for uncut stone. Right off, even without consulting my chart, I spotted the one that capped the vault. Dan and Father McGiffert had scraped an X on it. Besides, when I tapped it with my poker, I thought the sound was somewhat hollow.

Setting the candlestick on the floor, I took off my coat and fell to work incontinent. But I was up

against a stiffer job than I had imagined. Old Jacques Cournot had put that flag in for keeps. The
cement in the seams between was hard as nails. Besides, being chary at the start of making much noise,
I pottered along ineffectually and lost a good half
hour. Then, chucking caution out the window, I
whacked away with my poker and andiron till I was
sweating like a butcher. Often I must rest; and
then I would get down on my knees and blow at the
cement dust and be rewarded with a slight deepening of the chink.

Altogether I must have worked at that flagstone
nigh on four hours; I know my candle played out,
so that I must fetch a fresh one; and in the end I
could have kicked myself for being such a dunce.
Let me tell you. You see, the slab of rock was
shaped like a rough triangle, and I had been pounding like a pile-driver around two of the corners and
the greater part of the three sides, but the third
point of the stone I had so far left untouched, thinking to get there by and by. I was going to be nothing if not methodical; lifting this rock was too important a business to attack haphazard. But
luckily my patience gave out at last, and I drove the
end of the poker into the third angle. The cement
cracked like an egg-shell, the poker popping down
through the crevice and all but escaping from my
grasp. Here was something funny. I knocked out
a bit more of the cement (it broke as easily), knelt
down and slipped my fingers between the two flags.

The cement was scarce half an inch thick, and the marked flag shelved back sharply underneath: Cournot had evidently chipped it thus for an easy purchase in prying.

Within a quarter of a minute I had smashed through the rest of the thin cement (quite eight inches of it), inserted my poker as a lever, and heaved down with all my weight. To my amazement (for I expected nothing to give, seeing I hadn't got through the thick cement) the big rock swung up as on hinges; a black mouth yawned momentarily at my feet; and then, ere I could stay it, the slab fell back into position. But in that brief space I saw what an ass I had been. The cement around the whole flag was of equal thickness; the adjacent flags were bevelled to support this one; and for four mortal hours I had been pulverizing pure limestone!

But I wasn't put out for long. Ass or no ass, I had got the stone loose anyhow. With another heave on my poker I pried her up again, secured a grip with both hands, and hoisted her over on the tower floor. My heart gave a jump at what I had uncovered! Below me was a pit black as ink—but at the bottom of it lay Domini's treasure.

Taking the candlestick, I peered down into the vault for the platform or top landing of the staircase. Sure enough, there it was, about five feet below the surface. Now for a plumb-line to hit the treasure. What could I use? So far as I knew nothing of the sort was available, or, if it was, excitement wouldn't let me stop to hunt for it. I just snatched a stone hatchet from the wall, and let myself down through the opening till my feet touched the platform. But here, when I shifted my weight, the whole staircase swayed beneath me. I caught my breath! To the bottom of the pit it must be twenty feet or so—no little tumble. Would the rickety old contraption hold together?

I reached up and got my candle. Very close on every hand gleamed gray rock, so close that I must crawl down the steps backwards. The wood creaked and popped ominously, but I made the third step without mishap, and turning, looked on down the staircase. The glare of the candle, though it didn't illumine quite the entire descent, showed the steps intact and the rock roof slanting out more horizontally. Below, apparently, the pit was roomier.

Calculating as nearly as I could the exact middle of the third step (as the chart directed), I held the tomahawk, head downward, against the outer side, let it swing to rest, then released it. It struck: not with a sharp crack, as I expected, but with a muffled kind of a sound, almost a thud.

Gingerly but swiftly I followed after. In such a taking was I, positively trembling in every limb, that I couldn't tell whether the staircase quaked or not —and didn't much care, either. Once on the bottom I whipped round with a jerk. The candle-flame snapped out, and darkness, like a thousand smothering blankets, enveloped me. I could scarce steady myself to strike a match; and when I re-lit the wick my hand shook like a leaf.

I turned and looked: my heart wondered, feared, and then began to taste a bitter thing.

Straight up from a hole in the floor of the vault was sticking two or three inches of the tomahawk handle.

I almost staggered forward. Dropping on my knees, I plucked out the tomahawk, thrust in my arm, and felt nothing but bare rock. The cache had been rifled; not a single coin was left!

I could have wept, the pang of disappointment was that keen.

But weep I didn't. Perhaps I was wrong, perhaps the treasure was in there anyhow. (I knew I was a fool for so thinking.) I held the candle closer. The hole was a perfect pocket in the rock, small at the mouth but wide at the bottom, like a fish-bag; the inside of it as smooth as your hand; and it contained absolutely nothing—not a copper penny. The treasure must have been lifted.

Then my eye fell on something that cinched the certainty of my loss. To one side lay a flat stone, some six inches square. I picked it up and set it in the opening. The glove on your hand couldn't fit more snugly. This was the place beyond a doubt. Some lucky dog had beat me to it.

I got to my feet. What would Dan and Father McGiffert say? What would Domini say? What would Domini *do?* She had nothing. . . . The candle in my hand was burning with a funny flame, all full of streaks and stars of fire. I winked my eyes, and brushed away the tears: tears couldn't help.

But still the flame behaved oddly: the sparkling radiance was gone, but the flame was bending over, then twisting upright with a little curl of smoke. Two or three times it did this ere I saw the reason.

The reason was simple: a draft of air. But if a draft of air, there was another outlet to this vault besides the one in the tower floor. Coming out from under the staircase, I looked around. The rock to my right was slit with a narrow fissure. I crossed over to it. Sure enough, a cool dampish air breathed through this opening. I could feel it, plainly, upon my cheek.

Shielding my candle, I slipped through this fissure and found on the other side a sloping corridor— dark walls, glistening with beads of water, gloomed high on either hand; the smooth floor tilted gently downward; but on ahead, except for the draft, the blackness like a solid seemed to choke the passage. It was no vault, this hiding-place of the old trader, but a cave. Perhaps he had meant to use it as a means of escape. . . . Why couldn't we use it for the same purpose!

Back I skipped through the gap, and began to mount the staircase.

. . ."Gerry!" whispers a voice.

Looking up, I saw Dan's face peering down through the hole in the tower floor.

"Come on up. Father McGiffert's gone. Slipped away nicely."

I reached him the candlestick, and pulled myself out.

"Where's your treasure?" says he, smiling at me over the candle-flame. Then, ere I could speak, he must have read the truth in my face. His strong arm came quickly about my shoulders. "Never you mind, Gerry, I was fooled as much as yourself. I *did* believe in the buried gold. I should be sorry for myself if I hadn't. Never you mind."

"But it was there, it was there!" I insisted fiercely. "Somebody took it. I can show you the place where it was hid."

"S-sh," he warned. (We were in the post-room now with the candle blown out.) "Speak lower. Of course I know it was there. And you deserved to get it, Gerry, old man. You put up the gamest, scrappiest fight I ever heard of. It's just tough luck, that's all it is."

"Dan," said I, cheered by his kindness, "I didn't find the treasure, but I found a way out of the house." And I told him briefly of the cave.

"Well," says he, "if it comes to a push we'll try it. Right now everything's going smoothly. If we can hold 'em off till daybreak, we're safe. Father McGiffert should be back by then." He paused, and we both stood there listening in the black silence.

From somewhere in the house came the ticking of a clock—tick-tock, tick-tock, tick-tock; the night was that hushed.

"Gerry," whispers Dan, "I'm sure they'll start something soon. I feel it in my bones. You go upstairs and rap on Domini's door. Tell her and Mary to dress and come down. Then hustle back to the billiard-room. I'll wait here."

I groped to the table and set the candlestick down. My fingers touching the dagger, I picked it up and stuck it in my coat-pocket. It might come in handy.

Just as I reached the stair-head, the door of my uncle's room opened, and a dark-robed figure stood on the threshold.

"Domini?" I whispered. "Why, I thought you were sleeping!"

"Oh, Gerard, I'm so afraid—not for myself, for him. If anything happens, what will become of him?"

I knew whom she meant.

"Domini," said I, "if it does come to the worst, you know they cannot harm him. He is gone. He is not there." Which, at the best, was mighty poor consolation.

"No," said she, "he is not there. His soul is in God's hands; we must leave his body in God's hands too."

I closed the door noiselessly.

"Dan wants you to dress now, Domini, you and Mary, and come downstairs. No, everything's safe

so far. But I found a way out of the house.
There's a cave under the tower. You see, I went
down there after the treasure. But—but I didn't
find it. Somebody was there before me. I'm sorry,
Domini; for your sake, I'm sorry."

Her hand just touched my arm—the merest
caress.

"Poor fellow!" whispers she. "And after all
your labor too! Ah, dear Cousin, your brave heart
is more to me than all the buried gold in the world."

I was glad she couldn't see my face. Sure, the
Lord, when He made me, must have thought He was
making a girl, for my tears come upon the least prov-
ocation; which shames me fiercely.

XXXII

THE ATTACK IS LAUNCHED

IN the billiard-room I resumed my post. For all Domini's tender speech, I felt mighty blue over losing the treasure. Yet, if it wasn't to be mine, neither was it to be Carver's—here was comfort (cold comfort, to be sure), and I grinned wryly. After all, it would be a good joke on Carver too!

But who in the world could have lifted the treasure? I wondered. Not Carver, that was certain. If he had, there would have been no parley. Not Iron—Iron was dead. But one other person knew of it—Silly Sim—and Silly Sim was dead too, or as good as dead. And yet, hold on! Whoever scooped the treasure must have been familiar with the secret passage of the cave; he must have come at it, not through the tower floor (that stone hadn't been touched since Cournot laid it), but from the outside, up through the cave; he must have hit the other mouth somewhere in the hills.

Soft footfalls sounded in the post-room, and the sibilance of whispered words; then, once more, stillness: Domini and Mary had come down.

320

Now, to my thinking, as Silly Sim had had the chart and as, being an old-timer in these parts, he would be acquainted with every nook and cranny in the hills, beyond doubt he had stolen a march on all of us.   He was the man!   As sure as this shotgun was in my hands, he was the man!   He might be crazy, but not too crazy to smell out buried treasure.   Yet, if he had got possession of it, how did this square with his hankering about Jack's House? Well, that just proved his insanity.   Perhaps, in his poor cracked head, he was obsessed with the idea that the people of the house had discovered their loss, and he must keep an eye on them.   A hundred to one at this very moment that treasure lay hidden away in the cavern on Eagle's Nest!

Suddenly I stiffened, all my skin a-prickle.

Though I saw it not, nor heard it, within three yards of me stood a presence.   I knew it; and the hair of my head lifted, and my heart quit beating for two seconds and then raced like an express.   How my attention was attracted I cannot tell; for my head had been full of the treasure and Silly Sim, and the room was dark as a nigger's pocket.   I could see simply nothing, not even the fireplace before which I sat.   And yet, all of a sudden, there it was, this presence—close, close! . . . but where?

Shivers ran up and down my back.   I listened; I peered.   But to my ears no sound came, nor to my eyes the vaguest form.

Was it fancy merely?

. . . Ah!

From the broken window stole the tiniest sugges-tion of a creak—a very pin-point of a sound.

All ears, I strained forward in the intense gloom, a tight pain across my chest for the suspense. So keenly I listened that even here I caught the small voice of the clock that was upstairs. A minute, per-haps, was ticked thinly off. Then the window spoke again, definitely this time: a faint but clearly audible scraping, like a cat's paw scratching bark.

I stood up, clutching my gun. (My palms were moist on stock and barrel.) With infinite caution I tiptoed to the window—to the edge of the drawn blind. My left hand touched first the wall, then the wooden jamb.

Gently I inserted a finger between the jamb and the shade: a pale hand lay on the bottom sash. It rose, and a gleam of something with it: the man was removing the jagged glass. Dimly I saw him, his dark head and shoulders and his stealthy hand, not an arm's length from my straining eyes. Then, through the slit, sight gave place to smell: a vagrant puff of air, heavily charged with gasoline, breathed against the window. Then, once more, the white hand with fingers spread like a monstrous spider, moved toward the sash.

What was I to do? Slip the muzzle of my gun behind the shade and blow his head off? I should have done it, maybe; but I couldn't. To shoot at Crowninshield in a whirl of desperation was one thing; to kill in cold blood was quite another.   All my soul revolted from it.

Meantime that ghostly hand, passing horribly under my eyes like a hand without an arm, had removed another fragment of glass.   And still through the window drifted the strong vapor of gasoline.

Yet this I could do, (for the man must be stopped at least).   Drawing the dagger from my pocket, I crouched and waited.   Slowly the hand re-emerged phantom-like from the dark and rested upon the sash.   With one swift blow I drove home the steel; through flesh and bone and wood it pierced, and stuck.

The shriek that tore the silence!   God save you from ever hearing its like.

Aside I had sprung.   Into the room leaped a tongue of flame, and my ears near split with the concussion of sound.   As though that revolver shot were a signal, a vivid yellow glare filled the night without; the black blinds of the windows were fringed with it.   In a flash I knew that Carver had set the house afire: he would burn us out.

All this happened in the droop of a lash, ere I could dart into the post-room.

"To the tower!" I cried.   "Fire! Fire!"

In the weird light I saw Dan and Domini and Mary, turned my way as in a tableau; their faces all eyes, wild desperate eyes, doubting, fearing, courageous.

Then, from the hall, in rushed William

"Fire!" he roared, his face aghast.

Mary uttered a piercing scream, and reeled.   I caught her.

"You better not faint!" I threatened savagely, and shook her shoulders.   "If you do, you're a goner!"

She looked at me, whimpering.

Already Dan, Domini, and William were in the tower chamber: I shoved Mary headlong through the door.   Dan slammed it behind us, and shot the heavy bolt.

"Down the cave!" he cried.   "Quick!"

At the same moment a thundering cataract of blows fell on the tower door.   It quivered on its hinges, but held fast.   A fierce babble of voices sounded without, but above them all a deep throat bawled.   "Up with the log, you hounds!   Ram her in!"

I turned.   The hole in the floor was no longer black; it was a figure of orange, like a giant pie slice. Next breath Dan had lifted Mary off her feet.   She let out a screech, and then went limp.   Like a sack of flour he let her down to the platform.   However William got her to the bottom I don't know.   But he was an age in doing it; and just as the dark mouth brightened again the door groaned under a shattering impact: they had got their battering-ram into action.

I dropped on one knee, whipping the shotgun to

my shoulder. Though the candle was below, a lurid purplish radiance streamed through the three narrow loopholes, illumining the room with eerie distinctness. I could see the iron bolt of the door; I could see it leap in its socket, leap and bend, and stay bent. Already a thin bar of golden light edged the jamb. Two more blows would finish the job.

My fingers hooked both triggers: the first man through would not get far.

A hand fell on my shoulder.

"You're next! For God's sake, hurry!"

I didn't even look at him.

"If you care for Domini, Dan," said I, "you'd better go down there yourself. I won't move till—"

The gun was wrested from my grasp; the next I knew I was swept bodily from the floor and jammed down through the hole. The platform wobbled beneath me. Fearing lest it should fall to pieces, I scuttled down the steps: but I was more angry with Dan Mitchell than I was with Crowninshield.

J as I hit the bottom (and glimpsed William holdistg high the candlestick and Mary lying on the ground with Domini bending over her) an explosion like a volcano shook the air. A fearful cascade of cries and curses poured through the opening above, and a second later a pair of legs was dangling.

It was Dan; but under his sudden weight the staircase lurched off its center, and hung. He must be quick, quick! Already he was crawfishing down the steps. Still they held together.

But not for long: another pair of legs shot down through the hole, and struck the platform. A momentary crackle of loosened beams, and the whole staircase collapsed with a crash.

The candlestick flew across the cave, rolling on the floor with sputtering wick. I leaped forward, snatched it up, and turned.

William lay on the ground stunned by a spar of the fallen wreck. Against the opposite wall was a picture I shall never forget: Crowninshield, his face like a demon's in the wavering candle-light, pinioned to the rock by Dan Mitchell. In his right hand, stretched at arm's length, was a pistol: but Dan gripped the wrist. With his left hand he tore and hammered at Dan's humped head and shoulders.

"Oh, Gerard!" sobbed a voice at my shoulder. "He will kill him!"

I took the wrong "him."

"Steady, Domini!" said I. "He'd better kill him. Not much show for us if he doesn't! Domini, can you hold this candlestick?"

She took it with brave, trembling hands.

I jumped across the pile of timbers. To come so near that awful struggle was a shock! I could all but feel the straining of their souls. Crowninshield's mouth was wide agape; his red tongue, flaked with spume, lolled out. His eyeballs seemed almost bursting. Dan's right arm, like a rod of steel, was driven into his throat.

I reached up and grasped the barrel of the revolver. I saw Crowninshield's eyes roll sideways in his head. The look he gave me! if looks could kill and damn too,—well.

With a tug I wrenched the weapon loose. Upon the instant fell a horrible swift movement: both men went down, writhing in a tangle. Over and over again they rolled; their muscles cracked, and the breath in their nostrils whistled. Dan's hold was broken.

Poised over that twisting mass, I waited for my chance. It came. Crowninshield's great head popped out. I struck. All limp he went—a senseless hulk of flesh and bone in Dan's terrible embrace.

Dan lifted a bloody face and grinned.

"Nice—work, Gerry," he gasped. "By George —I—I think—he nearly had me!"

XXXIII

WE EXPLORE THE TOWER CAVE: AND I MAKE
ANOTHER TRY FOR THE TREASURE

DAN staggered to his feet. Blood, glistening like ink in the yellow glare, trickled from a gash in his forehead.

There was a sob behind me. I turned as Domini thrust the candlestick into my hands. Stooping, she ripped a flounce from her skirt.

"Oh, Dan, Dan!" cried she; and right there in that gruesome spot, with Crowninshield lying starkly at her feet, she dressed his wound.

She dressed it quickly; but in the interval I could hear the roaring of the fire above and the clamorous shouting of our foes. The house was doomed. Even were the staircase still standing, it would have been sure death to climb back to the tower. But one way was left: we must find the other end of the cave.

That there was another exit I knew now beyond a doubt. The air, under the suction of the heat above, was whistling and singing through the cave like a gale. The dust of the wrecked staircase whirled in bright clouds through the hole overhead.

The flame of the candle twisted and smoked; I could hardly shield it with my coat.

"Beg your pardon, Miss Domini, but if you could turn your attention to Mary here. She do seem quite in a faint and a man can't rightly handle her."

It was William, cool and proper. His face I could see, was haggard with the pain of his wounded arm. But never a word he spoke for that.

Already Domini was on her knees beside the girl's prostrate form. I placed the candlestick by, in a sheltered corner of the wall, and turned to Dan.

"We'll have to explore this cave, Dan, if we want to get out. We can't climb up there again."

"Of course, we'll explore it," says he. "I'm up to anything now. Wow! Ned Buntline in his palmiest days never had anything on us." He touched Crowninshield with his toe. "What are we going to do with this old boy? Leave him here, I guess."

I stooped and felt the bushy head: the hair was moist, but the skull was solid as a chunk of granite. The pulse was going, too.

"Plenty of kick in him yet," said I. "It won't be murder to leave him here. There's lots of air. He'll come round by and by. We've got his gun, so if he follows us he can't do much anyhow."

"Now you're all right, dear," said Domini; and turning, we saw Mary sitting against the wall, the tears streaming down her chalky face.

"Come on, Mary," cried Dan cheerfully. "The

show's all over. We've got to leave now. Gerry, give me that gun. You and Domini lead the way, and I'll pigtail the procession."

"No, you don't," I declared. "You've played me one dirty trick to-night. You rammed me down that hole. I guess I'm going to share some of the danger."

"Why, Lord, man!" cries he. "There's the danger—in front!"

"Well, I'm afraid of it then," said I doggedly.

Whereat he smiled, took up the candlestick, and squeezed through the narrow gap. Domini followed, and then William and Mary. Before I went I cast a last glance at the sprawled figure on the ground. Darkly it lay there, one great arm flung out and the ugly bestial face upturned to the down-misting light. How soon would consciousness come back? There was no telling. But one thing was certain: that when it did, unarmed as he was, he would rush after us.

I slipped through the crevice, and our flight began. Little was said. Even Mary ceased to whimper, and clung to William's sound arm, terrified into silence. Indeed, that dismal gloom was enough to daunt a stouter heart than Mary's. The candle, owing to the strong current of air, shed but a flickering light, which was, I think, more awesome than total darkness. Huge shadows went wavering along the walls—high walls of cragged, shiny rock. And over the heads of those in front I could see the throat of inky blackness that kept swallowing us. Always the passage sloped downward, winding; always the same grim walls rose frowning on either hand; always the shadows glided, fearful and grotesque, looming like monstrous spirits, and beckoning with futile gestures, and flitting in despair away.

Suddenly Dan halted. Before him towered an immense wedge of rock, with the passage forking to either side.

"Which way?" said he, and then moved warily to the left.

At once I saw he had picked wrong: the candle in his hand was burning with a flame vertical and steady. But, ere I could speak,

"Back, Domini!" cries he. . . . "Good Lord, look at that!"

We clustered cautiously forward. At our feet gleamed a rocky brink. Below a black void yawned —bottomless, horrible.

And then, from behind, fell a sound that shook my heart. Above the low moaning of the wind we heard what might have been a loosened rock strike and roll on the floor of the passage!

We said nothing, only looked at one another: a ring of anxious faces in the candle's yellow glare.

Dan broke the silence.

"Well, this isn't getting us anywhere," said he briskly. "Let's back up. Look sharp, Gerry. You're in front."

Any moment I expected Crowninshield to come

bursting down upon me. I had the revolver ready for him, but nothing of the kind happened. We gained the other passage and pursued our way.

And by and by I thought I began to feel a warmer air. We rounded a sharp turn, and then came a cry from Dan.

"Bushes, by George! Hold on! . . . Yes, sir, there's a tree, and the sky with a peep of dawn in it. We're out of the cave!"

"Thank God!" said Domini, with a little gasping sob.

Hurrying forward, I struck my foot against a metal object. I heard the ring of it. Stooping, I picked it up: a coffee-pot. A sudden intuition pierced me.

"The light, Dan!" cried I. "Look around! Do you know where we are!"

He held the candle high, as the others gazed on with wondering faces. There was the pine-box, and the jug, and the dead ashes of the campfire.

A soft whistle was his only answer.

"The kidnappers' cave!" cried I. "Lord, if they had only known where it led to!"

"Well, let's clear out double-quick," said he. "I've had fighting enough for one night. There's not much scrap left in any of us, I imagine. Mum's the word now, and watch your step. Good-by, old candle, you did a good job. Come, Domini."

We were in darkness again, creeping through the hedge of bushes at the mouth of the cave. But once

on the other side, I knew it was not the flush of dawn
Dan had seen: and so did he.

"Hold on," he whispered. "Look at that light.
That's not the day. That's—"

"That's Jack's House," said I. "It's behind us
somewhere."

Up through the trees the sky was all ruddy with
reflected fire; and straight ahead down the valley
thick stocks of oak and maple stood up darkling in
the elfin light.

"I know the way," said I; and assuming the lead,
started off in the same direction Carver and Blue
Island had taken two days before.

For perhaps a hundred yards we skirted the curving base of the hill; then came a sharp turn, and lo!
away up yonder on our left, behind the pine-trees—
a netted screen woven of jet and gold—glowed the
conflagration.

We gazed together in a kind of awe. We all
knew what was being reduced to ashes up there before its time. Christian burial had been denied it,
but Christian Sacraments had not. Between the two
(I thought) when my own hour came, I could well
dispense with the former were I but sealed with
those last sacred rites.

Out of the corner of my eye I stole a glance at
Domini. Her head a-tilt, she was staring tearless
at the hilltop. Her lips were moving—trembling,
I fancied at first, but not so: I, too, said a prayer for
my uncle.

"I wonder if they've come," said Dan's voice at my ear. "If Father McGiffert got away safe, he should be back by now. It's three o'clock. Dawn will be breaking soon."

"I tell you," I whispered, "you all get in those bushes and sit tight. I'll sneak on up the hill and see what's what. It won't take me long."

Slyly I dodged up through the trees, skipping from pine to pine, all on the alert for the least hint of our enemies. The nearer I approached the larger grew the fire, fierce spouts of flame blazing straight up into the dark sky; and the noise of it was like a low roar, with dull crashes now and then as some supporting beam gave way. The whole hilltop was illuminated like midday; even where I was, still a good piece down among the pines, you might have read small print. A lump of gum on the bark near my fingers glowed like a sapphire. Overhead the branches stirred and rustled in the strong suction of the air.

Closer still I ventured, till I came almost to the open lawn. Not a soul was to be seen in all that brilliant space—only the ring of tall black trees, like grim spectators, and the great fire burning in the midst. No human sound at all, no cries of men— only the hungry, growling crackle of the blaze.

The walls and roof were still intact. But from every door and window furious tongues of flame were shooting forth, curling, and quivering, and licking upward. So splendid a spectacle it was that for minutes I clean forgot myself; forgot my comrades below the hill, forgot our enemies, forgot even the treasure; utterly lost in the biggest, most glorious bonfire I had ever seen.

Then, presently, began a loud, rending noise, like the first rip of a near-heard thunderbolt, and all of a sudden, with a huge smothering crash, the whole roof caved in. Up rolled enormous clouds of smoke, spangled with a million red sparks. Then, once more, the flames soared out of the four gaunt walls, a solid sheet; and high above it, belched forth from that blazing furnace, floated flakes of fire big as your hand. I tell you, it was a gorgeous sight!

But by and by I returned to earth. Remembering my mission, I again looked around; but seeing no one, slunk back down the hill.

Dan spied me yards off; his head popped out of the bushes. When I came up,

"What luck, Gerry?" he whispers.

I crawled under the leafage.

"No luck," said I. "Didn't see a single person. Carver and his crowd have gone, I guess. Father McGiffert hasn't come, though. I couldn't see anything of him. Nobody's up there. But, O boy, you ought to take a look at that fire!"

"Well," counseled Dan, "the best thing we can do is to wait right here till daylight. Then, if Father McGiffert doesn't show up, we'll just have to hoof it to McGregor, I reckon. With Crowninshield out of the way, I don't think those other chaps are spoil-

ing for a fight.   They haven't anything left to fight
for.   House gone, treasure gone, leader gone—you
can bet they're not hanging around here; they've
beat it.   But we'll stick tight, anyhow, till daybreak;
and keep mum."

In the silence I fell to thinking on the treasure,
and what the chances were of its being in Silly Sim's
cavern: or rather, because I made sure it was there,
what the chances were of my slipping off, unbe-
knownst of the rest, seizing the precious stuff, and
springing on Domini the surprise of her life—crown-
ing all our hazardous adventures with the rich
gleam of gold.   The prospect thrilled me, I tell you.
And as I sat there in the dark, I could see myself
laying at her feet a great bag of glinting coins, all
solid gold, with here and there in the yellow heap
the fiery flash of a priceless gem.   It would make
no difference that now I was as poor as she (my
purse I had left in Jack's House) all should be hers.
And she would thank me, and say—well, she would
say something to make my heart glow; but it
shouldn't start my tears—that I swore.

Edging over, I peered out of the bushes.   The
light was no longer just a reddish glare; a sober
grayness filled the quiet valley; the dawn was come
at last.   I craned further out—and snapped back
like a gopher: I could have sworn to a sudden movement yonder behind that clump of brush.   I peered
again.   Nothing stirred in the thicket; the leafage
hung motionless; on every hand the dim, still woods

slept on under the stealing dawn. After all, it might have been the hop of a rabbit, or the flirt of a squirrel's tail; it might have been—but the ardor of my plan cooled mighty suddenly.

"Hello!" whispers Dan. "It's daylight, isn't it? I reckon I dozed a bit. Anything doing yet?"

"Dan," said I, "I was going up to Eagle's Nest for the treasure without telling you. But now I think I'd better let you know, in case anything happens."

"Why," says he, "you think it's there?"

"I'm sure it is. Silly Sim's the only one could have taken it. I'll bet he swiped it years ago and hid it in his den. Anyhow, I'm going up there to find out."

"Well, nothing like trying. But I'd better keep the gun. Good luck, old chap."

I crawled out of the bushes and put off. Silently and quickly I went. In the graying woods, windless and heavy, all was a dead hush. Just the same, a kind of fear kept twitching at my heart. I could not rid myself of the fancy that I was being shadowed. Often I wheeled suddenly in my tracks; but the trick never worked; there was nothing behind there but solemn trees and mounds of brush, and maybe a sleepy bird hopping on a bough. And all the while the dawn spread blankly across the ashen clouds.

At last, descending the bluff, I reached the railroad track. No mist on the river this morning;

leaden like the sky above, the water glided, noise-less and spiritless, on its long journey. Cold it looked and drear, that river. I took my eyes away and glanced up at the huge bluff; drear it looked, too, for all its greenery, and somehow menacing.

Then, chucking fancies overboard, I struck out stoutly down the track.

Crowninshield's boathouse I passed on the run, and brought up panting a hundred yards below it. But nothing had happened; the place, like its owner, lay like dead.

Before and behind the track was empty. If any-one was dodging me (and, as I say, fancy or no fancy, I could not but feel the prying of a pair of eyes), he was certainly making a good job of it. But my goal was looming closer every step; almost above me now frowned the stern brow of Eagle's Nest. Higher it seemed in this sad dawning light, higher and grimmer and hinting more mysteriously at something dread.

After a little search I hit the path Carver and I had climbed three days back. With my heart beating thickly, not only on account of the ascent, I nimbly scaled the bluff and came out on the ledge that led to the front of the cavern. Again I got that shock of the sudden emptiness all about; the slag sky above, the vast waste of air before me, and below, so far below! the lead-hued river.

Quickly, then, I made for the cavern's mouth.

I reached it, started to enter, and was all but

knocked off my feet by a rushing cloud of huge dusky wings. Flat on my face I fell, as the vultures, stinking fearfully, flapped away. What these ghouls had been about I knew ere I raised my eyes. Straightway, before aught else, I sought the pallet of pine-twigs and covered it with scraps of blanketing and canvas.

Then I began my hunt for the treasure.

The cavern consisted of two rooms, as you may recall. First, I would examine the outer one, though I had a hunch the treasure wouldn't be there. Nevertheless, out I went, almost to the mouth, turned and took a survey.

Then something befell that cut off my breath like throttling fingers: a shadow leaped in and lay beside my own!

XXXIV

DAWN ON EAGLE'S NEST

"STILL after the treasure?" said a quiet, deadly voice.

Round I span.

There stood Carver with folded arms and cap jauntily cocked; but the pale cheek and hollow burning eye told a different story.

All trembling as I was, I measured my chances at a glance. Carver was perhaps six feet away.

"Mr. Carver," said I, stepping toward him; and next breath had darted past, and was shooting round the corner of the cavern.

But I didn't shoot far. The ledge narrowed abruptly. With a gasp I fetched up short. I was on the south side of Eagle's Nest; the ledge to safety lay on the north.

"What's the matter?" said a voice behind me. "Aren't you going any further?" And turning, I saw Carver coolly straddled on the rock, his arms still folded. Out of the corner of my eye I glimpsed the mighty depth below: glimpsed it and shuddered. Already a giddiness was creeping over me; but I flung it off, and inching round in my tracks, faced the cold gray cliff. In a cranny before my eyes was a little white flower; it nodded under my tremulous breathing.

"You must be afraid of me," said Carver.

A sudden hope leaped in my breast.

"Then you will not kill me?" I cried.

"Oh, don't put it that way," says he. "I just can't allow you to swear me to the gallows."

My heart sank: but rose again, wildly fluttering.

"But I promise you," I panted desperately, "I swear to you, I won't breathe a word of it!" A cowardly speech, maybe; but ah, it was a cruel thing to die!

Carver laughed. "If I were in your fix, I'd probably say the same. But then," he added, "you'd be certain to change your mind. I would."

"No, no, no!" I cried. And then I grasped at another straw. "If you let me go, I'll tell you where the treasure is!"

He chuckled grimly.

"Ah, the treasure," says he. "I'm beginning to think that treasure's all a fake. It's not in the tower. Oh, don't look surprised. I was leather-headed there, I grant you; it wasn't till last night— a little before that idiot Crowninshield set fire to his own property—that the cave way dawned on me. But I found the boodle already taken. You hadn't taken it; I could hear you pounding on the stone overhead. Then, like yourself, I tried Silly Sim's here. If he took it, the old loon hid it where neither you nor I nor anybody else will ever find it. No, no, kid, you won't tell me where the treasure is." Smiling, he uncrossed his arms and counted off, finger against finger. "Promises, no go. Treasure, no go. Anything else? I'm open to persuasion."

I lifted my head. "Help!" I called at the top of my lungs. "Help! Help!——"

"Stop it!" he commanded fiercely. "Another yelp, and you'll get a bullet through your heart."

A pistol was in his right hand, and his dark eye glowered.

A weariness came on me then, almost an indifference. The void below no longer plucked at my heels; my tormenting murderer there no more dismayed me. I had given up—that was the reason; there wasn't any hope, so I just didn't care.

"Why don't you shoot me?" said I. "Have it over with. I'm tired."

His revolver was already back in his pocket, but his hand jumped for it.

"Yell again, and I will," said he.

But there I stuck. I would sooner be shot than fall, but I hadn't the nerve to pull the trigger.

I looked at him, my cheek lying against the cold rock. With no thought of pleading—that was gone—I began to speak:

"I don't see how a man like you can be happy even with all the treasure in the world. You have murdered Iron; now you are going to murder me.

What for? To cover up the first murder. All right, suppose no man ever finds you out. Those two murders are hanging around your neck day and night. You know them, and God knows them. Life is short, they say; I never dreamed how short till now. When your time comes, and you die, won't it be a fearful thing to face your Maker? You must know He will ask you about us two, and why you robbed us of the most precious thing we possessed. When you have killed me, and are far away some-where, remember what I've said."

He pulled a wry face, and then grinned.

"Well, I like your cheek! You stand there as cool as cool, and read me a lesson like a minister. But I'll admit this much. I'll admit it won't be pleasant to remember you on dark nights—when I'm by myself. You touched a weak spot there.— You see that ledge; you see how it runs out into single footholds. If you can reach the top that way, I'll let you go. But you must make up your mind in two minutes."

He lit a cigarette, tossing the match over the bluff. Then, squatting on one knee, he pulled out his watch. "Go!" said he, as if starting a race.

I didn't need two minutes to make up my mind. A chance had been offered me—how slender I didn't stop to consider—and at once the hope of life al-most choked me with joy. The blood rushed to my heart, and my knees shook. Momently I faltered, trying to get a grip on myself. Then, hugging the face of the cliff, I began to edge along the perilous path.

It was but a foot or so wide, and presently dwindled to inches. I stopped. Beyond were slight juts of rock; even a hawk would feel giddy there. Giddy! God help me, I must not even think of the word! I swallowed hard, shutting my eyes tight. I must not look below; I must keep my soul riveted here on the gray rock.

Drawing a careful breath, I turned my eyes aloft. Five feet above my head was the soddy brink of the cliff (the grasses, sharp as sword blades, pricked against the velvet clouds), and a span below it, like a shepherd's crook, the up-curving stock of an elm sapling.

I felt out with my left hand, then with my left foot; and got a higher hold for both. My right hand clutched a crag, and I raised myself slowly, carefully, but visibly nearer. A little more, and the sapling would be within reach. A thought began to rise in my heart; if I couldn't make that sapling I should never be able to return to the ledge, even though Carver might allow it; I had burnt my bridges. But this fear I fought down, panting; and renewed my climb.

At last, however it was done, my right arm stretching its full length, I seized the slender shoot. But to move another inch I must put my whole weight on it. Would it be equal to the drag? I

couldn't tell. With a gasp I strained upward. The
fingers of my left hand closed round the stem. My
legs dangled. But the sapling held.

I dropped my eyes, seeking a purchase for my
scraping feet. God, shall I ever forget that sight!
A patch of the crawling river, and treetops like
squat shrubbery, and a glimpse of two black threads
that was the railroad. The pit of my stomach sank;
black horror, like a hundred snatching hands,
reached up for me. I sobbed aloud; then clench-
ing my teeth, lifted wild eyes into the bright dawn.

"Well," said Carver (but his voice came as from
a distance), "you're a first-rate acrobat. But I'm
afraid you'd better find a place for your feet. That
little tree can't stand the gaff .   .   .   You'll just
hang by your arms, eh? Ah, you won't be able to
hang long. You'll soon tire and drop off. Dear
me, you'll have a terrible drop. Look below and
see. When they pick you up, they won't be able to
say I did it. They'll think it was just an accident."

I saw now why he had given me this chance, the
cunning devil. Like a fool, I had played into his
hand. But I shut my eyes, ground my teeth, and
held on. Never, never would I let go; my arms
should pull from their sockets first. If Carver
wanted to kill me, he must kill me with a bullet.

Then along my straining mind, straining like my
arms, gleamed a ray of hope. I remembered Dan.
I had told him, hadn't I, of my purpose. He must
know I was up here on Eagle's Nest. Maybe he

would come. Oh, if he could but see me now, how quickly he would come! Still, had I only the strength to cling on—cling on—cling on—he might save me yet.

Something of my thoughts Carver must have divined, for quite suddenly,

"You're too damned obstinate," says he; "or else you haven't any more imagination than a crawfish. Mere fancy should have tumbled you long ago. Well, I can't wait. I'll tumble you with one of Silly Sim's fish-poles."

Can you match barbarity like that! He would poke me off the face of the cliff, as you reach up with a stick and twitch an apple off the tree.

I heard his footfall on the ledge, and despair began to numb me. Why not let go, and cheat him of his game? . . . But would that be cheating him? That's what he wanted!

Something fell lightly upon my chest. I opened my eyes. Down against the scaly rock dribbled crumbs of clay. I looked up. On either side of the sapling's stock, just beyond my fists where it stuck out from the soil, two tiny streams of earth were trickling.

I knew what that meant. Within one minute, a little more or a little less, the sapling would rip loose; and then— A nausea seized me; out of my heart a weakness crept, and stole up my arms; the grip of my fingers seemed to slacken; cold sweat

beaded my forehead; by turns my body was fire
and ice.   Yet, somehow, I did not fall.   Yet, somehow, I had the nerve to look up again.   No longer
trickled bits of clay; it was cracking off in cakes.

I was to die.   Sure, the good God in that last
moment spoke to my heart, for up to then I had had
no thought of Him.   But a sweet calm stood suddenly in my soul; and,

"O Lord Jesus," I prayed aloud, "You will judge
me soon.   By Your passion and death, forgive me
now all my sins.   I am sorry for them because by
them I offended You.   Forgive me.   I forgive all
my enemies.   I do, I do!   I forgive Carver—"

"Oh, never mind about me," said a voice, somewhere.   "I'm not any enemy of yours.   I'm not even
going to pry you loose.   I see I don't have to.
Good-by, old top, remember me to the angels.   You
can tell them all about Iron—he probably didn't
join their company himself."

As though I had been shot from the mouth of a
cannon I whirled through the air; but not downward—upward; and a great voice roared,

"No, by thunder, he didn't!"

I rolled, half crazed, upon the grass.   A shot
rang out.   Laughing, I looked up through my tears;
and saw something flash back over the giant's head
above me and then streak down over the bluff like a
silver spear.   Rose a single cry—like a bleat: and
then silence.

I turned on my belly and chewed the turf, and dug my fingers into it, and laughed again; and my tears fell on the grass like rain.

I don't know whether I swooned or not, but the next clear recollection I have is of looking up into Iron's enormous face.

"Well, sonny," says he, "them open deadlights is a good sign. You're all right now, don't tell me you ain't, hey? A little white 'long about the cutwater, but that's to be expected more or less."

I sat up, feeling pretty limp and washy.

"There, now, that's right," he boomed on. "I lay you'll eat your breakfast yet. But shiver my sides! you was sailin' mighty close to the wind, you was, mighty close. Another p'int, and I reckon you'd a fouled your gear consider'ble."

"I thought you were drowned," said I, staring at him. "You told Carver you couldn't swim."

He threw back his head and roared. Then, giving me an admiring look, "Dash my buttons, was you that nigh!" he cried. "Well, now, don't that beat the Dutch! Come, I like your style, sonny. You fooled me good, but I ain't bearin' no grudge for that. And as for that fox—his name were Dick, he said—well, he's got my dirk through his gizzard now. Hereafter, I lay he'll prob'ly savvy parties don't tell his kind the straight-cut truth." He paused and batted me a cunning wink. "Swim!" says he. "Sonny, I could swim like a petrel, a'most afore I shed my di'pers. But was I goin' to blab it

to that swab? I knowed the trick he were up to—
drown Iron and hog the blunt; and I had my steel,
and I was ready. But souse my scuppers, he were
too quick for me. Well, he won't never be quick
no more, and you may put a dot to that."

"But how *can* you swim?" said I. "You've only
got one arm!"

"What's an arm!" says he. "Why, I could keep
this old hulk afloat with *all* the riggin' chopped
away. But I'm a-tellin' you, sonny, I got more
swimmin' than I bargained for; more walkin' too,
blast my bulwarks!" He lowered his voice. "But
you look here, sonny, you've got the chart—"

A shout went up in the woods behind us. Iron
sprang to his feet, his face working in alarm.

"What's that?" cries he.

"Those are my friends from Jack's House,"
said I. "They're coming to my rescue."

"Good-by, sonny," he began hurriedly. "You
skinned Iron; but remember, he thinks mighty high
of you. You've got the chart, and you've got the
treasure too—leastways you'd ought to have it. But
there's Dick below the cliff with my dirk through
his middle. And—"

"And here I am, Mr. Iron," said I, 'your only
witness to swear you slew him in self-defense. Are
you going to run off and leave your only witness?"
(The hallooing among the trees was growing
louder.)

He gave me a wondering look. Then, his small

eyes suddenly flashing, he fetched his thigh a mighty thwack.

"Well, there now!" he exclaimed. "Ain't you got a head on your neck! And you just hopped out o' the cradle, in a manner o' speakin'. Self-defense! Self-defense, you says. And self-defense it were, too, by thunder! He fired at me, he did; fired point-blank as I was a-fishin' of you up. And you'll swear, you will, that Absalom Iron were defendin' hisself. You'll say, it were killed or be killed, and Iron heaved his dirk in self-defense, that's what you'll say." His voice sank almost to a whisper, as though he were about to impart a secret. "They won't swing a man for self-defense, will they, sonny?" I told him, no; but saw as clear as day that he had meant to slay Carver, self-defense or no self-defense. But I kept my own counsel: whatever the old rogue's intentions, self-defense was the fact. Besides, he had saved my life.

At that moment, out of the belt of trees further back on the bluff, darted the first of the rescuing party. Spying us, he stopped dead and dropped his rifle into the crook of his arm; and then came slowly forward. A tall man he was, quite unknown to me; but, I supposed, one of the posse fetched by Father McGiffert.

"You're the boy, I guess," says he. "Why, you're all right. Ain't nothing happened to you. Who's he?" with a nod at Iron.

"He's a friend of mine," said I. And then, as I

was about to launch into details, here comes Father McGiffert with three or four more, and behind them Dan and Domini; she panting and leaning on his arm, and her cheeks like roses.

My heart sang to see all my friends again; especially to see her.

"Hello, Father!" I cried. "Hey, Dan and Domini! Come and meet the man who saved my life. This is Absalom Iron."

You should have seen their faces; puzzled is no name for it. Iron smirked and made a leg.

"Well, I'm blowed!" said Dan. "I thought you were after the treasure!"

The old sailor's face was one huge smile; or rather, half a dozen of them.

"So I was," says he; "in a manner of speakin', I was. But this here boy, he's smarter than paint, he is. Mind, I says it—smarter than paint. Why, I'd liefer try to come over all the admirals in the British navy as him. He played rings around Iron, he did. He's took and got the treasure; but shiver my timbers! I'm kind of hankerin' after a peep o' the gold anyhow."

"O Gerard, did you find it after all?" cries Domini.

I shook my head. "There wasn't any treasure, Domini," said I. But, ere I could tell of Silly Sim's hiding it again,

"What!" roared Iron, and whopped down on the grass as if I had dealt him a knockout—as indeed I had. There he sat, the very picture of staggered amaze; so that I had to smile.

"Well," said he slowly, gazing around, "you may keelhaul Iron for a dod-gasted, soap-brained, bunglin' lubber!—savin' the lady's presence. 'Treasure,' says Tom Donkin to me, 'treasure your great uncle's granny!' And he were right, by thunder! I reckon they ain't no treasure nowhere, except in story-books."

"Oh, but you're wrong there, Mr. Iron," says Dan, and (the nerve of the fellow!) took Domini's hand.

"Yes, Mr. Iron," says she, "there's one treasure not in any story-book." And, though she let Dan keep her hand, her dear eyes were given to me.

Then (and this may look like a framed-up way of ending my narrative—but it isn't) Eagle's Nest was suddenly flooded with golden light. Over the Wisconsin bluffs the morning sun was streaming through the clouds at last.

THE END

EPILOGUE

I HAVE written "The End"—and about-time! some of you may say. Well, and so it.is; all that was worth telling is told. Except, perhaps, that Crowninshield's kinsfolk came a-tearing out to McGregor vowing a fell vengeance; but shut up pretty quick when they discovered the real state of affairs, and shut everybody else up, too, official and unofficial. I, of course, was for pitching into them to the hilt.of the law; but Dan said no, and Domini on her side shrank from the notoriety.

But, ere I can put a proper period to this relation, I have yet to exercise a corporal work of mercy: I must bury the dead. As to Crowninshield, the less said of that hulking moron the better. He was found with a broken neck at the bottom of the pit which we had so nearly stumbled into the night of our escape. His kinsmen planted him hugger-mugger, as well they might. I do so now, and, though I can but wish him well, being dead, I fear he will sprout no lily.

Carver.was picked up at the foot of Eagle's Nest, with Iron's big knife driven clean through his right lung. A pitiless, snaky crook, whose name was neither Carver nor yet Reed, but Charley Price,.he was "wanted" at the time of his death in both San Francisco and New Orleans. A man of many shady dexterities, a profound rogue, a subtle mind fast fixed in evil, he has appealed to my imagination ever since as the type of the educated criminal—a trained intellect and the heart of a thug.

The bog in the bungalow glen never yielded up its victim. Though I insisted Blue Island was there, I was hardly believed; the glossy surface, like a sheet of satin, showed not a trace of him. Even when long rods were thrust into the slime, nothing was felt; so that the attempt to extricate the body was given over. To this day, somewhere deep in that deadly ooze, his bones lie weltering. But the rest of that gang, Jonas, to wit, and Short and Fiddles, made good their escape. Short, indeed, turned up later. But the other two must have fled the country. Nothing has been heard of them since. They may be running yet for aught I know; if they get a glimpse of these pages I am sure they will crack their wind.

What the buzzards left of Silly Sim was decently interred by Father McGiffert. With this good man, who was later removed to another parish, I still keep in touch. When I told him I was going to write this book, he asked me to give him a *nom de guerre;* but upon my protesting that this was impossible (seeing I was to chronicle the history of the case) he begged me at least to scant his own part. Well, I have tried to consult his modesty;

but I fear when he reads my narrative the ruddiness of his cheek will mount to his forehead; and I shall be in for it.

Absalom Iron, for the first few days after the affair on Eagle's Nest, was in a terrible taking; thought he should have a devilish hot time of it, if indeed he were lucky enough to get off with a whole skin; and declared to me (with a bang that near split the hotel table) that "he were a born fool for beating into port in the wery teeth of the law— like flying in the face of Providence." But he went scot-free, the old rascal. There was nobody to prosecute; even the State, when Carver's record transpired, refused to act: and of course my oath that the killing was done in self-defense cinched the matter.

I wish I knew whether that queer old bird is still alive, and where he is now. He gave me his address before he left—some little fishing-town on the English coast—but I have long forgotten it. He went away with his faith in Tom Donkin's sagacity quite up in the air; that able seaman's opinion on ghosts and treasure was enough to whirl one's head like a capstan. As to ghosts, he were a lubber; but as to treasure, "he predicked the whole hash, he did, a-lookin' at me o'er a pint of ale and his finger a-pressin' of this wery button on my shirt."

Indeed, as far as the treasure goes I was more disappointed than Iron himself; and I rather fancy you are, too. I know how it is when you read a treasure story, and in the end fail to strike the doubloons. That isn't right poetically, or even morally. You give an author chap hours of your time, and then on the last page he cheats you: it isn't fair. And you may take my word for it, if I didn't have to stick to facts, I would have found the gold on Eagle's Nest and whacked it up among Domini, Iron and yourself. Domini, I make sure, would have agreed gladly.

But, as I tell young Gerard Mitchell (who has a most amazing appetite for pieces of eight and the Jolly Roger), that treasure of Silly Sim's was still to play an exciting part in my life. You see, a few years later— But that is another story.

Lightning Source UK Ltd.
Milton Keynes UK
UKHW022230291218
334664UK00009B/1360/P